RIGHTEOUS SNIPER

A World War II Novel

DAVID HEALEY

INTRACOASTAL

RIGHTEOUS SNIPER

A World War II Thriller

By David Healey

Copyright © 2024 by David Healey. All rights reserved. No part of this book may be used or reproduced by any means without the written permission of the publisher except in the case of brief quotation for the purpose of critical articles and reviews.

Intracoastal Media digital edition published 2024. Print ISBN 979-8-9872808-3-6

Cover design by Streetlight Graphics

Editing by Castle Walls Editing

This book is a work of fiction. Names, characters, places, and incidents are products of the author's imagination or are used fictitiously. Any resemblance to actual events or locales or persons, living or dead, is entirely coincidental.

BISAC Subject Headings:

FIC014000 FICTION/Historical

FIC032000 FICTION/War & Military

If I have to choose between peace and righteousness, I'll choose righteousness.

— THEODORE ROOSEVELT

CHAPTER ONE

Seven roads converged on Bastogne, and Caje Cole was on one of them, in the back of an open truck with several other men, rushing toward the fighting at the encircled town.

On second thought, the idea that the truck was "rushing" anywhere was more like wishful thinking, considering the rough condition of the forest road. Even the term *road* was a stretch, since this was little more than a one-lane track through the woods.

"Beats walking," said a soldier on the bench opposite him.

"If you say so," Cole replied.

"You think the Krauts are done yet?" the soldier said, looking concerned. "As soon as we get some tanks up here, that's got to be it for them."

Cole gave the GI a harder look. The fresh-faced soldier in his new uniform was definitely a replacement sent to the front line, and Cole knew damn well that greenbeans didn't last long.

Not in this cold. Not against SS troops. Not against battle-hardened Wehrmacht soldiers either. And definitely not against Tiger tanks.

Cole just snorted and shook his head. He knew that any further conversation would be a waste of breath. The poor son of a bitch didn't know he was dead yet.

Ignoring the GI, he kept his gaze focused on the surrounding forest that the road passed through. Grime and gunpowder darkened Cole's face, but his bright eyes, clear as cut glass, stood out in the winter gloom. He kept a good grip on his sniper rifle. The cloth swaddled around the telescopic sight—an effort at camouflage—had once been white, but the fabric was now muddy and stained with dried blood.

Winter wind whistled in Cole's ears, and a few stray pellets of sleet stung his cheeks. He tried rearranging the scarf, covering the lower part of his face, but it didn't do much good against the frigid onslaught. The sun had dared to emerge that morning but had long since retreated behind a wintry gray veil.

Against the cold, he wore a ragged pair of gloves that he'd cut the fingertips out of, the better to work the rifle. He wiggled his fingers to keep them from getting too stiff.

Meanwhile, Cole surveyed the landscape.

He knew that the Krauts were out there somewhere.

They might be around the next bend in the road.

Or maybe the one after that.

If he saw them first, just maybe he'd be able to keep this GI across from him alive for one more day.

Hell, maybe he'd even be able to keep *himself* alive.

The rest of their sniper squad rode with him in the back of the truck. He glanced at Vaccaro, who was slumped against Hank Walsh, the young soldier they called "the kid," both sound asleep.

Either that or they were dead from hypothermia. In this weather, Cole reckoned it was a toss-up.

Still looking at Vaccaro, Cole shook his head and grinned, lips curling back from sharp-looking teeth. In the dim light, the smile gave his face a wolfish appearance.

That damned Vaccaro. He was a real idiot sometimes, but Cole reckoned that Vaccaro was the only buddy he had in the whole damn army. He'd better do what he could to keep him alive.

Cole kicked Vaccaro's boot. The other man stirred but didn't come fully awake. Still alive, then.

He recalled how Vaccaro had caught up to them at the last instant and had barely managed to climb into the truck.

"What the hell are you doing here?" Cole had demanded.

"Yeah, yeah, I missed you too."

"You dumb bastard. You ought to have stayed in the hospital."

"I wanted to make room for somebody who needed it."

"Some people ain't got any sense. Vaccaro, maybe you ain't the dumbest guy in the world, but you better hope he don't die."

"Aw, stuff it in your corncob pipe, hillbilly."

Then Vaccaro promptly fell asleep.

Cole, Vaccaro, and Hank were all that was left of their sniper squad, not including the lieutenant. They had lost Rowe and McNulty just days ago. Cole hoped to hell that they didn't lose anybody else. But you couldn't go into battle hoping that you would survive. Just the opposite. In some strange way, a sense of fatalism helped keep you alive.

Lieutenant Mulholland rode up front with the driver, which was his prerogative as an officer. The cab provided shelter from the wind, but the bouncing truck would be punching him in the kidneys just like the rest of them.

For troops on the move, it would have been better if the road was completely frozen, but the passage of vehicles had turned the surface into a sticky brown stew of slush and mud ladled out into endless potholes.

There had been a tattered canvas cover on the back of the truck, which had initially blocked some of the wind but did nothing to keep the cold at bay. The cover had been so shredded that it had finally given up the ghost and blown off a couple of miles ago, leaving the men exposed to the elements.

Riding in the truck wasn't any joyride, given that it jarred Cole down to his bones. Maybe the cold made those bones feel more brittle. The driver was sure as hell managing to hit every tree root and pothole, the jolt of each bump telegraphing its way up through the stiff frame of the truck, to the wooden benches, then directly into Cole's spine. Hell, even his teeth threatened to rattle loose.

All available vehicles had been pressed into service to move troops to where they were needed. Following in the wake of the truck was a jeep, so heavily laden with men that the top-heavy vehicle kept threatening to tip over.

Every hundred yards or so, the truck rolled down into a hole so deep that the odds came down to a coin toss for whether they would be getting out again. Then there would be a tremendous jolt, from which it seemed unlikely that their forward momentum would recover.

But each time, after a tense moment in limbo, the truck would continue bouncing down the rutted road.

Worse, Cole couldn't shake the feeling that they were sitting ducks as they crept along.

He kept his eyes on the woods.

There were few good roads through the Ardennes region, a fact that the fighting armies on both sides had come to know all too well. The terrain was hilly, even mountainous, punctuated by stretches through mountain valleys and fields, all dormant now and covered by drifts of fallen snow. In the bare patches, the ground showed through, frozen and brown with dead grass.

Narrow bridges crossed the winding mountain streams, where there were often villages that had grown up around the bridge or around a mill powered by the stream.

Considering it was December 1944, the scenery should have been right out of a Christmas card, but war had spoiled it. The charred hulks of burned tanks marred the crossroads, and dead bodies lay semi-frozen in the snow at the roadsides. Instead of the smell of spiced cider or baking cookies that so many GIs remembered from the Christmas season, there was an occasional sickly-sweet odor of burned flesh and the stink of spilled fuel.

As they passed one of these grisly vignettes of death and destruction, the GI across from Cole leaned over the side of the truck and vomited.

Cole couldn't blame the poor bastard, but he was used to such scenes by now.

As a reminder that the Germans were far from beaten, a flurry of shots rang out. A pattern of bullet holes appeared like stitchwork in the sides of the truck. A man cried out in pain as he was struck by a bullet.

"Everybody out!" Cole shouted, reaching over to shake Vaccaro and the kid, who were still groggy after being awakened by the sound of gunfire.

The men spilled out of the truck, some instantly falling and finding themselves sprawled in the mud. Their clumsiness may have saved their lives as bullets passed over their heads. The tracer rounds glowed devilishly in the gloom.

Others leaped into the slushy ditches, ignoring the fact that their trousers and boots were immediately soaked through.

A few men chose to use the truck for cover, which proved to be a mistake. A well-aimed round from a Panzerfaust struck the truck and exploded with spectacular effect. The men spun away, screaming torches of flame. If the Panzerfaust round had struck a few moments earlier, when the truck was still full of troops, they would've all gone up in flame—Cole included.

Cole had taken refuge in the nearest pothole, with Vaccaro and the kid nearby. He spat out a mouthful of cold slush, not quite getting the taste of grit out of his mouth.

"Kraut bastards," he muttered, then shouted over at Vaccaro and the kid. "You two all right?"

"We were better a minute ago. You see him?"

"Yeah."

Down the road, he had spotted the German wielding the spent Panzerfaust, which fired a single round. The weapon was intended to knock out tanks rather than transport trucks, but it had done its job with spectacular effect.

Instantly, Cole lined up his sights on the German. His crosshairs automatically went to the man's chest—an easy shot at this range. The German had been waiting in ambush, hoping for the truck to get close. No wonder he hadn't missed.

Cole wouldn't either.

But it was also much too easy of a death for an enemy who had just reduced several of the GIs that Cole had been sharing the truck with to burned sausages. Pausing with his finger on the trigger, he lowered his aim to the German's kneecap and fired. As the shattered bones gave out, the man collapsed in the road, screaming. Far from any real medical attention, in the bitter cold, what remained of his life wouldn't be pleasant.

It was a form of casual cruelty that came all too easily now to the GIs.

Cole's expression as he worked the bolt wasn't quite a grin, but something more like a snarl.

Vaccaro had seen Cole shoot and thought at first that Cole had missed, since he hadn't instantly killed the German.

"Aren't you gonna finish him off?"

"Nope," Cole said.

Vaccaro glanced over at him, probably wondering what Cole meant, but he knew better than to say anything when he saw the expression on Cole's face.

"Let's get the hell off this road and into the ditch," Cole shouted.

Cole went first, rolling out of his hole and running at a crouch for a roadside ditch. He tumbled in with Vaccaro and the kid right behind him.

To his relief, he saw that Lieutenant Mulholland had also made it into the ditch. He looked around for the greenbean from the truck and spotted him, dead in the road, his new uniform soaking up the mud and blood.

Poor bastard never had a chance, Cole thought.

The fusillade of enemy fire increased. Bullets plucked at the dry winter twigs overhead, making them dance and twitch like the fingers of a guitarist moving over his chords. Bits of clipped branches dropped onto their heads or fell to the road.

Sheltering in their holes, they returned fire.

But the column wasn't here to fight Germans. Their orders were to get to Bastogne. Getting bogged down now fighting a small unit of the enemy wasn't in the cards. The front part of the column hadn't been hit, and those trucks started rolling out, leaving the sniper squad to deal with the attack and fight a rear-guard action.

"There can't be more than a handful of those bastards, but they've been waiting for us to show up," Vaccaro said. "They're dug in like my old girlfriend's fingernails grabbing my arm at the Spook-a-Rama ride on Coney Island."

"You sure it was the ride she was scared of?"

"Yeah, yeah, very funny. I keep forgetting that your idea of a date was taking your sister to a hog butchering. You're such a damn hillbilly."

"Hey, fellas, what are we supposed to do about these Germans?" the kid asked, watching nervously as the rest of the convoy slowly disappeared from sight around the next bend in the road.

Nearby, the lieutenant was shouting something about suppressing fire. It was going to take more than that. As Vaccaro had pointed out, the Germans were simply too well dug in from hidden positions. Meanwhile, they had the Americans right where they wanted them—cowering in a ditch. It didn't help that the slush and mud had soaked through their uniforms. Even though they were down low, the cold wind had still managed to find them.

As soon as the sun had disappeared behind the hills, the temperature had dropped steadily. Without doubt, the slush and mud on the road would freeze solid tonight.

Beside him, Cole could hear the kid's teeth chattering. Staying in this ditch too long meant the cold would kill them if the Krauts didn't.

"I've got an idea," Cole said. "Pop some smoke and cover me."

As soon as enough smoke began to screen his movements, Cole slipped back onto the road and made a beeline for the dead GI from the truck. It looked as if the man had been unlucky enough to be killed as soon as he had leaped down from the vehicle.

"Sorry, buddy," Cole said, then grabbed the dead greenbean by the back of the collar and dragged him the short distance to the still-smoldering wreckage of the truck. He positioned the body under the truck, using the man's helmet under his chin to prop up his head. He found a rifle and tucked it into the man's grip. From a distance, it would look as if the GI was making a valiant last stand.

Cole had long since given up any notion about being disrespectful of the dead—as long as he didn't know them. Nonetheless, he found himself offering the dead man an explanation. "Sorry about this, fella. But if killing a few Krauts after you're dead ain't revenge, I don't know what is."

Cole skedaddled back into the ditch.

Once the smoke started to clear, the Germans began firing at the corpse. As their muzzle flashes in the twilight's gloom revealed their positions, Cole and Vaccaro picked them off one by one. Soon the enemy fire ceased altogether. Either they had finished them off, or the survivors had managed to slink away into the trees.

"All right, I think we got them," Mulholland said. "Let's go catch up to those trucks. I sure as hell don't want to hoof it to Bastogne—or be out here on our own once it gets dark."

Crawling out of the ditch, dripping wet, they double-timed it. It didn't take long before the column came into sight. The trucks weren't exactly speeding down the road, but the convoy would keep moving through the night. It was a maddening snail's pace, but it was progress. Cole had to admit that the dead greenbean had been right about something. Riding in the trucks sure beat walking all the way to Bastogne.

Incredibly, the jeep that Cole had spotted earlier was still gamely trailing along in the wake of the convoy. By some miracle, it still hadn't capsized, even though it had picked up a couple more men, survivors of the ambush. The thing had picked up so many men that it looked like a bunch of grapes with wheels.

But there was no room for the snipers on the jeep, so they kept going.

They ran to the back of a truck and were pulled inside. The lieutenant joined them this time.

"Where the hell were you guys?" a soldier asked.

"Christmas shopping," Vaccaro wisecracked. "Better late than never, right? I hope you wanted Santa to bring you some ice and snow, because that's all that was left."

The GI was too exhausted to process that Vaccaro was kidding. "What the hell are you talking about?"

"Ignore him, he ought to be in the hospital anyhow," Cole said. "Let's just say we were takin' care of business. The business in this case being some of Hitler's buddies. They won't be bothering us again."

It was crowded in the back of the truck, not a terrible situation in this cold. The residual body heat was welcome, and some guys even broke out blankets. They settled onto their seats, trying to get some rest and stay warm. This truck still had its canvas covering, which did zilch to keep the heat in, but it did break the worst of the wind.

"Sleep if you can," Mulholland said. "Once we get to Bastogne, there won't be much of that."

CHAPTER TWO

OBERSTURMBANNFÜHRER INGO BAUER considered his options.

For days now they had been pushing through the hills and forests as the Germans advanced. He had called a brief halt while he got his bearings.

Bauer was a tall man in his forties, with dark hair and blue eyes that stood out in a face that seemed permanently tanned and lined from the summer months spent fighting across French fields, despite the fact that it was now winter.

Looking around, he saw that his men were cold and tired, some slumped in the snow or on patches of bare ground. The lack of discipline nagged at him, and he thought the men would be warmer if they had remained standing instead of resting upon the frozen ground, but he held back the command—*Steh auf! Get on your feet!*—that had already begun to form at the back of his throat.

He had to remind himself that some were only teenagers, pressed into service. There were still a few veteran soldiers, and he depended on them to keep the youngsters in line.

Toward the rear was a small group of American prisoners that they had swept up in the advance. The prisoners slumped to the snowy road, much like his own men.

What had happened to the unit that had set out so confidently from Germany just a short time ago? *The cold and snow and constant fighting, that's what.* It had all taken its toll on the men.

Truth be told, it had taken a toll on him as well.

Had it really been just a few days ago that he had listened as Der Führer unveiled this plan to advance through the Ardennes Forest? Hitler and his planners had made it all sound so certain. Here in the cold and snow, with Allied forces digging in and not giving up, the plan seemed nothing but foolhardy, the Obersturmbannführer thought.

At least they were well equipped, with plenty of food and ammunition. The Germans also knew all about winter gear, and they were much better outfitted than the Allies. They were used to the constant gray of a European winter. The Achilles' heel of the German campaign was proving to be fuel for the panzers and the tanks' ability to traverse the narrow forest roads.

The sound of a throat being cleared interrupted his thoughts.

"What are your orders, Herr Obersturmbannführer?" asked Hauptmann Sepp Messner, who had appeared at Bauer's elbow.

Bauer waited a moment before replying. It was just like Messner to address him formally, even though it was just the two of them talking, in the middle of a forest. He had encouraged the use of first names, but Messner definitely had an iron rod up his ass in that regard.

Bauer wondered whether he would ever hear the sound of his first name again.

He knew that Messner didn't like him, and the feeling was mutual. Messner was a few years younger, but he was two inches taller and far more handsome than Bauer, not to mention that he came from a much wealthier background—just the sort of young officer who caught the attention of all the young ladies in Berlin. Messner resented the fact that a mere peasant such as Bauer outranked him. Bauer's surname, in fact, meant "peasant" or "farmer" in German—a fact that Messner surely had not overlooked.

Perhaps it was petty, but it felt good to keep Messner waiting for a reply. He took his time studying the map he held, although he had long since memorized it. Their destination, the town of Bastogne, lay ahead.

"We move forward," he said finally. "We will see if we can join up with the panzers. They can't be too far ahead."

"What about the prisoners?"

Bauer shrugged. The prisoners were the least of his concerns, considering that his unit had lost contact with the larger panzer force ahead as the result of having to sweep a couple of villages that the tanks couldn't be bothered with. In the process, they had picked up a dozen American GIs who had basically been lost in the forest. "We will take them with us."

"They require watching," Messner said, disapproval apparent from the tone of his voice.

Bauer glanced over at the prisoners. He doubted that they would give anyone much trouble. They looked to be in even worse shape than his own men, if that was possible. The Americans lacked real winter gear, wrapping themselves in blankets and even burlap feed sacks to fend off the damp cold. Bauer supposed that he should let them eat something, but there wasn't time. The expressions on the Americans' faces ranged from blank to fearful. None of them looked defiant.

He turned back to Hauptmann Messner. "What else would you have me do with them, Sepp? Tell them to keep up. I want you at the rear to watch for stragglers."

Of course, he knew very well that Messner was hoping that his commanding officer would order him to shoot the prisoners. Bauer had no such plans. He wasn't sure how much of his reluctance to shoot the Americans came from a sense of simple decency toward enemy soldiers —and how much was inspired by the urge to annoy Messner.

There was also the fact that the rules of war had remained somewhat gentlemanly between the Germans and Americans. Sometimes there were regrettable incidents where prisoners on both sides had been shot, but those were isolated cases where passions had gotten out of hand or there was no expedient way to deal with prisoners other than to shoot them.

The truth was that the Allies *wanted* the Germans to feel comfortable surrendering—preferably in large numbers, as had happened at the Falaise Gap and other battles. The reasoning seemed to be that every German who surrendered was one less to fight.

In any case, these prisoners on the road weren't Russians. Bauer would have been glad to shoot any Russians himself.

Through gritted teeth, Messner replied, "As you wish, Herr Obersturmbannführer. I will keep them moving."

The Hauptmann walked off, and Bauer sighed. Having a malcontent as second-in-command only added to his headaches.

He felt that Messner was too reckless by far, taking chances and gambling with the lives of their men. For his own part, Bauer had begun to wonder whether there was a chance, even a slim one, that life would go on after this nightmare of a war was over. That hope was a bit like the faint light you saw on the horizon that hinted at dawn, even while the dark of night still enveloped you.

Of course, survival seemed to be a coin toss at the moment. They still had this day to get through. And if they were lucky, the next one after that. In war, you couldn't think too far ahead.

Bauer hadn't given up—he was a good German, after all—but he believed that only a fool could think that Germany would emerge triumphant after the beating they were now taking on two fronts. The way that Bauer saw it, the best option for Germany was some sort of conditional surrender or treaty. He suspected that the window was closing for any kind of negotiated peace, but if this battle in the Ardennes was successful, they still might get at least that.

Hauptmann Messner was one of those fools who still believed that total victory was possible.

Soon Messner was shouting at the prisoners to get on their feet. The unit began to move up the road.

From his maps, Bauer knew that their destination, the village of Bastogne, still lay several miles ahead. The crossroads town was essential to capture. The heavy tanks couldn't manage the narrow roads through the hills, so the only way forward was through the town. Bauer had been told that, unfortunately for the Germans, the 101st Airborne and other units were putting up a stiff resistance. It would be vital for Bauer's men to catch up with the panzers to create a more effective attack force.

With the panzers out of sight, the only vehicles that Bauer had at his disposal were a couple of Kübelwagen. Small but sturdy, these vehicles, manufactured in the tens of thousands by Volkswagen, managed to traverse the hilly roads no matter how much mud and slush the winter threw at them.

The Kübelwagen were currently serving as their ambulances, and Bauer had long since given up his seat to make room for the wounded and the worst cases of frostbite. The second Kübelwagen had been Messner's, and it had taken a direct order for the Hauptmann to give up his vehicle—and then only reluctantly. Messner made the point that Germans who allowed themselves to get frostbite were no different from men who shot themselves in the foot to avoid duty.

"Duly noted, Messner," Bauer had said, his tone far from patient. "But you need to get out and walk."

Bauer was not ready to go so far as classifying frostbite cases as dereliction of duty. Nonetheless, he was not happy about the frostbite—those men should have known better than to let their feet get wet. In this cold, wet feet were as effective as a bullet in neutralizing a soldier. He made sure that the sergeants reminded the newer men to change their wool socks whenever they could.

Bauer now had little choice but to plod along at the head of his men. He even carried a rifle taken from one of the wounded.

They left the open ground and moved back into the forest. As the trees closed in around them, Bauer felt a sense of uneasiness. He'd been told that there shouldn't be any Allied troops between here and Bastogne, but who really knew?

Something flickered just at the corner of his vision. He turned that way, rifle at the ready, but there was nothing to see. Perhaps it had been some winter bird or foraging animal? Looking at the barren trees, he couldn't help but think that they resembled the rib bones of the dead he had seen piled up in Russia.

He recalled hearing stories about the old days and how there had once been wolves roaming these woods, preying on the local peasants during the coldest months. Men went off to cut wood and did not return. Children went to bring the cows home and disappeared.

The wolves grew fatter.

Stories to scare children, not soldiers.

He shook his head and turned his attention back to the road.

He set a brisk pace, and after an hour his men were strung out along the road despite the efforts of the sergeants and corporals to keep everyone moving. He had lost sight of the end of the column around a bend in the gloomy road.

Bauer was about to call another halt so the column could regroup when he heard a burst of automatic weapon fire toward the rear.

His first thought was that the Americans had found them after all. He shouted orders for the men to get off the road, but it was unnecessary. His men knew what to do. They were already sprinting into the underbrush, getting behind trees, pointing their weapons toward the rear.

Bauer strained to see what was happening, but whatever was going on back there was hidden from sight. The flurry of gunfire was followed by a series of pistol shots, spaced apart like the ellipses at the end of a sentence.

It didn't sound like an attack, because there was no return fire. He had been in this war long enough to know the different sound that American weapons made, and he had heard only what sounded like German weapons. Then he remembered that Messner was back there bringing up the rear and shepherding the prisoners.

The prisoners, he thought. *He's gone and done it, damn him.*

Frustrated by the fact that his view was blocked, and with a growing sense of anger, Bauer jogged back along the column. Of course, the rest of his men were now on edge and watching the woods nervously.

When he finally reached the rear, he saw the curtain closing on the massacre.

Most of the prisoners lay dead in the snow. Hauptmann Messner walked among the bodies like he was out for a stroll, inspecting the cabbages in his garden with delight. When he came to a prisoner who was still moving, a cabbage ripe for the picking, Messner paused and shot the American in the back of the head with his pistol. The sharp crack echoed across the snow-covered hills.

Messner wasn't the only one with unfinished business. Miraculously, one of the prisoners seemed to have gotten away. Bauer could see him in the distance, running through the trees. He was limping badly and probably wounded, but he had somehow managed to get away from the road.

But he would not escape. One of his men raised a rifle equipped with a telescopic sight. *That would be Dietzel,* he thought, one of his Jaeger, or scouts, who had a reputation as a crack shot.

Bauer found himself holding his breath as the Jaeger took aim, even surprising himself by willing the prisoner to run deeper into the trees. Yes, the man was an enemy soldier, but he had so much fight in him.

Then the rifle fired, and the fleeing man tumbled into the snow and did not move again.

Bauer stood alone in the abrupt silence, clenching and unclenching his fists. He had the odd sense that the wintry hills and trees were somehow looking on in disapproval.

Hauptmann Messner walked toward him, brandishing a happy smile. Behind Messner came two soldiers. One was Obergefreiter Gerhard Dietzel, holding his sniper rifle, and the other man carried an automatic weapon. He recognized him as a soldier named Gettinger. Both were men who had found the Hauptmann's favor and had become quite loyal to him. In their sullen eyes, Bauer saw mirrored Messner's disapproval of their commander.

Over the Hauptmann's shoulder, Bauer could see the prisoners' bodies sprawled at the edge of the road. Several soldiers had come from the front of the column to see what all the shooting was about.

"They could not keep up, Herr Obersturmbannführer," Messner said. Even Messner seemed to hear the lie in his voice, because he shrugged dismissively.

"Is that so?" Bauer fought down the anger that he felt because he did not want to shout at his second-in-command in front of the men. It was not the prisoners that Bauer cared about so much as the fact that Messner had intentionally thumbed his nose at Bauer's orders.

Dieser Hurensohn. That son of a bitch.

Bauer took a deep breath to calm himself.

"For pity's sake, Messner. What have you done?"

Like a lawyer, Messner laid out his case. "The prisoners were slowing our advance, perhaps intentionally. Some of them even tried to get away into the forest." He turned to the soldier with the sniper rifle. "Isn't that so, Dietzel?"

"Yes, sir."

"What's done is done," Bauer said. "Just make sure that there are no survivors."

"There were none. I think you saw me make sure of it." By way of emphasis, Messner patted the pistol at his belt. Then he commenced to pull his black leather gloves back on.

"Good. Because if the Americans find out what you have done, none of us will survive, either, if we are captured. No German will."

Bauer turned away, his one consolation being the look of realization crossing Messner's face.

A die had been cast; a line had been crossed.

Also, none of them knew it yet, but Messner had been wrong about killing all the prisoners.

There had been one survivor.

Hidden under the corpse of one of his buddies, a GI named Charlie Knuth held himself very still to avoid receiving a coup de grâce at the hands of the German officer. He held his breath until his lungs felt ready to burst, although he wanted to cry out in pain from the bullets that had torn through his body. Lucky for him, before the German officer had made a closer inspection, attention had turned to the GI trying to escape through the woods.

The man would survive to tell the bloody tale of what had happened on that road through the forest.

And there would be hell to pay.

CHAPTER THREE

On the morning of December 19, General Dwight D. Eisenhower, officially the Supreme Allied Commander in the European Theater but known to the common soldier and the public simply as Ike, summoned his command staff to Verdun.

His mood and those of his high-ranking officers were just as gloomy as the surroundings. The town was gray and drab, the streets filled with slush, offering little sign that it was the Christmas season. There were a few wreaths and swags of greenery tied with ribbon, but they appeared dried out by the winter wind, the ribbons faded.

He had made his temporary headquarters in that French town, in an old stone barracks that dated to at least the seventeenth century. Ivy clung to the mortar along with an air of history repeating itself.

After all, it was near this spot that one of the bloodiest battles of World War I had taken place against German forces, resulting in more than three hundred thousand men killed on both sides. Some of his generals had been young officers back then. Now, twenty-eight years later, the Germans had once again upset the applecart by refusing to be beaten and launching an offensive through the rugged Ardennes region.

The German offensive had taken everyone by surprise. Since

coming ashore on June 6, 1944, Allied forces had been making mostly steady progress against the Germans, pushing them across France and back toward their fatherland. There had even been optimistic predictions that the war would be over by Christmas. However, Hitler's offensive had blindsided the Allies.

The inability to detect any signs of the German plan was a complete failure of military intelligence and downright embarrassing to Eisenhower. The intelligence failure was partly due to the overall assumption that the Germans were on the ropes and incapable of an offensive operation. The complete secrecy with which Hitler's generals had carried out their plan put it on par with the secrecy surrounding the D-Day invasion itself.

To make matters worse, there were rumors flying that none other than Otto Skorzeny, the daring SS commando, had hatched a plan to kidnap or kill Eisenhower. Perhaps the rumor was far-fetched, but it wouldn't have been the first time that the Nazis had attempted something so outlandish. Consequently, Ike had been slinking around Verdun, coming and going through side doors, while a double rode around in his staff car.

To say that Ike wasn't happy might have been an understatement.

"Do you think we can get some fresh coffee around here?" he grumped.

"Right away, sir," replied no less than a full-bird colonel, who went hurrying out of the meeting room to fetch a fresh pot of coffee.

Ike had looked like hell since the planning for D-Day began, thanks to the stress that weighed upon his shoulders and a lack of sleep. The bad news of the last few hours hadn't done much to improve his condition.

It also didn't help that the fifty-four-year-old survived mainly on a diet of cigarettes, black coffee, hot dogs, and two fingers of bourbon nightly. He preferred not to waste time on food and was well aware that his troops in the field didn't eat any better.

A haze of stale cigarette smoke already filled the room. A couple of the British officers smoked pipes, which only added to the fug, along with the smell of wool uniforms, damp from the rain and releasing the smell of stale perspiration.

The bare stone walls and small windows set deep within them did little to add any sense of warmth to the room, heated by a rusty potbelly stove that burned damp chunks of scrap lumber and struggled to throw off any real heat. Easels displaying maps had been set up around the perimeter of the room, though that was somewhat unnecessary, considering that most of the men here spent several hours daily studying maps and could have drawn these from memory. The tobacco smoke hugging the ceiling continued to thicken like an approaching storm front.

Outside the room, the guard had been doubled as a precaution, with at least two burly MPs standing beside each doorway. They were doing a thorough job of questioning anyone who wasn't wearing a general's stars.

Present for the meeting were all the key players in Allied military operations, including Air Marshal Arthur Tedder, General Omar Bradley, General George Patton, Lieutenant General Jacob Devers, and Field Marshal Montgomery's deputy, Freddie de Guingand. Conspicuously absent was Montgomery himself, who preferred not to meet personally with those he deemed of lower rank—such as Eisenhower. Nonetheless, it was Eisenhower who was in charge—and who would be blamed if the German offensive proved successful.

Accompanying these men were several staff members. Most prominent among them was the recently promoted Lieutenant General Walter Bedell Smith, who served as Eisenhower's chief of staff. He was known to all by his nickname, Beetle, which not only was a play on his actual name, but which also reflected his hard-shelled personality. With so many demands for the general's time and attention, he guarded access to the busy general like an armor-plated sentry.

On smaller matters that weren't worthy of Eisenhower's scrutiny, his decisions carried all the weight of the Supreme Allied Commander. Consequently, he was not a man to be trifled with. This morning he looked even more worried than usual, which for Beetle Smith was definitely saying something.

The room filled with high-ranking officers was unusually quiet. The matter of the German counteroffensive was serious business. They all watched Ike expectantly.

It was clear that the Supreme Allied Commander was disgruntled. To start with, Ike disliked the name that the press had given this defensive fight, having dubbed it the Battle of the Bulge. It was an apt description, considering that on the map, the German offensive had created a deep bubble through the Allied lines.

However, Ike thought that "Battle of the Bulge" sounded like a diet plan or, worse yet, a hernia repair operation.

Ike was determined not to turn this meeting into a blame game. He looked around at the room filled with anxious officers. However it had come about, they now had to deal with the situation.

The colonel returned with the coffee, and Ike nodded his thanks.

"Gentlemen, let's get started. We have some business to discuss," he said. He nodded toward a young officer, who hurried to close the double doors to the meeting room. "The Germans are apparently headed for Antwerp. Maybe even back to Paris, if they can. The question is, What are we going to do about it?"

"I say we should open the gate and let them come all the way in," Patton said, jumping right into the fray. Out of all the officers in the room, he was the most immaculately dressed, from his tailored tunic right down to his gleaming riding boots. He somehow managed to have more stars on his uniform than the rest of the generals combined. "Once the Germans are really spread out, we hit them with a meat grinder. I'll be happy to work the handle."

For emphasis, he used his right hand to slowly make a cranking motion, showing how he would turn those panzer divisions into sausage.

"That's not going to happen, George," Ike said. He agreed that letting the Germans get strung out and then pulverizing them wasn't a bad military strategy, but the American public might not see it that way. "We can't let the Germans get that far. The question is, How do we stop them, right now?"

"If the weather wasn't so bad, our planes wouldn't be grounded, and this would be a different story," an officer pointed out.

"We can wish all we want to, but that doesn't change the fact that it's foggy, snowy, and goddamn cold," Patton said. He snorted gruffly.

"Our planes can't fly. My tanks don't give a damn what the weather is like."

Ike fixed Patton with a baleful glare. He knew that he should have welcomed Patton's can-do attitude—it was what won wars. The trouble was that, coming from Patton, such words always sounded more like a taunt—as if everybody else had their heads up their asses and it was up to Patton to save the day.

Ike poured more coffee to allow himself a moment to rein in his temper and gather his thoughts.

If there was one general who had been a source of constant headaches for Ike, it was Patton. The problem was that Patton had a knack for making rude comments in speeches, bragging, and otherwise making himself unloved by the rest of the officers' club. Only Montgomery's ego was possibly bigger, but at least Montgomery conducted himself like a gentleman.

For the most part, the show that Patton put on resonated with the average soldier. He was like the army's equivalent of Admiral Halsey, who was always making spirited comments. He meant them too. There was no general with more of a fighting spirit than Patton. But as was typical, Patton often went too far.

Nearly the final nail in Patton's career coffin had come just a few months before, when he had slapped young soldiers hospitalized for shell shock and called them cowards. The incidents had incensed Eisenhower, and he had briefly sidelined Patton.

Then again, Patton was just the man you needed in a fight. And a fight was what they now had on their hands.

Perhaps Patton's hour had finally arrived.

Ike sighed. "George, how long will it take you to get your tanks into action against these panzers?"

"I can have them killing Krauts the morning after tomorrow," he said.

The other generals stared. Pivoting the entire Third Army that Patton commanded seemed like an impossible task. What they didn't know yet was that Patton had already set the wheels in motion, issuing orders before he had even left for this meeting. He had bet that Ike would be desperate for help and so had planned ahead, unwilling to waste precious hours.

"Don't be fatuous, George."

"Nothing of the kind," Patton said. "Hell, it's not really the Boche that worry me. I'm more concerned about this snow and fog. That's the real enemy."

Quickly, Patton revealed his plan to send his troops and tanks to turn back the Germans. He spoke with such confidence that he seemed to consider the outcome to be a foregone conclusion.

As exasperating as Patton could be, it was a reminder of the man's talents.

Soon after that the meeting broke up. There were other details to be set into motion, but in the end, Patton's men would provide a key piece of the plan to fight back against the Germans.

Ike might not have cared much for the name—Battle of the Bulge—but more than anything else, he didn't want anyone to call it a German victory.

* * *

IKE HAD good reason to be worried.

Germany's bold Operation Christrose was coming closer to success as the Germans made a move to reach Antwerp and deliver a setback to the Allied advance. The port city of Antwerp remained vital to Allied supply lines. Fortunately for the Allies, the weather that enabled the Germans to attack without fear of retaliation from the air was a double-edged sword.

In addition to the winter weather wreaking havoc with German logistics, the poor roads and staunch resistance by US forces had slowed Hitler's plans. However, the advance had not been entirely thwarted. There was a narrow window of opportunity before either the skies cleared or the Allies could respond in greater force.

While the prong of the German advance led by Kampfgruppe Friel was running into trouble, it didn't mean that the Germans had been defeated or turned back everywhere. Case in point was the crossroads town of

Bastogne. The German advance couldn't go around it because there weren't any roads in the countryside big enough to support the passage of their armor. No, the Germans must go *through* Bastogne. What they had not counted on was stubborn resistance by the beleaguered forces there.

Reinforcements had arrived in the form of the 101st Airborne. They were putting up a good fight, but they didn't have any armor of their own. The battle for Bastogne had heated up as the Germans threw everything they had at it. Now US armor and personnel were rushing toward the fight—Cole and the men in the trucks included.

* * *

COLE'S EYES roved across the dark stretches of forest they rolled past. All that he could see were trees and more trees across low rolling hills carpeted with snow. It was the sort of landscape that Cole was used to from the mountains back home. However, the deep shadows among the trees gave the forest a sinister feel. Lucky for the convoy, they had not encountered any other Germans since the skirmish in which the Krauts had blown up one of the trucks with a Panzerfaust.

Nonetheless, he knew all too well that danger might lurk around the next curve in the road.

As a reminder of that, over the noise of the truck motor could be heard the occasional chatter of a machine gun in the distant hills and the deep thump of artillery. As the miles passed, the sounds gradually grew louder, indicating that they were headed toward the action.

"You'd think what we did at La Gleize would have been enough," Vaccaro grumped. "Isn't it someone else's turn?"

"Hell now, city boy. You know they're just sending us because they know we'll get the job done."

Still, Cole had to agree that they had already done their part, and then some, in the fighting around La Gleize.

At that village, Cole and the other members of his sniper squad had helped turn back the German panzer unit that had reached La Gleize before running out of fuel and ammo. The German commander Friel and nearly eight hundred of his men in Kampfgruppe Friel had escaped back toward Germany.

By some measures, allowing so many experienced SS troops to escape and fight again another day seemed like a disaster. The Germans had used a clever ruse of lighting cooking fires and giving the appearance of holding their position, but had slipped away in the hours before daylight.

You had to hand it to the Krauts for pulling that one off, he thought.

Had allowing the Germans to escape been a failure? Cole didn't feel that way, because the truth was that the American forces had managed to end the advance of Kampfgruppe Friel. Also, the Germans had been forced to abandon their tanks and support vehicles—they'd nearly all been out of fuel, anyway.

Then again, not all the Germans had escaped. Cole had set a trap for the German sniper known as Das Gespenst and had caught him in the forest outside La Gleize. Das Gespenst had been attached to Kampfgruppe Friel, helping them cut a swath of destruction as the Germans advanced.

But no more.

Das Gespenst kaput.

Cole smiled at the thought, cold lips curling back from his teeth in a feral grin. The smile did not reach his pale eyes, which were thoughtful, remembering the moment when, with a single bullet, he had finally ended a feud that had begun on the bloody beaches of Normandy.

There was no telling how many Americans Das Gespenst had targeted in his crosshairs, but it had certainly been a terrible toll. The German sniper had finally been paid off in American lead.

Although one prong of the advance had been blunted, the Germans were far from done. They were still pushing hard at Bastogne. The American holdouts were blocking their advance but hanging on by the skin of their teeth. Whatever reinforcements could be rounded up were being rushed toward Bastogne before the Germans could break through.

Rushing was more like wishful thinking, considering the slow pace of the truck making its way through the muck and mire, the slush. The truck drivers and crew were the real heroes today, hunting for the best traction on roads that were little more than muddy tracks.

Some of the men jammed into the back stood up and stomped

their feet from time to time to stay warm. Others sat motionless, hugging themselves, afraid to move and let any heat escape from their ragged clothes. It was hard to say which method worked best.

Cole figured that the best strategy was to ignore the cold. He had to admit that wasn't working so far.

He turned to Vaccaro, who was hunkered down on the bench beside him, and said, "Ain't you glad that you didn't stay in that hospital? Hell, you'd be under a warm blanket right now, drinking hot soup. You wouldn't know what to do with yourself."

Vaccaro snorted. "Don't remind me. At least we're better off than those poor bastards at Bastogne. I heard the Krauts bombed the hell out of them."

The truth was, Vaccaro looked more than a little worse for wear, which was understandable, considering that he'd been wounded during the fight at La Gleize. By any sensible measure, Vaccaro should have remained in the makeshift hospital in a church. But like many of the walking wounded, Vaccaro had decided that he wasn't going to sit this fight out.

Their recent skirmish on the road hadn't helped. But Vaccaro wasn't about to give up.

There was still too much at stake, and the truth was, every American soldier now had a burning hatred against the Krauts for the Malmedy massacre, where nearly eighty US troops, held as prisoners of war by Kampfgruppe Friel, had been murdered in cold blood. At La Gleize, they had also seen an innocent young woman gunned down as she tried to help the wounded. For many GIs, the fight now felt personal.

It certainly did for Cole.

As he watched the shadows lengthen among the trees and the forest grow darker, the thought crossed his mind that it was one helluva way to spend Christmas Eve.

* * *

THEY WEREN'T the only ones experiencing a miserable holiday. In the embattled town of Bastogne, the commanding officer, General McAuliffe, had issued the following statement to his men, written out on a typewriter that typed unevenly and copied onto thin paper using a mimeograph machine that needed more ink. The results weren't pretty, but the message warmed the hearts of the defenders.

December 24, 1944

Merry Christmas! What's merry about all this, you ask? We're fighting—it's cold—we aren't home. All true, but what has the proud Eagle Division accomplished with its worthy comrades? Just this: We have stopped cold everything that has been thrown at us from the North, East, South, and West.

In his own words, the general related the soon-to-be-famous story of how he had rejected German demands to surrender. It was a story that had grown and spread among the beleaguered troops in Bastogne, giving them a sense of pride at their ornery general. Just when the situation had been at its bleakest, the Germans had attempted to get the American defenders to surrender. Under a flag of truce, a German envoy had delivered the offer to General McCauliffe.

McCauliffe's reply had been a single word: "Nuts!"

The response left the Germans scratching their heads. They didn't understand what the unfamiliar term meant. Once they figured out that the American general was basically thumbing his nose at them, the firing recommenced. From the hills and forests surrounding Bastogne, more German shells fell like the snow.

CHAPTER FOUR

THE BOLD STRIKE by Germany had originated in the mind of Adolf Hitler and had been a closely held secret, even as he'd gathered troops, trucks, tanks, and planes all through the autumn of 1944, moving them into position using the mental chessboard of his mind. When German troops finally surged into the Ardennes, it was a single-minded projection of Hitler's will.

He had unveiled the plan at his secret lair, called Adlerhorst, German for "Eagle's Aerie." This hideout was located near Koblenz, a town on the Rhine riverfront, roughly fifty miles from the Belgian border.

Der Führer had summoned dozens of generals and other key officers there to reveal his plans. Under cover of darkness, in a cold rain, they had arrived, not knowing what to expect. Among these officers was Obersturmbannführer Ingo Bauer, a veteran of the monthslong struggle to halt the Allied push across Europe. Bauer spotted General Manteuffel and the chillingly blunt Sepp Dietrich, even Field Marshal Gerd von Rundstedt, and felt out of place in such exalted company.

What in the world was he doing here?

Some officers, Bauer included, half expected to be shot. There was some precedent for that.

After all, it had been only six months before that Claus von Stauffenberg had tried to assassinate Der Führer by detonating a briefcase filled with explosives during a meeting. Hitler had survived and launched a savage purge of anyone even slightly connected with the plot. Rumors spread of basements with meat hooks, or buckets of water and electrical wires, as the Gestapo and SS dealt with the traitors.

The assembled officers were informed rather brusquely that they would soon be addressed by Der Führer himself.

The secrecy surrounding the meeting and the security efforts did little to alleviate their fears. They were relieved of their briefcases and any sidearms. The officers were then brought to a large room and seated by rank. And yet they were treated more like prisoners than Germany's command staff.

Young SS guards with MP 40 submachine guns stood around the edges of the room, watching the officers with open disdain, as if hoping for some excuse to pull the trigger. They seemed to view the gathered officer corps not with respect, but with disgust for a group of balding fat men who seemed intent on losing the war.

Perhaps their thinking mirrored that of Der Führer.

"No one in the audience dared move or even take his handkerchief out of his pocket," one general later recalled.

Bauer held himself stiffly at attention in his chair, scarcely breathing. Like the others, he hadn't ruled out the possibility of mass execution.

However, he found himself excited about seeing Hitler. Although he was tired of the war and wondered how it could possibly go well for Germany in the end, he had always found the German leader inspiring.

Then a side door opened and the leader of the Third Reich appeared.

A barely audible collective gasp filled the room.

Hitler's appearance shocked them. He looked stooped, pallid, and he dragged one foot as he walked. Even his voice was low and hesitant. It was hard to believe that this was the same man who had rallied the German people and enthralled millions with his energy. Bauer had to admit that he had fallen under Hitler's spell as much as anyone.

However, each military loss that Nazi Germany had suffered in the last few months must have been like a body blow against its supreme leader.

Only when he warmed to his subject and the possibility of victory did some of his old fire and confidence return.

Before the spellbound—and captive—audience, Hitler revealed his plan. He had been working to gather these forces since September. It was to be a multipronged effort.

Several divisions of troops that included the Second SS Panzer Division Das Reich and Volksgrenadier divisions, more than one hundred transport planes carrying paratroopers, hundreds of panzers, nearly two thousand heavy artillery guns, mortars, and V-1 rockets.

Under the direction of Otto Skorzeny, specially trained infiltrators who spoke English and wore American uniforms would wreak havoc behind enemy lines. These men were taking a huge chance, knowing that they would be shot as spies if captured.

At least a thousand of the Luftwaffe's remaining operational bombers and fighters would take to the air, including a handful of the new Messerschmitt 262 jet fighters that crossed the skies at 525 miles per hour. Nothing that the Allies had could keep up with them.

Hitler was gambling everything.

But even Hitler wasn't so mad that he didn't grasp the enormity of the gamble he was making.

"You must know that we are besieged," he said bitterly. "Surrounded on all sides by our enemies. The forces of the Russian dogs snarl at us from the East. Here against die Alliierten we have our best chance of success, or at least of driving a wedge between our enemies. We must exploit their natural suspicions and jealousies."

Here Der Führer paused. He seemed to gather himself for what he was about to say.

Eventually he continued: "It will not be possible to assemble such a force again. If we should fail here, there will be dark days ahead."

Hitler was not someone who ever wanted to speak about the possibility of defeat. To hear Der Führer make this admission was incredible.

All that the stunned officers could do was listen—and think of a thousand reasons the plan would fail. Bauer could certainly think of a few.

Hitler did not ask for questions, and no one dared to ask any.

Once Der Führer had finished, there was an opportunity for the officers to filter past him for a quick handshake and a few words of encouragement. They had seen a glimpse of their old leader, but given his physical condition, and the hard fight ahead that they all faced on the battlefield, it was hard not to feel as if this might be the last time they saw their leader, or vice versa.

Bauer had never met Hitler in person. Normally Bauer didn't lack for confidence, but in Hitler's presence he found that all he could manage was to stammer, "Mein Führer."

Nonetheless, he felt Der Führer take full notice of him, even if it was for the briefest instant. It was like stepping from a dark room into the full glare of the sun. Then Hitler's attention turned to the next man. A little shaken, Bauer moved on.

Some of the bolder officers even took the opportunity to lobby for changes to the plan, but Hitler would not hear of it. He simply brushed off these concerns. With thoughts in the backs of their minds of those rumored cellars where the Gestapo waited with meat hooks on which to hang troublemakers, the generals were in no position to argue.

Good career soldiers tended to be pragmatists. They weighed the odds. The odds of defying Hitler and surviving were not very good.

Although Bauer could not have known it, the situation was completely different from the one at Allied headquarters, where some debate was expected, even if Eisenhower ultimately made the decisions. Even from the top, FDR and Churchill might cajole, but they did not dictate—they delegated.

"The reasoning is sound enough," one general confided to another on the ride back. Bauer overheard him, although the general was keeping his voice low so the driver couldn't eavesdrop. Gestapo spies were everywhere. "We might just manage to drive a wedge between the Allies."

"Yes," the other general agreed. "And perhaps more time will enable us to deploy our new weapons and turn the tide. But the Ardennes? In wintertime?"

His companion just shook his head. Curiously, he then quoted from a poem called "Charge of the Light Brigade," written by an Englishman, Lord Tennyson. It was a poem about bravery and duty in the Crimean War, even in the face of a fatal military blunder.

"Theirs not to make reply,

"Theirs not to reason why,

"Theirs but to do and die."

Bauer didn't say anything, but he thought that summed up the situation perfectly.

Just four days after that mysterious and fateful meeting, the attack began.

* * *

THE SHEER SCOPE and fury of the attack immediately put American forces in disarray.

There was good reason for that. First, the Ardennes region was thinly defended, not seen as a priority. The mountainous terrain seemed like all the defense that was needed.

To that end, the sector was jokingly called both a nursery and an old folks' home. It served as a training ground for new units before facing the enemy. On the other hand, several units that had been worn out in the long months of fighting across Europe had been sent here for rest and relaxation. The theory was that they could expect plenty of both.

A bonus was that at its best, the snowy villages of the region looked picture perfect as winter weather arrived. Here and there, hidden châteaus and even crumbling castles were tucked into the valleys. There wasn't much to do except sleep, eat, and admire the scenery.

That was just fine with the weary GIs.

From the German perspective, the choice of the Ardennes region had as many pros as cons. The Germans knew well enough that the Ardennes region was only lightly defended. But there were good reasons for that.

There were no highways that ran directly from Germany into Belgium. The hilly terrain created a natural barrier. Advancing troops would be forced to use the narrow mountain roads that linked one town to another, hopscotching from one village to the next. Along the way, it would be necessary to cross mountain streams spanned by small bridges.

None of it was ideal, especially for moving heavy tanks, including the new sixty-ton Tigers. But once free of that terrain, upon crossing the Meuse River, it would be nothing short of a glorious race to Antwerp across wide-open territory.

* * *

THE ATTACK BEGAN before dawn on December 14, with a massive artillery barrage and German advance. Taken by surprise, the thinly spaced and unprepared American defenders were quickly overwhelmed. The roads soon became choked with retreating soldiers, moving away from the German advance at a snail's pace. The thin frozen crust on the roads quickly turned to mud due to the sheer number of boots and vehicles. The mud made the retreat even more of a slog.

Many of the demoralized soldiers lacked winter gear, not even coats or gloves, and several didn't carry weapons. It was not a force that was ready to turn and fight. They were just concerned with placing one foot in front of the other, putting as much distance as possible between themselves and the Krauts.

Retreat was a mindset, or possibly a disease. Once it took hold, it spread like a fever. Some who caught it became close to panic. It took leadership to turn that around, and in the confusion caused by the German attack, leadership was lacking.

Corporal Brock Sumner was among those caught up in the rout, not that he was happy about it. Brock was a big man who used his size to bully others. He was only a corporal, but he lorded it over mere privates like he was a general.

"Last time I checked, we were here to fight the Krauts, not run from them," he grumbled, looking around at the long lines of retreating soldiers. He saw lots of scared faces, although some were just dead tired. He sure as hell didn't like to think of himself that way.

"Nobody seems interested in that," the soldier slogging along next to him pointed out. That man's name was Lavern Barr, but naturally everyone called him Vern.

"I just wish to hell one of these so-called officers would actually take charge," Brock said. "We're supposed to fight, ain't we?"

"I don't think most of these fellas have got much fight in them," Vern pointed out.

Brock looked around again at the sea of retreating soldiers, the line of troops stretching in front of him and also behind as far as he could see.

"Yeah, but with this many guys we ought to be able to knock the hell out of the Krauts, if we could just turn around and fight," Brock said. "We are sure as hell going the wrong direction."

In many ways, Brock was simply echoing his training. Army philosophy was to advance. Maybe it was football thinking. The best defense was a good offense.

Advancing sure as hell beat running, as far as Brock was concerned.

Up ahead he could see commotion. There was a tank—actually, a line of three tanks—plowing right up the middle of the road. The Sherman tanks were forcing the retreating soldiers into the ditches. Jeeps, trucks, whatever else was in their way, were also being forced off the road. A handful of support infantry traveled in the wake of the tanks.

"What's going on?" Vern had seen it too.

"Looks to me like somebody has finally got the right idea," Brock said. "They're moving toward the fight, not away from it."

The tanks traveling against the current of the retreating column were causing more than a little consternation. A few arguments broke out, but nobody was going to win an argument against a Sherman tank. Any truck or jeep that refused to move out of the way found itself nudged into the ditch.

The bully in Brock liked that.

Off to one side, avoiding the mess on the road, a jeep was driving across the field, heading toward them. Brock could see an officer in the passenger seat. Suddenly the jeep came to a stop, close enough that Brock could hear a major shouting orders to the advancing tank unit.

"Take no orders from anyone who's not Seventh Armored!" the major shouted. "I don't care if they've got stars on their collar. If anybody gets in the way, run them over!"

As the Sherman tanks approached, Brock made up his mind. He gathered up his squad and told them, "Enough of this retreating shit. We're hitching a ride with these tanks."

If the men in the squad disagreed, they knew better than to argue.

The tanks were forced to move slowly, but at least they were moving in the right direction. Their pace was slow enough for Brock and his men to climb aboard. In the hatch, the tank commander made it clear in no uncertain terms that he didn't want Brock bumming a ride.

"Corporal, get the hell off my tank!"

"We're going with you. We're in this war to fight," Brock shouted over the revving engine. "We're sure as hell not here to run!"

The tank commander gave him a nod, then grinned. "In that case, welcome to the Seventh Armored. Now hang on!"

CHAPTER FIVE

DARKNESS ENABLED the convoy of reinforcements to slip past the Germans and get into Bastogne. For Cole and the other snipers, it was a relief to finally get off the truck.

"I hope I never have to ride on a truck again," Vaccaro groaned. He stretched his arms over his head and walked stiffly away from the vehicle. "That thing bounced around so much that my legs hurt, my spine hurts. Hell, even my teeth hurt. As for my ass, it's gonna be sore for a week."

"At least we were better off than those poor bastards who had to ride in the jeep," Cole said. "They couldn't even grab some sleep because they had to hang on for dear life the whole way."

Lieutenant Mulholland gathered the men, taking charge of the group that had ridden up in the truck, not just the snipers. "Listen up, we're going to bed down in one of the buildings and get our orders in the morning. Meanwhile, I'll see if I can find us some hot chow."

They would be spending the night in the cellar of an old furniture shop. In the dim light of an oil lamp, they descended well-worn wooden stairs, brushing against ancient stone walls that exuded dampness. There was no heat, but they were out of the wind. More importantly, the cellar provided shelter from the shells that the enemy occasionally lobbed into the town just to keep anyone from getting a good night's sleep.

The electricity had long since gone out, and the only light came from candles and lanterns. A few lucky residents still had enough coal to heat their homes, but others were forced to huddle under blankets or put on all their sweaters to fend off the cold. Families sheltered in basements between bombings, praying that this nightmare would end sooner rather than later. Food and clean drinking water were getting scarce.

Cole took off the sheet that he had been using as improvised camouflage. It had once been a blinding white but was now soiled, spotted with mud and blood. He spread his blankets on the hard-packed dirt floor of the cellar, with Vaccaro and the kid doing the same.

"To be honest, it's not much of a place to bed down," Vaccaro said.

"I've slept in worse," Cole said. The dirt-floored cellar reminded him of how he had slept under the porch back home when his pa was on a bender. "We all have."

"I guess it does beat a foxhole."

Cole stood up and stretched his stiff arms and legs. Vaccaro wasn't the only one who felt sore right down to his bones. It had been a miserable trip, made worse by the constant threat of attack. At least here in the cellar he felt as if he could finally let his guard down, no longer having to worry about being ambushed by Germans hiding in the woods beside the road.

Exhausted though he was, Cole set to work cleaning his rifle. He slid the bolt out and ran a patch through the barrel to clear any fouling.

Watching him, Vaccaro just shook his head. He'd made no move to clean his own weapon. "Hillbilly, you must already have the cleanest rifle in Bastogne. They don't give out medals for that, you know. Why the hell don't you relax a little for once?"

"I don't need a medal," Cole said. "I just need to hit what I'm shooting at tomorrow."

"You haven't missed yet," Vaccaro said. "That's what they should give you a medal for."

"I'm just doing my job, city boy. Shooting things is what I do best."

Cole returned his attention to the rifle. He knew that his life depended on the Springfield functioning properly. It hadn't let him down yet. Vaccaro had told him to relax, but truth be told, cleaning the rifle *did* help him relax. He found going through the ritual of breaking down the rifle and cleaning it to be soothing, a way to clear his mind before turning in. Other men might dip into a paperback or read a letter from home for the umpteenth time if they weren't too exhausted, but that wasn't an option for Cole. Even if he could have read them, he never got any letters.

Vaccaro was just about the only one who knew the truth, which was that Cole was illiterate. Anybody else who figured it out and made fun of Cole for being a dumb cracker risked having his teeth bashed in.

He'd never had much of a chance for book learning back home in the mountains. The nearest school was miles away, and it always seemed like there were more chores to do. Besides, Cole had always preferred spending his free time wandering the woods and hills, usually with a rifle in his hands. The woods had provided the only education he'd needed.

He could read signs in the woods the way most men could read a newspaper. Words just looked like so much chicken scratch on the page to him. Hell, he could pick out the shapes and patterns of the constellations in the clear night sky better than he could make sense of a jumble of letters.

His parents hadn't put much stock in book learning, especially his pa. Cole's old man had been what folks called woodsy, in that he scrounged a living from the hills and forests of the Appalachians by cutting firewood, trapping, and making moonshine. Unfortunately, his pa had been a bit too fond of his own product. He was a mean drunk, and it was best to keep out of his way if you didn't want to get your head busted by his hard fists.

But when he was sober, Pa had been a good teacher in the ways of the mountains, showing Cole and his brothers how to shoot, hunt, and trap. Being a good shot meant the difference between meat for supper —or just some eggs and potatoes fried up in lard.

Cole reckoned that some of his best memories were of his pa—

along with some of his worst. He supposed that was like most people in that there was often good with the bad, like a tiny vein of silver running through rock.

Pa's hardscrabble occupations meant that the Cole family had been dirt poor, living in a shack near Gashey's Creek on land they couldn't rightly say they owned except by the fact of living upon it. They were just squatters when you got right down to it. A lot of mountain people didn't rightly know if they owned the land they lived on, but it was mostly land nobody much wanted anyhow.

The shack was hammered together out of discarded lumber with a roof made from scrap metal. That roof leaked when it rained, but Cole still missed the sound of the rain drumming on the sheet metal as he slept under the eaves with his brothers.

When he hadn't been hiding out from his drunken pa, sharing the space under the porch with the hound dogs.

This war had been an escape from that life.

He might return to it someday and build himself a little cabin all his own back in the mountains where he could live off the land.

Something to think about after the war.

If he survived.

* * *

Lieutenant Mulholland returned with hot grub. He'd found a pot full of what was purported to be stew. As the icing on the cake, he had somehow procured a couple of bottles of red wine—just enough for each man to have a cupful.

Mulholland didn't say how he had come into possession of the stew, and nobody asked. For all they knew, he had taken the stew and wine from one of the town residents at gunpoint. It might not have been Mulholland's style when he had come ashore on D-Day, but long months of combat had hardened the young officer.

The food cheered the men. It had been a long time since they had eaten anything other than cold rations.

"Now this is the way to fight a war," Vaccaro said, taking a healthy slug of wine.

But not everyone was as convinced.

"What is this?" somebody asked, peering with suspicion at a chunk of meat on his spoon. "I hope to hell this isn't horsemeat."

"Don't matter if it's horsemeat or filet mignon—it's warm, ain't it?"

Nobody could argue with that. The stew was quickly devoured. For the first time in several nights, the men went to bed with full bellies, warmed by the wine.

The distant thump of artillery lulled them to sleep.

* * *

By the gray light of a winter's morning, what they found when they ascended from the cellar was a battered town under siege. The slush-covered streets were churned up from the passage of vehicles and pockmarked with shell holes. Both the commercial and residential buildings were mostly covered in stucco, but the intermittent bombardment had opened spiderweb patterns of cracks across their facades.

Hasty defenses had been set up to stop the Germans if they did make it into town. Side streets were blocked with overturned wagons, dining room tables and sofas, even the carcasses of burned automobiles. Household goods and debris from bombed houses were strewn across the sidewalks. The overall effect was as if there had been a riot at a rummage sale where a fire had broken out.

"I'll be right back," Cole announced.

"Where you going?"

"Shopping."

Most of the houses were empty, their owners having fled—or else they were hiding in their basements. He picked a house a couple of blocks down from the main street, figuring it wouldn't have been as picked over. It was a neat and tidy two-story town house, its stucco exterior untouched so far by war. The only hint at the beating that the town had taken from the Germans was a wooden shutter hanging askew.

Although the house was modest by most standards, it seemed impossibly palatial compared to the shack where Cole had grown up.

Keeping his rifle ready, he pushed through the door, which was unlocked.

"Howdy?" he called.

There was no answer. The house had that air of stillness that comes from being empty. With the house left unheated, the winter cold and damp had crept in, making the interior feel even chillier than the outside air. Away from the noise and activity of the troops, he might have been the last person alive in this whole damn place.

He moved deeper into the house. Whoever had lived here must have left in a hurry. There were dishes still on the dining room table, set out on a cheerful tablecloth the bright yellow of buttercups. A couple of dirty dishes sat in the sink. On the counter stood a cup of tea with a skim of ice and curdled milk.

A framed picture of an old couple wearing fancy clothes stared down at him from the wall, their eyes disapproving.

Damn, if this don't feel spooky.

He was pretty sure he would find what he needed upstairs. He started up them, leading with the muzzle of his rifle. Each creak of the stair treads sounded as loud as a gunshot in the empty house.

He poked his head into a bedroom and saw just what he needed.

White bedsheets. He stripped them off and went to the next bedroom and did the same.

The bed had been neatly made as if whoever lived in this house had fully expected to be sleeping there. Cole hoped they would again—although they might wonder what had happened to their bedsheets.

He went down the stairs and back out of the house, then found Vaccaro and the other soldiers where he had left them. He gave a sheet to Vaccaro, then another to Hank and the lieutenant, and he kept one for himself.

"Fresh camouflage so we blend into the snow," he explained.

Vaccaro nodded his thanks, then nodded around at the battle-damaged town. "I'm surprised you found anything. This place is a damn mess," he said.

"You won't get no argument from me," Cole agreed. Bastogne looked like many towns they had passed through where war had taken its toll.

"Maybe we just ought to let the Krauts have it if they want it so bad," Vaccaro said. "It's sure as hell not much to fight over."

Lieutenant Mulholland had overheard. "I agree it's not much to look at right now, but you know what they say in the real estate business, right? Location, location, location. This town is smack-dab in the middle of the path that the Krauts need to take, and they can't go around it because there aren't any decent roads. The bottom line is that we're not letting the Krauts have it. Now everybody back on the trucks. We're being moved to where they need us."

Everyone groaned. Nobody was looking forward to another joyride in the back of an open truck.

"Lieutenant, can I ride up front with you?" Vaccaro asked. "I promise not to ask if we're there yet."

"Just shut up and get in the truck, Vaccaro."

Groaning and cursing at their stiff bodies, the men climbed back in. It was a rare infantryman who turned down a ride, but today was an exception.

As their truck drove through town, Cole spotted a skinny boy rooting through a garbage can for something to eat. The boy froze as the truck approached, caught in the act like a foraging raccoon. Cole fished in his haversack and tossed the kid a tin of rations. The boy pounced on it, then scurried away into the gloomy shadows of an alley.

"You might regret that later if they can't get any supplies in here," Vaccaro said.

"I'll take my chances. Besides, that was lima beans and ham," Cole replied, identifying one of the least favorite C rations. Having grown up hungry, Cole was never all that particular about what he ate, but even he had his limits.

"In that case, you should have thrown him two cans," Vaccaro said. "Better yet, throw one at the Krauts. It'll be just as deadly as a grenade —it just takes longer."

The squads of soldiers they passed looked muddy, cold, and exhausted. Then again, Cole figured that their own group of so-called reinforcements weren't in much better condition. They could hardly be called fresh troops.

The soldiers in Bastogne had been fighting for days on end without relief. In addition to the artillery fire, on Christmas Eve the Luftwaffe had made an appearance, bombing the town and even strafing it with machine-gun fire. It had been one hell of a Christmas present.

At the edge of the town, the truck stopped, and they all piled out once again, joining a larger group of soldiers assembling there. Some of the men had already been fighting in Bastogne for several days, and others, like Cole's own squad, had been rushed in to hold off the German attacks.

A veteran of the Bastogne fight wandered over to bum a cigarette. Those had become scarce. Supplies had been dropped from the air, but ammo and medical supplies had been the priority, not cigarettes.

"Here you go, buddy," Vaccaro said. "Take the rest of the pack. It looks like you could use it."

"Thanks," said the soldier, who was muddy and had a large patch of what looked like dried blood down the leg of his britches. Considering that he wasn't limping, it probably wasn't his own. He lit a cigarette and inhaled deeply. "Welcome to the circus," he said.

"It's quite a show," Vaccaro agreed.

"The Krauts won't quit and neither will we. Did you hear what we said to the Germans when they asked us to surrender?" the soldier asked.

He spoke with a pride as if he had personally negotiated with the Germans.

"From the looks of the place, I'm guessing you told them to forget it. The Krauts are still pounding away."

"You've got that right, buddy. General McAuliffe had one word for them, that's what. 'Nuts!'"

"Boy, are we glad to see you," another soldier said as the reinforcements jumped down from the truck. "It's about time you ladies got here."

"Yeah, yeah, we already licked our Germans south of here in La Gleize, so they sent us up here to help you handle your Krauts."

The soldier snorted. "Be my guest. The thing is, the Krauts don't like being handled by you or anything else."

"We'll see about that."

The soldier noticed their rifles. "Are you guys snipers? That's a good thing. The Krauts like to set up in the hills or in one of the church steeples outside town and pick us off. It's about time we had somebody who could shoot back."

"That's what we do."

As it turned out, their skills as snipers wouldn't be put to use right away.

Lieutenant Mulholland gathered the men to be addressed by a captain who seemed to be in charge.

"All right, I know you men are from different units and some of you just got here," the officer said. "I'm Captain Brown. We appreciate the help, believe me. Since this group is kind of cobbled together, you're now officially part of Team SNAFU."

Several of the men chuckled. SNAFU was a popular military acronym for "situation normal, all fouled up." The name Team SNAFU seemed to fit the circumstances. The unit had been thrown together by order of Colonel Roberts as a way to get every possible soldier into action. Meanwhile, the 101st Airborne anchored the defense of Bastogne.

"SNAFU sounds about right!" someone yelled.

"Listen up," the captain said, raising his arms to tamp things down. "The first job for Team SNAFU is to hold back the Germans who will be coming along this road soon enough. They want to get into Bastogne, and we're not going to let them, are we?"

"No, sir!" several men shouted in unison.

Cole had to hand it to Captain Brown. He was managing to rally tired and exhausted troops in time to face a new threat from the enemy.

"We're going to follow this road here and then get into the trees and dig in. Remember that if the Krauts get past us, this road takes them right into Bastogne. So don't let them by, goddammit."

That was it for the speech, and it was too damn cold to stand around listening to speeches anyway. Captain Brown climbed into a jeep that rushed up the road, and the infantrymen followed on foot.

CHAPTER SIX

HOLDING Bastogne against the Germans was a bit like the Dutch boy trying to stop all the holes in the dike by using his fingers. In this case, they might need their toes too.

"What I'd like to know is, Where the hell did all these Krauts come from?" Vaccaro wondered. "They're supposed to be beaten—or close to it. That's what everybody says, anyhow."

"I reckon Hitler had other plans," Cole said.

"You have to hand it to those Kraut bastards," Vaccaro said, offering the enemy some grudging praise. "They just don't know when to give up."

"How do you know they don't think the same thing about us?" Cole pointed out. "It's got to gnaw at them, us putting up such a fight."

The weary soldiers of Team SNAFU were trudging beside elements of the 101st Airborne, being rushed to plug the latest hole in the dike. All of them were cold, weary, muddy, and hungry. Their C rations did little to quell their deep hunger.

The only consolation, at least as Cole could see it, was that the Germans couldn't be in much better shape. Not if they had been advancing in these same conditions.

Cole looked around at the column of men, all moving along the slushy road. Nobody talked much, as if trying to conserve energy. Most of them had boots soaked through, no match for the snowy conditions, leaving their feet white with cold and their toes numb. It was amazing how a man could get to fantasizing about dry socks. Once they stopped moving and the sun went down, frostbite would set in.

Below the knees, the men's trousers were wet from melted snow and speckled with mud. Many wore jackets that were not adequate for the winter conditions, not having been issued real cold weather gear yet. A few didn't have coats at all. The weather was as much of an adversary as the Germans.

Soldiers did whatever they could to buttress themselves against the cold, developing a strategy to reduce their shivering as much as possible. Around their necks, some wrapped makeshift scarves cut from blankets they had scavenged in Bastogne. Still others stuffed old newspapers, mattress ticking, or even straw under their clothes in a desperate attempt at insulating themselves.

Some men wore cloths tied under their chins and tucked under their helmets to protect their ears, looking as if they wore old-fashioned bandages for a toothache. Vaccaro wore a strip of cloth torn from a flowered bedsheet from his chin to his helmet, making him look utterly ridiculous.

So far Cole had made few concessions to the cold, but even he had his limits and found himself shivering whenever he stopped moving for long. He still wore the bedsheet that he'd found as camouflage. The makeshift poncho didn't offer any protection against the cold, but it would help him blend in against a snowy background when the time came.

They didn't have far to go before they were ordered into the woods along the roadside, where they commenced to dig in. They were on high ground at the top of a low hill that overlooked a large open field below, through which the road continued. From this position, they had a commanding view of the road as it passed through the field. The entire area would be within their field of fire. It was clear to everyone that this spot had been chosen because the Germans were expected to make an appearance soon.

The men proceeded to dig in, but getting their entrenching tools to bite into the frosty ground wasn't easy. The stubborn ground spit chunks of frozen earth back at them as it bounced off their shovels. The tree roots didn't help either. Some men resorted to stabbing at the ground with their bayonets to loosen the soil. Once they had dug down about six inches, past the frost line, the digging became easier.

Cole didn't need to be told twice to dig deep. The metal blade of the entrenching tool jolted his arms each time it bit into the rigid ground. He swiveled the blade so that he could use the tool more like a pick than a shovel, hacking at the soil knitted with crystals of ice.

They were really exposed here. The ground beneath the trees was so barren of underbrush that it was like a park, with no cover other than the trees above.

From time to time, Cole glanced with apprehension at the stark bare branches overhead. He had seen how an artillery burst could transform trees into whirling deadly splinters.

"What am I, a soldier or a farmer?" Vaccaro complained.

"Shut up and dig," Cole said. "The deeper, the better. You heard the officers. Sounds like we'll be facing tanks. Those panzers will tear us apart."

Like aircraft, a tank was one of those machines that sparked joy in the heart of an infantryman—as long as it was one of their own. When it was an enemy tank that they were facing, the emotion was quite the opposite.

And so they burrowed down into the frozen ground, grunting with the effort.

But no sooner had they made some progress laboriously hacking through the frozen ground than orders came to move out. A chorus of groaning went up from the men.

They took up new positions, still on the hillside, even closer to the road, but beyond the trees. That was fine by Cole, who hadn't liked the thought of being shelled while under those branches.

The lack of tree roots made the digging that much easier, although the frozen ground still made them fight for every inch. The digging warmed the soldiers, who were almost grateful for the exercise because of that, but it created a new problem.

"Take it slow," advised Captain Brown, walking among the foxholes being excavated. "You don't want to break a sweat or those wet clothes will chill you to the bone once you quit. You've got time—the Germans aren't anywhere in sight."

Once the captain had moved on, Vaccaro said, "Damn, that's the first time anybody in the army has told me to take my time."

"Don't get used to it," somebody said.

"Just make sure it's deep," Cole said. "If there are Krauts headed this way, it's gonna get ugly in a hurry."

They had a good view of the road and the open field beyond. Given that their flanks were covered by wooded, rugged hills, the Germans would have little choice but to follow the road through the field, where they would be caught out in the open.

Cole touched his rifle and smiled.

However, the grin faded as he looked around him. He hadn't noticed it before, but there was a distinct absence of any real firepower other than GIs with rifles and a few machine guns. He reminded himself that they would likely be facing panzers. German armor would chew them up and spit them out fast as a mule went through sweet clover.

"I got a bad feeling about this," he muttered.

"You and me both," Vaccaro said. "I sure wish we had some tanks of our own. The Krauts will sure as hell have panzers."

Vaccaro wasn't wrong about that. Bastogne was still cut off and isolated, the Germans attempting to punch holes through the dike. US armor was still nowhere to be seen. Cole had the dismal thought that they'd be fighting enemy tanks with rifles.

Once the foxholes were dug, the men settled in to wait. They lay in their holes, shivering, as a new layer of snow covered them, eventually melting to soak through their clothing and make them even colder.

The waiting proved to be almost as nerve-racking as an actual battle. Time passed slowly in the cold holes they had dug.

There was nothing to do now but be patient. The cold settled over the men like an icy blanket, with the dampness seeping into joints and bones still sore from the marathon truck ride. Hardly any of the soldiers were past thirty years old, but the raw cold made their knees and elbows ache like they were a bunch of grandfathers.

Worn down from exhaustion, many of the men were getting sick from the cold, and the sounds of sneezing and coughing carried through the still winter air. It was a lousy, miserable place to be getting sick.

The worst part was how a man's thoughts gave way to his imagination. Every flicker of a bird among the trees became a German. Shadows in the gloom appeared to be menacing tanks. The distant boom of artillery surely meant that a shell was headed their way.

To make matters worse, a freezing fog had rolled in, blending with the snowy landscape to create a world of whiteness. The fog reduced visibility and skewed their perspective to the point where the trees opposite them seemed to be like so many tall marching soldiers.

The damp air had a way of carrying sound long distances, and odd noises seemed to come at them from all directions at once. Cole could hear a man in a foxhole a hundred feet away talking to his buddy, and it sounded like they were right next to him.

"Keep it down," Lieutenant Mulholland ordered in a hoarse whisper. "No sense letting the Krauts know exactly where we are."

The fog was more than a little unnerving. They were all relieved when the fog began to lift, but it stopped at the level of the treetops.

When they finally did hear the rumbling of engines, it was coming from their rear.

"What the hell is that? The Krauts are behind us!"

"Goddammit!"

Everyone spun around, fearing that the Germans had somehow gotten behind them. A cheer went up when they realized that it wasn't German armor, but their own.

The cavalry had arrived in the nick of time.

However, the tanks soon stopped, as if unsure whether the men in the foxholes were Germans or Americans. A figure appeared in the lead tank, gazing at the men through binoculars.

You couldn't blame him. Many of the soldiers had donned sheets for camouflage or whitewashed their helmets, trying to blend in with the snowy background. Considering that the Germans also wore white camouflage, it was hard to tell them apart.

Lieutenant Mulholland stood up and waved, but the tank

commander wasn't buying it. They had good reason to be wary of German Panzerfaust. Plus they didn't seem to have any supporting infantry, making the tanks more vulnerable.

"Cole, go down there and let those tankers know whose side we're on," Mulholland said.

"You got it, Lieutenant."

Cole shucked off his improvised white smock so that whoever was in the tank could get a look at his US uniform. Next he slipped his rifle through the sling and walked down the slope to meet them.

He was surprised to see that the lead tank was bigger than the others. He decided that it must be one of those Jumbo Shermans that he'd heard rumors about. They were supposed to be big enough and tough enough to tangle with a Tiger tank.

The name *Cobra King* was painted on the side. A single white star on each side of the turret identified it as a US fighting tank.

This battlefield beauty had been built at the Fisher Tank Arsenal in Michigan, one of fewer than three hundred M4 Sherman "Jumbo" tanks. Powered by a Ford V8 engine, theoretically it could reach speeds of around twenty miles per hour, but that wasn't possible in the rugged terrain of the Ardennes region.

He wasn't one to be nervous, but Cole couldn't seem to keep his eyes off the machine gun on the front of the tank, not to mention the black maw of the 75 mm main weapon. If that tank crew didn't like his looks and decided to open fire, Cole knew there wouldn't be enough of him to bury in a shoebox—if they found anything at all. His mouth went dry at the thought.

Lieutenant Mulholland could have sent anyone, but he had decided to send Cole. Why? Cole could only guess, but he suspected that Mulholland still harbored a grudge about Jolie Molyneaux. Jolie had been a French Maqui, or freedom fighter, assigned to be their guide way back in Normandy.

She had been an excellent guide, tough as nails, and beautiful to boot.

Conflict had arisen in the squad because, in wartime, men fought over a single filly like wolves fighting over a scrap of meat.

The lieutenant had figured that as an officer and educated man,

Jolie would naturally go for him. Much to his surprise—and to Cole's—she had quickly shown that she preferred the company of the sniper. That had been months ago, but Mulholland still seemed to hold it against him, which explained why Cole was now crossing the open field.

When Cole got closer, the tank commander visibly relaxed. He lowered his binoculars and climbed down from the tank.

The lieutenant stuck out his hand. "I've only seen Germans these last few days. I thought you might be more of the same."

"Glad to see you," Cole replied, shaking the lieutenant's hand.

"I was worried about infiltrators too. Rumor has it that a lot of Krauts are wearing US uniforms and raising all sorts of hell." The lieutenant paused. "Say, you're not really a German, are you?"

"I reckon not, Lieutenant," Cole replied in his mountain twang. It was not an accent that a German would bother to learn.

"Well, it would be one hell of a dumb infiltrator who walked right up to a tank, so I figured you weren't a Kraut. Also, no offense intended, but you sound pure cornpone."

"If you say so, sir."

The lieutenant nodded at the men dug in on the slope. "What's going on?"

"We're a welcome party for the Krauts headed up this road into Bastogne. When we heard your engines, we reckoned it was the Germans arriving. They're supposed to get here any minute now."

The lieutenant grinned. "Mind if we join the party?"

"That would be right nice of you."

"All righty, then. Sounds like there's no time for proper introductions. Tell your CO that we'll set up in those trees off to your flank, closest to the road. The Krauts will have to get past us if they want to get into Bastogne."

"Yes, sir."

The lieutenant took a long look at Cole's rifle. "Sniper, huh?"

"Yes, sir."

"I've got to say I don't care much for snipers, present company excluded. I've only been in command of this bucket of bolts for three days. That's because a Kraut sniper picked off the previous lieutenant when he stuck his head out of his hatch to have a look around."

Falling prey to snipers was definitely an occupational hazard for tank commanders. Cole realized that he had picked off a few German tank commanders doing the exact same thing, but he didn't say anything about that to the lieutenant.

"I'll go let our CO know your plans." Because he was feeling ornery, Cole couldn't resist adding, "Oh, and keep your head down, sir."

"Very funny."

The lieutenant turned back to his tank, and Cole made his way back up the slope to report where the tanks would be positioned. Already, the Jumbo Sherman had revved up its engine and was hightailing it for the woods near where the road emerged into the field. The two smaller tanks followed along in its wake like puppies following the mama dog.

Captain Brown had come down to hear what Cole had to say. He nodded and added a small smile. "I'll be glad to have their help. If three tanks got through, that means more will be on the way. Things are starting to turn around for Bastogne."

The tanks weren't the only card up the captain's sleeve. Dug in on the hillside, Team SNAFU had their rifles and a handful of machine guns, but no heavy firepower. However, they would not be hung out to dry.

Out of sight back in Bastogne, the artillery had the coordinates of this field dialed in. When Captain Brown gave the word, the artillery would open fire on the Germans in the field. The Krauts would be in for a deadly surprise.

CHAPTER SEVEN

THEY DIDN'T HAVE to wait much longer for the Germans to appear. The guttural sound of straining engines announced the approaching panzers and the arrival of the German advance. However, the Germans did not immediately cross the field as expected.

It was as if they smelled the trap that had been set for them.

The panzers stayed within cover of the trees on the opposite side, their engines growling like a pack of mechanical wolves preparing for the hunt. It was clear that the enemy had spotted the US troops dug in on the hillside. They were likely trying to determine the strength of the unit opposing them.

"What the hell are they waiting for?" Vaccaro wondered.

"The Krauts are always smarter than we give them credit for," Cole replied. "They're not gonna rush out into the open."

He had the telescopic sight to his eye, hoping that a target would present itself.

For now, the German troops kept to the cover of the trees and tanks. None of the tanks had its hatch open. These tanks meant business.

Vaccaro seemed content to let Cole do the shooting for now. "See anything?"

"They're keeping to the trees," he said. "If there's infantry with 'em, I can't see them. Ain't nothin' to shoot at yet."

Like the Americans, the Germans also had a few tricks up their sleeves. Instead of crossing the field, the panzers opened fire from the edge of the forest opposite the US position. Shells from the German guns began pummeling the US line. Due to the angle of the slope, some of the high-explosive rounds hit the frozen ground and ricocheted to explode in the forest behind the men. Even above the detonation of the rounds, they could hear the cracking and splitting of the wood.

Glad we ain't in them trees, Cole thought.

Plenty of shells found their target. The German gunners had good aim and at this relatively close range were able to zero in on individual foxholes. Shells hit, exploding with such force that whatever had been in that foxhole was obliterated. Clods of earth—and worse—came raining down. Every man on that slope wished he had dug his foxhole deeper. They gripped their helmets tight and pressed their faces into the cold ground, willing themselves to sink deeper. Dirt clogged their nostrils and got into their mouths, but nobody cared. Meanwhile, shrapnel whistled overhead.

Every man had already been reminded not to fasten the strap of his helmet. This was because the concussive force of an explosive shell could get cupped inside a helmet like a pail scooping up water. The sheer force of it could take a man's head clean off. Cole had seen it happen to more than one greenbean. With the strap left undone, the blast might blow the helmet off but leave his head attached to his shoulders.

More shells struck as the bombardment by the panzers continued. So far their own three tanks hidden nearby had held their fire.

The jeep that had carried Captain Brown out from Bastogne was parked within view near the boundary with the woods. A shell hit the jeep, and it was hurled skyward before its carcass went rolling away, fire pouring from the wreckage. Fortunately, there was nobody aboard, the driver having taken shelter in a foxhole.

"Holy hell!" the captain exclaimed, watching his ride reduced to a burning hulk.

After several minutes, the Germans seemed to determine that they had done enough to soften up the US defenses. The firing stopped, and the panzers came roaring out from the shelter of the trees on the far side of the field.

Cole lifted his head up enough to determine that there were eight panzers. One of them was bigger than the rest—a Tiger tank. No wonder the world had felt like it was coming to an end.

The panzers were not alone. As they churned across the snowy field, lines of infantry emerged. Cole was shocked at the sheer number of enemy troops. Most of the time in combat, he'd seen only small squads of Germans. There must have been close to a hundred soldiers advancing.

Team SNAFU didn't have nearly that many men, and they had already taken a beating from those panzers. The tanks fired more shots as they advanced across the field.

Still, there was no response from the American side. No artillery shells fell, and the Shermans remained silent, hidden among the trees.

"Hold your fire!" Lieutenant Mulholland shouted, loud enough for them to hear over the ringing in their ears.

Cole did as he was told, although he had already picked out a target. Some damn fool tank commander had finally stuck his head out of the hatch. Cole put his crosshairs on the Kraut and waited for the lieutenant's command.

He wasn't the only one. Every rifle and every machine gun were now trained on the Germans.

"Let them get closer," they heard the captain shout in the distance. "Open up on them at four hundred yards."

To Cole that seemed foolishly close. The panzers would quickly close that distance and push them off the hill. He kept his rifle on the target, itching to pull the trigger.

"Fire!"

His sights still lined up on the panzer, Cole squeezed off a round and watched with satisfaction as the tank commander slumped over.

He worked the bolt, searching for another target.

All around him, the roar of rifles and machine-gun fire filled his ears.

It was a slaughter. The first burst of fire decimated the German infantry. Caught out in the open field, they had no cover as the hail of bullets clawed at them. The snow began to turn red with German blood.

Then the air itself seemed to shatter as the artillery in Bastogne opened fire, the shells screaming overhead and landing amid the line of panzers. Geysers of earth soared skyward.

The trio of tanks hidden in the woods opened fire as well, targeting their counterparts. Soon at least half the enemy tanks were ablaze. A few members of the tank crews ran from the burning tanks, but for them it was too late. They were on fire, human torches that danced macabrely before collapsing in the field. Watching them, Cole felt a little sick.

The remaining tanks retreated, either reversing or making lumbering turns back toward the cover offered by the trees. Often they ran over their own dead or wounded in the process. Fire from *Cobra King* chased the enemy tanks and troops the whole way back across the field. As the Germans disappeared into the trees, a few final shells rained down into the forest, shattering the trees and raking the men beneath with deadly splinters.

"Cease fire!" Mulholland shouted.

It turned out that Captain Brown wasn't content with simply holding the hill and turning back the Germans. He gave the order to advance and follow the enemy into the trees, intending to annihilate them completely.

Cobra King and the other tanks roared out from among the trees, leading the counterattack.

Cole heard the order and thought, *Holy hell*. If the Germans rallied in those trees, they could easily return the favor if they opened fire on the advancing Americans.

Cole had no choice but to crawl out of the foxhole and start down the hill, Vaccaro and the kid right behind him. They passed the burning carcass of a panzer. Even as a wrecked hulk, it was hard not to be impressed with the sheer size of that behemoth. The burned bodies of the tank crew lay smoldering in the snow, filling the air with the sickly-sweet smell of burned flesh.

He hurried past, running for the trees, hoping against hope that the Germans didn't wise up and start shooting.

* * *

Bauer watched in disbelief as the German troops were cut to pieces.

Not just any German troops, but *his* troops.

Smashed and broken.

It had seemed like such a small thing to push the Americans off the hill—so far, the disorganized US troops they had encountered in the Ardennes Forest had put up little fight. He recalled that the prisoners they had taken—the same prisoners that Messner killed—had surrendered without so much as a shot fired. These Americans on the hillside had been far different. They had been dug in and equipped with machine guns. Bauer's men and the other troops hadn't stood a chance.

Then the world had seemed to end when the artillery shells rained down and the tanks added their deadly fire to the mix. Where had those tanks come from, anyhow? The Americans weren't supposed to have tanks yet.

He could see that to try to advance any farther would be suicide. He ordered the men around him to retreat.

"Back to the woods!" he shouted.

Nearby, Messner seemed angry about the order, scowling, but even he wasn't so much of a fool that he wanted to run right toward the machine guns. It was a killing field like something that Bauer had heard described from the Great War. He kept low as tracer fire stitched the air overhead.

Once they were back in the trees, even that proved to be no mercy as the American artillery found them there. Men dove to the ground, scratching at the snow in a futile attempt to dig themselves deeper. Mercifully, the artillery stopped firing.

"Rally to me," he shouted, trying to organize the tattered troops. He pushed a soldier toward a man who struggled through the snow, dragging a bloody leg. "You there, help that wounded man."

Bauer had experienced doubts previously about the folly of Operation Watch on the Rhine, as the German offensive was called. What had started out as a promising venture had quickly bogged down due to the bitter weather and the poor supply chain. The Americans had staked their claim on Bastogne, and they meant to keep it, as evidenced by that fierce defense of the hillside overlooking the road into the town.

He felt a sudden sense of hopelessness and the utter futility of it all seemed to wash over him like a storm wave. He looked around at the men. Most wore winter-white camouflage, but so many were wounded now that almost every smock was flecked with blood. Advancing yet again into that killing field, or even trying to go around it, now seemed impossible.

The panzers that had accompanied them had almost all been destroyed in the shelling. Even one of the tanks that had made it out of the field was smoking badly—some sort of engine malfunction—and it had to be abandoned. The tank crew got out and joined the infantry, looking dazed and lost outside the confines of their steel beast.

The sight of these torn and bloody men broke his heart. They were all good men who had done their duty to the fatherland. The best he could hope for was to help as many of his men survive as possible. If he could just get them back the way they had come, dodging the enemy, they might be able to reach the relative safety of the German border.

But his plan fell apart as quickly as it had formed.

"Herr Obersturmbannführer, they are crossing the field!"

"What?"

"The Americans are coming after us."

Bauer had to see for himself and ran to the edge of the forest. Sure enough, the line of US infantry was advancing. Even three tanks had appeared and were heading for the trees where the Germans sheltered.

It was fight or flight.

With so many wounded and exhausted men, fleeing was out of the question. They would have to turn and fight.

The order was forming on his lips when Bauer realized that he had a third choice.

He drew his knife, the beautiful blade decorated with the swastika and eagle on the hilt, and used it to cut a strip from his white winter camouflage smock. He found a suitable stick and knotted the white strip to one end.

Messner came running up to him.

"Herr Obersturmbannführer, what are you doing?" asked Messner, looking horrified. As usual, he was accompanied by Gettinger and Dietzel, who had managed to survive the bloodbath.

"I am going to surrender and save as many of the men as possible," Bauer said. He added bitterly, "With any luck, they won't shoot us all, like you did to those American prisoners."

"But sir, you cannot surrender!" Messner protested.

"I can and I will. It is our best option," Bauer said matter-of-factly.

"Herr Obersturmbannführer, I forbid you from doing this!"

"You forbid me?" Bauer wondered. He felt anger, then consternation. "May I remind you that I am the commanding officer here."

But Messner was so furious that spit flew from his mouth as he shouted, "This is a betrayal of the Reich and of the Führer himself!"

Bauer thought, *It is the Führer who has betrayed us.*

Many of the men nearby were listening to the exchange, some of the wounded slumped in the snow, so Bauer stopped short of speaking his thoughts out loud. The men had suffered enough.

Finally, he sighed in exhaustion. Messner could obey orders, or he could go to hell. "I am going to surrender, Messner. It is the best way to save some of these men."

"Herr Obersturmbannführer, you must not do this."

"Look around you, Messner. Do you see all the wounded? Without supplies, we can do almost nothing for them. The ones who aren't wounded are nearly dead on their feet with exhaustion and the cold."

"You are a traitor!"

Messner's hand drifted to the flap of his holster. Next to Messner, he could see Dietzel grow tense, his grip tight on his sniper rifle. So far the barrel hadn't swung in his direction, but all it would take was a word from Messner.

Bauer ignored them and began walking through the trees toward the field. He half expected to hear a shot—it would be the last thing he ever heard—as Messner moved to stop him. He kept walking, hoping that shooting his commanding officer in the back would be too much, even for a zealot like Messner.

One of the men saw him with the white flag and stopped him with tears in his eyes. It was one of the enlisted men who had been with him for a long time. The man was bleeding heavily from several wounds suffered in the attack across the field, his makeshift bandages seeping blood. "We can still fight them, Herr Obersturmbannführer!" he said.

Bauer squeezed his shoulder. "You have done enough, old friend. We will get you some help soon."

Before moving on, Bauer looked behind him, half expecting to see Messner or the sharpshooter taking aim.

But Messner was gone, along with his henchmen and several of the more able-bodied soldiers. He caught sight of the last of them disappearing into the trees. Apparently they were not going to surrender.

It was their choice. Some part of him felt proud of them, but this would not be his own path. He would do what he could to save what remained of his men.

Bauer took off his smock to reveal his officer's uniform, then squared his shoulders and walked out into the open, waving his white flag.

CHAPTER EIGHT

Cole and the others did not get much of a break after defeating the German attack toward Bastogne. They were pulled back after the German attack had shattered upon the hillside like waves upon the rocks. The field was littered with German dead, the snow stained red, the corpses of the destroyed panzers still smoking. As terrible as it was, no man present would ever forget the gruesome tableau before them. Decades later, it would be a story to tell their grandchildren. But for now they simply felt numb from the cold and glad to be alive.

Already more snow was falling, as if nature wished to hide humankind's sins. If you got close enough, you could hear the snowflakes sizzle as they melted on the hot metal. If hell froze over, Cole reckoned that this was what it would look like.

"That's a lot of dead Krauts," Vaccaro remarked.

"Dead, stupid Krauts," Cole emphasized. "They marched across that field like they owned it. What the hell did they expect?"

"They expected us to run, that's what."

"The Krauts got that part wrong."

"Fine by me," Vaccaro said. "Word is that they're sending us back to Bastogne. Maybe we can find some more hot grub. A fire would be nice too. I'm not sure that I'll ever feel my toes again."

Nearby, young Hank was doing jumping jacks to get his blood moving.

Cole shook his head. Where the hell did the kid get that kind of energy? Cold as it was, now that the fighting was over, Cole was half-tempted to crawl back into his foxhole, pull a blanket over himself, and go to sleep.

To their surprise, several of the Germans had surrendered, including their commanding officer. Many of the new POWs were wounded. The Germans looked battered and broken after the punishing attack and the harsh weather conditions that took a toll on both sides. Given the appearance of the vanquished, it was hard for the surrender to feel like victory. Close up, the enemy simply looked like regular human beings.

But more than a few of the Krauts, along with their remaining panzers, had managed to slip away. Perhaps hoping to put the Americans at ease, the captured officer claimed that the survivors of the attack were on their way back to Germany. At least that was the rumor flying around.

"Too bad we didn't wipe them all out," Cole said. "We'll just have to fight them later."

They left their foxholes and returned to Bastogne. This time there were no trucks, and they had to walk.

Although the arrival of the Sherman tanks indicated that relief forces were finally about to break through, German troops still ringed the town. The ring was no longer impenetrable, but it was there all the same.

More than a few artillery shells still fell from time to time, indiscriminately killing soldiers and civilians, a reminder that the Germans were not ready to abandon their assault on the town. So far the Luftwaffe had not returned for another bombing run like the cruel Christmas Eve pounding they had delivered. That much was a relief.

Artillery wasn't the only indicator of the German presence. A sniper had set up on the edges of the town, in an area that US forces did not yet control. From there, the sniper was able to pick off troops seemingly at will. His bullets always seemed to arrive when least expected.

When a fella stood still a moment to light a cigarette. When a tired GI leaned against a wall.

Death reached out and found them from an impossible distance.

The constant sniper fire wasn't helping morale any. When it came to Bastogne, between the bombs and the bullets, there just didn't seem to be anywhere that was safe from the reach of the enemy.

For that reason, it shouldn't have surprised Cole when he was called in to deal with the problem.

He found himself summoned to headquarters with Lieutenant Mulholland. They brought Vaccaro along as a mascot.

Cole followed the lieutenant into a cramped house that had been commandeered as HQ. Outside, a clerk was using a hatchet to break apart a bomb-damaged chifforobe, which he carried in to fuel a huge fire blazing in the fireplace. More pieces of furniture stood nearby, awaiting their fate like cattle at the slaughterhouse. Despite the clerk's best efforts, the fire couldn't seem to warm the air.

A harried captain quickly explained the situation.

"Just when we think we've got the bastard, he moves on us," the officer complained.

"That means he knows his business," Cole replied. "It's how German snipers are trained, sir. They don't sit still for long."

The captain didn't look impressed. "Look, I don't give a damn what they trained him to do. Hell, maybe they taught him to play the fiddle and knit socks too. I just want him gone. I understand that you're the man to do it."

"Yes, sir."

The captain opened his mouth, perhaps to express his doubts, but he took a moment to look Cole up and down. His gaze lingered on Cole's battered sniper's rifle, then moved to Cole's gray-blue eyes. Their eyes met briefly, but the captain looked away, unable to hold Cole's gaze. He wouldn't have been the first man to detect something chilling in those eyes.

When he did speak, it was to say, "All right, if you say you can nab this Kraut, then I believe you. The only help I can give you is to have one of my men point out where this Kraut sniper has been operating."

Back outside, Mulholland had no words of advice except "Be sure and get that bastard. Oh, and try not to get shot."

With that he trudged off and disappeared.

Cole had to wonder if the lieutenant had meant that last part. He recalled how Mulholland had sent him down to parley with the tanks. That had been a somewhat dicey situation.

The message seemed to be that Cole was seen as expendable.

He had to wonder just when the hell Mulholland would get over Jolie—if he ever did.

Cole and Vaccaro weren't alone for long. The captain had promised to give them a guide, who appeared soon after in the form of a scruffy sergeant named Gifford, who looked as if the last time he had shaved was late summer. He was leading a couple of other men who hung back.

Gifford was about average height but solidly built, his cheeks covered in reddish-brown stubble. He looked to be in his early thirties. He had two greenish eyes, one a slightly different color than the other. Both eyes burned with intensity as they first swept over Vaccaro and dismissed him, then settled on Cole.

"So you're the sniper who is gonna solve our problem," he said, not sounding particularly convinced.

"I reckon."

Gifford shook his head like he'd just bitten into a lemon. "You reckon? From the sounds of it, you're a goddamn hillbilly. It just figures. Everybody in this army thinks you have to be a hillbilly to be a good shot."

Vaccaro spoke up. "Hey, take my word for it, this fella can shoot."

"If you say so," Gifford said. Keeping his eyes on Cole, he dipped his chin and spoke over his shoulder to the men behind him. "What do you think, fellas? Twenty bucks says this peckerwood gets himself shot by the end of the day."

One of the GIs snorted. "Nobody is gonna bet against that, Sarge."

Gifford turned his attention back to Cole. "The thing is, we don't need any help to get this sniper."

Cole shrugged. "Fine by me. Sounds like you can handle it."

He started to turn away.

"Hold on. Where the hell do you think you're going, huh? The captain gave an order, and we're gonna make sure it's carried out. Now, follow me, and when I say to, keep your head down."

Following the prickly sergeant, they headed for the northeastern quadrant. The town itself soon gave way to more widespread buildings and a few stone walls that enclosed small fields. In the distance stood a church, the tall steeple providing an ideal vantage point for a sniper. Surrounding the church was more open ground broken up by stone walls and some barns or cowsheds. The forest lay beyond, showing itself as a brooding gray presence.

"This would be a good time to keep your heads down," the sergeant said as they entered the backyards of small houses on the outskirts of town. "He'll have seen us by now if he's looking."

"I reckon he's looking," Cole said, keeping low. "Wouldn't be much of a sniper if he wasn't."

Right away Cole was impressed by the sniper's obvious skill in being able to reach the steeple without being seen. According to the sergeant, the sniper was also a tremendous shot.

"The son of a bitch never misses," the sergeant said. Having taken Cole's measure, he had changed his tune a bit and seemed friendlier. "He's already shot a few of our guys. This is personal. Think you can get him?"

Cole looked toward the church steeple in the distance. "I'll get him. I need to get closer to him, which means going out there in no-man's-land. Make sure your boys don't shoot me."

"I'll pass the word. Listen, when you come back in, the company password is 'black strap.' The countersign is 'molasses.'"

The sergeant left them alone, scurrying back through the alleys and along stone walls to avoid falling under the sniper's sights. For all his talk, he seemed glad to be getting out of there.

Vaccaro was already studying the church steeple through binoculars. "Not so bad," he said. "What would you say, three hundred yards?"

Cole studied the distance and gave a slow nod. "Give or take."

"I know you weren't blowing smoke just now when you said you could get him. But, you know, *can* you get him? You'd have to be able to see the son of a bitch, and right now all I see is a church steeple with solid stone walls. Maybe we could just bring up some mortars and blow the shit out of that church."

"Where would the fun be in that? No, I'm gonna get him. We're gonna get him. You and me, city boy."

"I was afraid you'd say that."

"I can thread the needle, all right. But you're right that I need to see the needle in the first place. Hand me those binoculars a minute."

Vaccaro carried Zeiss field glasses, taken off a deceased German officer. The optics were superior to any US Army–issued binoculars. Back home, they would have cost the average working man at least a month's salary.

Cole studied the church steeple through the binoculars, looking for something, anything, that indicated where the sniper was hiding. Like many of the buildings in Europe that they'd come across, the age of the church seemed to be somewhere between old and ancient. Even the oldest buildings back home were nothing compared to structures that dated back centuries.

The square tower offered a cold facade, topped with a slate roof. At the very top, beneath the roof, were several long slits. They were intended to let out the sound of the church bell used to summon worshippers, or perhaps to warn of danger, but the openings also happened to make perfect firing slits for the hidden sniper.

The only real sign of age and decay exhibited by the church was that the cross at the top of the steeple was weathered and missing pieces, perhaps thanks to the recent bombardments, with cracks running through it from years of exposure to the elements. One more strong windstorm and it looked as if the damn thing might blow down.

"What are you thinking?" Vaccaro asked.

"We'll have to get closer."

"That's just what I was thinking. But how do we do that without getting our asses shot off?"

"Let me think about it a minute."

The two men began to strategize quietly, using gestures as much as words. They had done this together before. Vaccaro would point out a path toward the steeple or a landscape feature. Cole would either grunt in reluctant agreement or shake his head in disapproval. It wasn't all that different from how a pair of cavemen would have planned their hunt.

Once again Vaccaro handed him the binoculars, and Cole studied the scene, taking in every detail. The church steeple loomed against the gray sky, its stony features brooding and somehow menacing. Above them in that steeple, the sniper would be hidden in the freezing shade, still as the stone around him, his rifle at the ready, waiting for a clear shot.

Cole thought about the differences between German and US snipers. First, he knew that he and other Americans had a lot to learn from their German counterparts. The US Army did not have a sniper training program beyond the basic marksmanship training that all soldiers received—or were supposed to. In the early months of the war, thousands of troops had been rushed through basic training without more than a cursory introduction to their rifles. The approach could be termed on-the-job training.

To be fair, not all these men were intended to be combat troops, and the army had desperately needed every warm body it could get its hands on for jobs from clerks to cooks to truck drivers. US snipers were men like Cole who had been found to be crack shots and kept their cool under fire. They were given rifles with telescopic sights and told to get to work.

It wasn't that easy. The enemy snipers they faced had often gone through specific training in the subtle art of targeting the enemy. He'd heard that to pass sniper training, the Krauts had to undergo a test in which they remained undetected by their instructors. They learned to camouflage themselves. They learned patience. They learned tricks to fool their prey. They learned to sleep and eat and relieve themselves in a hole in the ground. If they failed these tests, they did not earn their Scharfschütze badge.

German snipers were not just marksmen, they were trained killers.

That's what we're up against, Cole thought.

Americans liked to see themselves as great hunters and crack shots, and there was some truth to the fact that compared to most Europeans, many Americans had grown up with rifles and firearms. Wasn't every American supposed to be a cowboy at heart, or maybe Daniel Boone and Davy Crockett all rolled up into one?

For every Cole who had grown up hunting, it seemed like there were just as many men like Vaccaro who had only known pavement under their feet.

However, the Germans and the Russians also had a great tradition of hunting and a culture around firearms. German snipers tended to have been hunters in their youth. Most had grown up in the countryside. Their skill with a rifle had been honed by training. Some of the sharpshooters had experienced battle against the Soviet Union, and that included taking on the highly skilled Russian snipers.

You either learned quickly, or you died.

Cole and Vaccaro had learned their trade the hard way—by trial and error. It helped that Cole also had a natural cunning.

Looking at that church steeple, Cole knew that he would need all his skills to nab the German hiding up there.

"Let's go have us a look," he said.

Cole started off through the space between them and the church steeple, moving cautiously across the yard and even small barnyards. He constantly kept something between him and the sniper's position, whether it was a stone wall or the corner of a building.

They moved carefully and quietly through the maze of narrow alleys that crisscrossed the town. The frozen ground was hard and uneven, dotted with rocks and clumps of torn earth from the shelling. These threatened to trip up Cole's feet, but even in the ruts he managed to move lightly. Vaccaro clumped along behind him, making enough noise for them both.

Cole exhaled a cloud of breath in the cold air, his stomach tight with anticipation. Battle-worn after these months of war, he had experienced more than a few moments like this, those moments where life and death hung in the balance. It wasn't fear but the thrill of the hunt.

As they inched closer, they passed through a dense thicket of rosebushes encircling a house, the branches bare and twisted, grasping with thorns, like the gnarled hands of ancient whispering souls. The scent of damp earth and decaying leaves filled Cole's nostrils, a reminder of the funk from which all men sprang and to which they would return.

Not that Cole was in any hurry for that. So he took his time working closer to the church steeple.

As Cole and Vaccaro continued to analyze the situation, they noticed a small group of civilians gathering in the distance, near the church, their heads bowed in prayer. It looked like a funeral. A sudden gust of wind blew through the town, sending a shower of snow across the ground. The townspeople turned up their coat collars and kept praying.

They would have made easy targets, but the sniper seemed content to ignore them, saving his bullets for American soldiers.

Vaccaro whispered urgently, "Even if we get close enough, we can't risk firing near those people. They'd be caught in the cross fire. The last thing we need is any collateral damage."

"Yeah," Cole agreed. "Let's go at him from the other side. Maybe he won't be expecting us then."

As they scoped out the situation, they spotted a civilian wearing a tweed beret, picking his way through the landscape of low stone walls and outbuildings. Clearly he was headed in the direction of the German lines.

"Where the hell does he think he's going? Maybe he's a German spy."

"No Kraut would be caught dead wearing a beret, even if he is a spy. That's one of the locals. He must be friends with the Jerries."

"We ought to shoot the bastard."

"Let him go. No point attracting attention to ourselves."

Their stealthy efforts weren't enough. A shot rang out and struck the corner of a house just as Cole slipped behind it. Dust and bits of stone chips flew.

"Dammit! Another split second and that bastard would have gotten me."

"You're lucky it's starting to get dark or he might not have missed."

Cole nodded, thinking that Vaccaro was right about the fading daylight. His eyes flicked back and forth between the church and the distant hills. He wasn't sure whether it was the movement or something else that had caught the enemy sniper's attention. All he knew was that his heart was pounding. The sniper's bullet had been close.

Keeping low, he eased the rifle scope up to his eye. He ached to return fire, but there was no target visible.

Another shot came from the direction of the tower. No bullets struck nearby, and Cole had the sinking realization that the sniper had probably just shot another unsuspecting GI on the streets of Bastogne. It was just what they had been sent to prevent.

They didn't have much time before dark. As the hidden sun began to dip below the horizon, the shadows deepened and the light faded, making it more difficult to see the sniper's position. The church steeple was being cloaked by the darkness. Darkness had come slowly, but it now seemed to accelerate like a flood tide.

Then, a small miracle. The setting sun sank below the level of the clouds, revealing itself like the smiling face of a lover under the covers. The final beacon of light illuminated the entire town, bathing the rooftops of Bastogne in glowing light. The church steeple stood out like a lighthouse. They were close enough now that he could see footsteps in the snow, leading away from the church across the fields. He followed the footsteps out and glimpsed a figure trotting across the field, carrying a rifle with a scope.

"I'll be damned," he muttered. He put his rifle to his shoulder, desperate to settle the crosshairs on the Kraut sniper, but the man was too far away.

It's still worth a try, he thought. He raised the sights to a point above the man's head, allowing for the drop of the bullet.

Then the sun dipped behind a hill. It was like pulling down a window shade.

The enemy sniper in the distance faded to a gray blur and was gone.

Behind the rifle, Cole grinned his feral grin, his sharp white teeth showing.

It was just as well that he hadn't fired and warned off the Kraut. The man must have thought that he'd made his getaway unseen.

He knew that the enemy sniper would return in the morning. It went against the rules to shoot from the same position again, but Cole suspected that the church steeple was simply too good to pass up.

No, the enemy sniper would be back in the morning, intending to claim more American lives. And when he returned, Cole would be waiting for him.

They made their way back toward the American lines. The winter darkness was falling, and he couldn't see the sentries, although he knew they were there. He and Vaccaro kept to cover just in case the sentries proved trigger-happy.

"Black strap," Cole called out, giving the sign.

After a moment he heard a soldier shout the countersign: "Molasses."

Cole stepped out and waved. The scruffy sergeant he'd met earlier appeared opposite him in the dim light and waved back.

"Did you get him?" the sergeant asked. Curious soldiers stood behind him. Word must have gotten around that a sniper had been sent to settle the Kraut's hash. "I didn't hear any shooting."

"Don't you worry none, Sarge," Cole replied in his mountain drawl. "First thing tomorrow, I'm gonna tree him in that steeple like a coon."

CHAPTER NINE

COLE'S TRAP was a simple one. He suspected that the enemy sniper would be back in position by first light, moving under the cover of darkness. That was, *if* the sniper returned, which was a big question mark. It was a standard rule of sniper warfare never to return to the same hide two days in a row. Another basic tenet was to avoid taking the same path to and from a sniping position. If someone knew where to expect you to walk into his crosshairs, your number would be up.

However, Cole felt confident that the sniper would be back and might not be overly cautious. The German would be thinking that he wasn't facing a Russian sniper well versed in the cat-and-mouse game of sniper warfare. No, he'd think these Americans wouldn't know *Schmalz aus Butter*—lard from butter.

The sniper's nest in the church steeple was simply too good for him to pass up.

He'll be back, Cole thought.

Cole had puzzled out how to get at the sniper. He knew well enough that there was more than one way to skin a cat. One option would have been to enter the church and go after him or even ambush him inside the church.

He had told the sergeant that he'd trap the German sniper like a coon up a tree. But the more Cole thought about it, he decided to give something else a try.

After sending Vaccaro back to town, he looked through the outlying sheds and barns until he found what he needed. He used quick bursts from his flashlight to search the buildings. He lucked out and found both items after looking through just a few outbuildings.

Next, he returned to the path that the enemy sniper had taken, following the German's tracks through the snow. Although it was dark by now, he avoided the flashlight as much as possible for fear that the light might bring unwelcome attention—from both sides.

When he reached the gap in the stone wall that the sniper had passed through, Cole paused. He looked around, taking his bearings. Just to one side of the gap stood a stone barn, creating a backdrop that would silhouette the sniper when the time came. There was cover where Cole could set up nearby. This would do nicely.

Working quickly, he strung twine across the gap, about a foot above the snow. He anchored one end of the twine by tying it around a stone in the wall. The other end ran under the legs of a milking stool that he'd found in a barn. He put a rock on top of the stool to weigh it down, enabling the stool to serve as a fulcrum of sorts. The final leg of twine ran to the wire handle of a milking pail that Cole set atop the wall. The bucket contained a few empty milk bottles and a pair of cowbells.

He was counting on the fact that, in the dark, the enemy sniper wouldn't see the twine. Its light color helped it blend into the snowy background, especially at night.

He'd been worried that the sniper might slip right past him when the German returned in the dark, enabling the sniper to turn the tables on Cole. Once the sniper hit that string, the resulting racket would let Cole know when the man was crossing through the gap in the fence.

All that he needed now was some luck.

Plus, he'd need a little help from Vaccaro.

* * *

"You're sure this will work?" Vaccaro wondered.

"Hell no," Cole said. "But if it doesn't, the way I figure it, you'll be the one who gets shot."

"Gee, thanks."

It was near midnight and the temperature was below freezing. They were in the no-man's-land on the outskirts of Bastogne between the American and German lines. There were a few scattered houses, outbuildings, and small fields—all appeared to be deserted at this hour.

The snow that had melted slightly during the day was now a frozen crust that crunched under their feet as they moved into position. A freezing fog had rolled in, through which sleet and a little fresh snow still managed to fall. Miserable though it was, the weather served their purposes well, the cold and darkness discouraging soldiers on both sides from doing anything but staying bundled in their foxholes.

They retraced their steps until they came to the spot where the sniper had shot at them yesterday. Cole could see where the bullet had struck, leaving a brighter mark against the drab stone. That had been a little too close for comfort.

Cole led the way to the hiding place he had picked out. He wormed his way beneath an old hay wagon with a shattered wheel, which caused one side of the wagon to nearly touch the ground. Once Cole got under there, no one could see him. He rested his rifle across one of the broken spokes. Wrapped in a white rag, the muzzle was all but invisible. From where he lay, he would have had a perfect view of the gap in the stone wall, no more than one hundred feet away. Would have had—if it hadn't been dark.

That was where Vaccaro came in. Cole had set up his spotter in the lee of the stone wall, no more than twenty feet from the gap that Cole hoped the sniper would come through. Vaccaro had his own rifle and a .45, but the only thing he'd be pointing at the enemy was his flashlight.

"When you hear that racket start, you light him up," Cole explained. "I'll do the rest."

"Dammit, hillbilly. That Kraut will start shooting as soon as he sees my flashlight."

"Ain't likely," Cole replied.

"Why the hell not?"

"'Cuz he'll be dead by then."

"What if he's not?"

"Then turn off your flashlight and shoot back."

"There's got to be an easier way to do this."

"Listen here, city boy. They say that son of a bitch has shot at least a dozen of our boys. Shot them smoking cigarettes, shot them walking down the street. Hell, he even shot them taking a leak."

"Yeah." Vaccaro had heard the stories.

"When that flashlight hits him, he'll know for a split second that I'm about to punch his card. That's why we're going to do it this way."

"All right then. Let's do it."

They waited in the foggy, frozen night, shivering. Despite the cold, Cole could feel some of the snow melting beneath him and starting to soak through his clothes, adding to his discomfort. He wished that he'd thought to bring a blanket. He doubted that Vaccaro was faring any better. It was going to be a long, cold wait for them both.

Deep down, Cole knew that his approach smacked of revenge rather than soldiering. He grinned at the thought. Sometimes you needed a little vengeance.

What they were doing, simply put, was setting a trap to catch the sniper—a fatal and deadly trap.

If the sniper had a split second in which to realize that he was a dead man, even better.

The thought warmed him so much he forgot the cold.

Cole had always loved traps and trapping. As a boy he'd spent long days working his trapline. He collected the animals he caught, then reset the traps or moved them to a different location. He was no John Colter, trapping beaver in the far reaches of the frontier, but deep in the mountains he could go all day without seeing another human being. He had liked that just fine.

Cole was not one to sit and watch the birds and clouds. Restless by nature, he had kept on the move, working his way along the mountain streams and across remote ridges. The steep landscape and the toil of carrying the traps had turned his lean body hard and wiry. Wind, cold, rain, heat—the weather was just something to be acknowledged, something to push through to the next ridge, the next bend in the creek.

He had learned to move without a sound, sometimes walking right up to an unsuspecting fox or deer, so silently had he passed through the woods, like a forest creature himself. If he could take a shot at any game, he took it. Often he had just one or two bullets, and they were not to be wasted. Those skills had served him well in this war.

The Coles always had lived off the land. While the rest of the country suffered through the Great Depression, the hard times never changed for the Cole family.

The animals that he collected in his traps varied. There were a few beaver in the more remote mountain creeks, but he also caught fox, possum, muskrat, and raccoon. The pelts weren't worth as much with the demand for fur being low on account of the Great Depression, but he would at least bring in enough to buy another handful of bullets and maybe some canned goods. Anything else, and the Cole family pretty much made their own or made do.

His trapping trips weren't only about making money. In the end, he just liked being alone in the deep mountain woods. Once he got to be a teenager, he would sometimes disappear into those woods for two or three days at a time. At night, he would roll himself in a blanket and sleep by his campfire, cooking whatever he had caught over the flames. The mountains, his rifle, a fire, a blanket, fresh water from a mountain stream, something to eat that he had hunted or trapped—Cole realized it was all a man needed in this world.

Some might say that he had been born a century too late, but the old ways still existed if you sought them out.

Now, on the outskirts of Bastogne, waiting for his trap to be sprung, Cole let the time pass over him like currents over stones in a mountain creek. He stayed alert even as one part of his mind drifted. Occasionally he heard Vaccaro fidget. That city boy was noisy as a herd of buffalo.

But his ears stayed sharp for other sounds. From the town held by the Americans came the grind of gears and sleepy curses. From the distant woods came the occasional guttural words of German, carried far on the chill, foggy air.

Then he heard the crunch of footsteps approaching across the frozen snow. The footsteps were coming from the direction of the German lines. He put his eye to the scope and his finger to the trigger.

He had no doubt that this was the enemy sniper.

As the sniper approached, the footsteps slowed and grew stealthier. It was almost as if he could sense the trap—and if the sniper was good enough, maybe he could. At one point, the footsteps paused, and Cole could imagine his quarry stopping to sniff the air for trouble.

The footsteps resumed, approached the gap in the stone wall, and passed through. Cole realized that he hadn't needed the trip wire at all, not with the crunchy snow.

But the enemy soldier hit the twine anyway, yanking the milk pail off its perch, spilling the empty bottles and cowbells onto the ground. The clatter made Cole jump even though he'd been expecting it. He supposed that the German sniper might be having a heart attack right about now.

But it wasn't his heart that was going to kill him.

Vaccaro flicked on his flashlight, catching the enemy sniper like a deer in the headlights.

Through the scope, Cole got a good glimpse of him. The man was bundled in winter gear, rifle slung over his shoulder, a scarf over his face—but Cole could see the man's eyes clearly. They were blue as they caught the light and wide open in surprise.

Cole put his sights over the man's heart and squeezed the trigger.

In the circle of light, he watched as the shot knocked the man backward into the gap in the stone wall.

Vaccaro clicked off the light. Seconds later, he was running at a crouch back toward Cole's position.

"Let's get the hell out of here," he said, panting from the effort of running through the snow. "Between that racket and that light, we're bound to attract attention. We don't want our own guys shooting at us."

Cole couldn't agree more. They were in no-man's-land. Not everybody knew they were out here, and the GIs in Bastogne would be jumpy. He crawled out from under the wagon, and in the dark they weaved their way through the outlying yards to return to the center of Bastogne.

CHAPTER TEN

OBERSTURMBANNFÜHRER BAUER DID NOT REGRET his decision to surrender. First, he and his men were alive. The Americans had not shot them outright. There had always been the chance that might happen.

But they had been lucky. It seemed as if no one had found out about the incident on the road where Messner had ordered the American prisoners to be shot. If anyone had known, he supposed that their reception by the Americans would have been quite different.

Second, his wounded men had immediately been taken into the care of the American doctors in Bastogne. While it was true that their medical resources were limited and they were working out of a drafty old church rather than a hospital, the conditions were far better than what the German wounded could have expected in the forest.

He had even been allowed, under escort, to visit his men in the hospital.

The makeshift hospital was far from ideal, being dark and cold. The interior smelled strongly of grimy clothing and unwashed blankets, rubbing alcohol, and something unhealthy—perhaps decaying flesh. Nonetheless, the American medical staff were doing the best that they could for the wounded Germans. There were no beds, so the wounded had been spread across the stone floor.

Bauer saw with surprise that his men were on the floor right next to the wounded GIs. The care that they were receiving was every bit the equal of what the medical staff gave to their own men. Also in the mix were several wounded civilians, including a few women and children. *How regrettable,* he thought.

Most of the cases in the hospital were men with severe wounds. Any of the so-called walking wounded were needed to defend Bastogne. Now that he was a prisoner, behind enemy lines, Bauer had seen just how undermanned the Americans were. And yet he and his comrades had been unable to push them out of Bastogne. The Americans were just too determined.

Some men were so badly injured that their entire heads were swaddled in bandages, except for holes left for their nose and mouth. For many their wounds had not been caused by bullets but by the cold. More than a few fingers and toes had been claimed by frostbite.

Walking down the rows of wounded, he knelt at the side of each man to give him a quick word of encouragement. The wounded men had the bitter taste of failure in their mouths after the disastrous attack, but they had done their part, and it was still possible that the overall German advance might still succeed elsewhere.

At last he came to the side of Feldt, the old campaigner who had been bleeding badly from his wounds following the attack across the field, when Bauer's troops had been surprised by artillery and tank fire.

"Ah, Herr Obersturmbannführer," Feldt said.

"Good to see you, Feldt. How are you feeling?"

"Much better, sir. Thank you."

"Are you warm enough?" Bauer looked doubtfully at the thin blanket covering the old Soldat. Then again, none of the patients, American or otherwise, had much in the way of blankets, which were in short supply.

Feldt grinned. "I am German, Herr Obersturmbannführer. I never feel the cold."

Bauer patted his knee. "Well, it looks as if the Americans are taking good care of you."

"I have no complaints, sir."

Bauer stood up, feeling his knees crack in the cold. "Take care of yourself, Feldt."

"I will, sir."

Bauer reached the end of the row and nodded at his escort, a clerk who spoke a little German, and then the two of them started their return trip through the hospital.

He was almost back to the door, looking forward to some fresh air after the stuffy air inside, when he heard a shrill shout.

"It's him! That's the German son of a bitch who had us shot!"

Startled, Bauer looked around and spotted a man on a nest of blankets who had managed to raise himself on an elbow and point accusingly at Bauer.

So there had been a survivor after all. He had warned that fool Messner about that.

Bauer's escort didn't seem to know what to make of it, and Bauer himself didn't know what to do except to keep walking. The wounded man was still pointing and shouting, "Someone stop that Nazi son of a bitch!"

As it turned out, the wounded soldier's outburst was not going unnoticed. A doctor went over to the shouting wounded man and crouched beside him. The officer seemed to quickly parse the story, because he looked up at Bauer with a scowl.

The doctor got to his feet and pivoted toward Bauer.

"You there!" he called.

Bauer realized that his situation as a prisoner had just taken a turn for the worse.

* * *

THERE WAS a brief respite for the soldiers in Bastogne when a few bags of mail managed to get through. So far there had been airdrops of medicine, food, and ammo. Now there was also mail, because the army understood that morale was a powerful weapon.

There was little else that gladdened hearts so much as a letter from home. The words might be written by a wife, by a sweetheart, or by a mother. It didn't matter. What really resonated was the idea that someone back home cared, had made the effort to write words on a page, and now the physical piece of paper that had been in their hands had miraculously arrived on the front lines. Many of the letters were written on the thin paper known as Victory mail, or "V-mail," to speed the process of delivering mail.

As they gathered in the street for mail call, a few soldiers were lucky enough to receive letters from home. This time, among the sniper squad that was now part of Team SNAFU, it was Hank who got mail in the form of a letter from his mother.

The faint whiff of ink and paper made its way to Hank's nose as he held the letter. It was a familiar, comforting smell that reminded him of home and simpler times. The words made home seem close and yet also a million miles away.

The letter had been written before Christmas, and his mother described the preparations back home, from plans for baking cookies to the perennial debate between his parents over what variety of Christmas tree was best. Balsam or fir? As he read it, tears came to his eyes. Nobody said anything about the tears.

"It all sounds so normal back home," Hank said. "Yet here we are fighting in the cold and snow. It doesn't even seem possible."

Yet it was that idea of life back home that kept them going. They remembered a place where you could pray freely, speak your mind, and not live in fear of being shot at. What was there to fight for, if not for that?

Other than a package that Cole had received that contained a bowie knife made by Hollis Bailey back home, Cole never received any mail. His family wasn't the writing type, and Cole wasn't the reading type.

Vaccaro sighed. He hadn't received a letter either. He looked on a bit enviously at the others savoring each word from home.

"I guess nobody in my family had time to write with the holidays," he said.

"What about all your girlfriends?" Cole prompted. The way that Vaccaro bragged, you would have thought that he had to fight off the girls back home.

"Maybe I broke their hearts and they can't bear to write to me," he said.

But as it turned out, the mail sack included a handful of letters and packages addressed to "Any GI." The corporal who had distributed the mail went around handing them out. He gave a package to Cole, who stared at it, not quite knowing what to do.

"Aren't you going to open it?" Vaccaro wondered.

"Who's it from?"

"I guess people back home haven't totally forgotten that we're out here fighting for them."

Cole slid a calloused finger under a loose corner of the brown paper wrapper and tore it open. There was a scarf inside hand-knitted in shades of brown and yellow, with a bold red stripe worked in. Against the drab, slushy backdrop of Bastogne, the scarf was like a bright bird glimpsed in a wintry forest.

Also inside was a letter.

He handed it over to Vaccaro. "Better read that," he said. "It might be from one of your girlfriends after all."

Vaccaro looked at the letter with curiosity. It was addressed to "Dear Soldier" in a neat, somewhat childlike handwriting.

"You better read that aloud, Vaccaro!" someone urged.

"All right, all right." Vaccaro shook out the letter with dramatic flair, cleared his throat, and began to read out loud:

Dear Soldier,

I hope this letter finds you well, even amidst the chaos of war. My name is Emily, and I am a fifteen-year-old girl from a small town in Ohio. Although we have never met, I want you to know that your courage and sacrifice have touched my heart in ways I cannot fully express.

As I sit by the window, watching the snowflakes fall gently onto our frost-covered fields, I think of you—far away from home, battling the bitter cold and the relentless enemy. It's hard for me to imagine the hardships you face, but I want you to know that you are not alone. We, back here in Ohio, stand with you in spirit, praying for your safety and victory.

The Battle of the Bulge—the name itself sends shivers down my spine. I've read about the fierce fighting, the freezing temperatures, and the unwavering determination of our troops. You are the heroes who hold the line, who refuse to yield even when the odds seem insurmountable. Your sacrifices will forever be etched in history, and I am grateful beyond words.

In our little town, we've organized knitting circles to make scarves and mittens for the soldiers. Every stitch is a prayer, every warm garment a token of our appreciation. We gather in the church basement, our fingers working diligently, imagining the warmth these gifts will bring to your frozen hands. It's a small gesture, but it comes from the depths of our hearts.

I've seen the newsreels at the local theater—the brave soldiers trudging through snow, their breath visible in the frigid air. Some of you are barely older than my big brother, and yet you carry the weight of the world on your shoulders. How can I thank you adequately? How can I convey the depth of my admiration?

Perhaps these words will reach you across the vast ocean, through the smoke and gunfire: Thank you. Thank you for defending our freedom, for standing firm against tyranny. Thank you for enduring hunger, fatigue, and fear so that we may live in a world where liberty prevails. I pray for my brother's safety every night and I also pray for you and all the soldiers fighting with him.

With heartfelt gratitude,

Emily

P.S. Enclosed in this package, you'll find a hand-knit scarf—a small token of our appreciation. Please wear it knowing that it carries our warmth and prayers.

Breaking the silence that followed, Cole was the first to speak. "I'll be damned," he said. "That girl can sure write a letter."

Cole was still holding the colorful scarf. He got up and walked over to where Hank was still staring at his own letter from home, as if willing each word to burn into his memory. Cole bent down and gave him the scarf. "Here, kid. You better take this. That girl who wrote us wouldn't want a mean bastard like me to have it. It will look a lot better on you—and keep you warm too."

Hank looked up and took the scarf, his eyes still damp. "Thanks," he said hoarsely. He held the scarf for a moment, then wrapped it around his neck.

The brief peace and quiet did not last long. It was as if the Germans had been waiting for this opportunity to catch them off guard. They heard the deep booms of artillery from the forested hills beyond Bastogne and then the sound of shells screeching in.

"Take cover!" Lieutenant Mulholland shouted, although the men were already scrambling to get out of the street.

Cole dove for a shell hole and landed alongside Vaccaro, who muttered, "Those goddamn Krauts must not have gotten any mail. I'd say they're jealous."

"Why don't you write them and tell them to go to hell?"

"That's not a bad idea."

Then the screeching reached a crescendo, and the artillery shells rained down on Bastogne.

The deafening sound of explosions and the continuous whistle of the shells filled the soldiers' ears, drowning out any other noise. The ground beneath them rumbled and shook like a giant's hungry belly. Through the roar of the barrage, they could hear screams of men who had been caught out in the open.

"Medic!" someone shouted. "Medic!"

Incredibly, some brave bastard of a medic dashed through the chaos to answer the cry for help.

Through it all, Cole stayed hunkered down in the hole while bits of rock and debris clattered onto his helmet. He prayed that a bomb didn't land on his head. With some amusement, he recalled the old saying that there was no such thing as an atheist in a foxhole.

If you're up there, Lord, spare me from these bombs, he prayed. *While you're at it, Lord, damn these Krauts to hell.*

CHAPTER ELEVEN

As THE LATEST bombardment rained down on Bastogne, a paratrooper from the 101st Airborne was risking his life on a highly unusual mission. The nineteen-year-old private ran down the street, dodging the bomb blasts, finally ducking into the shattered remains of a tavern.

It was a favor for a friend who had brought him there. Just minutes ago, he had been visiting a buddy at the hospital.

His friend had made a simple request. "Listen, won't you do me a favor? I'm dying for a drink. Can't you find me some booze?"

"Gee, I don't know—"

"Come on, won't you at least try?"

How could he refuse the wishes of a wounded buddy? He patted his friend's shoulder in reassurance and minutes later found himself outside on the streets of Bastogne.

Looking around at the bomb-blasted buildings, he wondered, *Now what?*

It couldn't be that hard to find some booze. He had to give it a try, at least.

From time to time a German shell whistled in and exploded, adding more rubble to the ruins. The air was heavy with the acrid smell of smoke and gunpowder, mixed with the stench of death and destruction. The earth rumbled and buildings collapsed. He felt the impact reverberating through his bones. He swallowed back the coppery taste of fear that he had become all too used to since the Battle of the Bulge had begun.

Through the smoke, he could see other soldiers running for cover. Only an idiot would be out on the streets by choice—and yet here he was.

The easiest thing would have been to give up—but that was not how he was wired. If he said he was going to do something, then he did it.

The young paratrooper thought back to when his father had seen him off at the train station. His father was an Italian immigrant and a proud American. Standing there on the station platform, his father had simply said, "Don't do anything to embarrass the family."

He hadn't so far, and he wasn't about to now.

He took a deep breath to steady his nerves, then headed down the street. He was looking for a bar or tavern that hadn't been smashed to bits. It wasn't easy to find. Building after building that he passed bore the telltale scars of the intermittent bombardments that Bastogne had endured. He passed the entrance to one bar whose shattered sign proclaimed it as UNE TAVERNE. Glancing inside at the fallen timbers scattered every which way like a game of pick-up sticks, he realized that the place would be a death trap to enter. He kept going.

Halfway down the next block, he found a more promising watering hole. The TAVERNE sign hung crookedly above the door like a broken wing, but the interior was more or less intact.

Might be something, he thought.

However, he was disappointed to discover that most of the bottles behind the bar had been smashed where they stood by some nearby bomb blast. Any intact bottles had long since been liberated by thirsty GIs.

He noticed that the beer tap appeared unscathed. When he pulled the lever, beer ran out and spattered on the floor. This discovery delighted the paratrooper, who couldn't wait to bring some back to his wounded friend. The question was, How was he going to do that? He looked behind the bar and around the floor for anything that might serve as a container for carrying the beer, but he gave up in futility. Everything was broken and smashed. He might have to hunt through the ruins of nearby buildings until he found a suitable container, costing him precious time. As a reminder that the bar might be reduced to rubble at any moment—and him along with it—a shell smashed into the street not more than a hundred feet away. The shock wave carried dust and the smell of cordite into the bar.

Rubble rained down and hit his helmet. That was when he got the idea.

Quickly, he took off his helmet and held it under the tap, filling it with beer. Once it was nearly overflowing, he started his return trip to the hospital. Mercifully, he seemed to have picked a time when the Germans were busy shelling another part of the city.

He reached the hospital and ducked inside, quickly locating his friend. No one bothered to question why a soldier was carrying a helmet slopping over with beer.

When his buddy spotted him, his eyes got big. "Is that helmet full of beer?"

"You said you wanted a drink."

"Boy, do I ever."

Kneeling beside the man, he helped him take a few gulps. He'd soon had his fill. That was no problem, because other wounded nearby had seen what he carried in his helmet, and they all wanted a drink from it. The helmet was soon empty.

"We need more!" the men cried. "Get more!"

The paratrooper found himself with no choice but to head back to the ruined tavern and fill up his helmet once again.

Coming back, he wasn't as lucky about the bombardment as he had been on his first trip. A couple of shells landed nearby, one so close that the blast knocked him off his feet. Still, he cradled the helmet as he went down, managing to keep most of the beer from spilling.

He was surprised to find himself being helped to his feet by a couple of soldiers.

"You all right, buddy?" one of the soldiers asked in a strong Brooklyn accent. "It's just a suggestion, but a helmet works a whole lot better when you wear it on your head."

The other soldier didn't speak right away. He was lean as a whip but strong, easily helping to pull the stunned paratrooper upright. "Why, I do believe this boy has got beer right here in his helmet. Sure smells like it."

The second soldier had a strong country accent, with the words *right here* sounding like *rye cheer*. The paratrooper was still swaying a little, so the soldier didn't let go.

The paratrooper could see right away that they were snipers, because both carried rifles with telescopic sights and they wore bedsheets over their uniforms in an attempt at winter camouflage. Both looked like tough customers, and he worried that they would help themselves to his beer.

"Listen, it's not for me," the paratrooper blurted. "It's for my buddies in the hospital."

"At the rate you're going, you'll either end up there yourself or get killed," the soldier with the country accent said. "Best follow us if you want to get there in one piece."

The two ducked down an alley, and the paratrooper felt compelled to follow. The alley grew narrower, seeming to press in on all sides, but the sound of the artillery shells impacting diminished. Minutes later they arrived at the hospital. He turned to thank them, maybe offer them a sip of beer, but they were already gone, having slipped quietly away into the darkness.

The paratrooper delivered his second helmet filled with beer, sharing it with even more soldiers this time. There was still plenty despite some of it having sloshed out during the shelling.

When that helmet ran dry, he made a third trip and shared the beer around.

With the praise of the soldiers ringing in his ears, he made yet another trip back to the tavern for more beer. Half of it slopped out on the run back, but it hardly mattered, because he never made it through the hospital doors.

Blocking his path was a very irate officer, who happened to be one of the doctors at the hospital.

He stabbed an accusing finger in the paratrooper's direction with so much force that it may as well have been a bayonet.

"Are you the one who's been giving my patients beer?" the officer demanded. He didn't wait for an answer before launching into a tirade. "I've got all kinds of bad wounds in here. Head wounds, chest wounds. Some are awaiting surgery. Giving these men anything to drink by mouth—beer, no less—is the worst thing you could do. You could kill them, dammit. I ought to have you shot!"

"Yes, sir," the young soldier stammered. The officer looked mad enough to make good on his threat.

"Now get out of here and don't let me see you again!"

Out of pure reflex, the chastised paratrooper slapped his helmet back on his head. The dregs of the beer that remained ran down over his ears, but he scarcely noticed because he was eager to get out of there. He wasn't going to wait around for the officer to change his mind. He followed the doctor's orders and got the hell out of there.

* * *

Back at Division HQ, Colonel Roberts was not a happy camper. It was bad enough that the Germans remained intent on pushing them out of Bastogne. Now he had the brass breathing down his neck to boot.

"You have got to be kidding me!"

"Sir?" asked a clerk who was busy at a typewriter. Paperwork continued for the army, even in the midst of war.

Ignoring the clerk, he glared down at the message in front of him. He worked at a makeshift desk that consisted of an old door set between two crates. Just days ago, the door had actually graced the front of a neighboring house but had been blown off by an incoming shell. One of the clerks had salvaged it out of the street.

A fireplace struggled to heat the room, but it seemed to be throwing off more smoke than heat. As a result, they had been forced to open the window to let in fresh air, which defeated the purpose of having a fire in the first place. A stack of papers on his desk threatened to blow away in the breeze, so he had set his .45 on top of the stack to weigh it down.

The colonel chomped hard on an unlit cigar. He would have liked to light it, but to do so would have endangered his ample sandy-colored mustache, because he had already smoked the cigar down to a stub. Cigars were in short supply, and the soggy nubbin of the last cigar that he'd smoked was all that he had left.

The message he had received concerned a German prisoner. In particular, a German officer named Bauer. The colonel had barely been aware of the existence of this officer beyond the fact that several Germans had surrendered outside Bastogne, but apparently *someone* knew about him—and they wanted to interrogate Bauer for a couple of reasons. The first reason centered on the fact that Bauer might have valuable information to share about the disposition of German troops or other battle plans.

The colonel shook his head. He knew that interrogating the German officer would be pointless. A German officer was a tough nut to crack, and there was no reason this one would be any different.

The second reason interest had been expressed in Bauer was that he was being considered a war criminal, responsible for the execution of American prisoners. The colonel had raised his eyebrows at that—he hadn't known anything about the incident until he had been informed by a surgeon who had treated a soldier who claimed to be the lone survivor of the incident.

The colonel had no reason to doubt that the account was true.

Perhaps the powers that be thought the accusation of a war crime would give them leverage with Bauer to get him to talk. For his own part, the colonel thought that the best solution would be to take Bauer out back and shoot him, if he had, in fact, been responsible for the murder of American boys.

But the decision wasn't up to him, and to make matters worse, he was being sent a British intelligence officer who happened to speak German. The colonel's orders were to make sure that the officer returned with the German.

It was this last part that left the colonel fuming. He would have to give up some of his soldiers to escort the German. He wasn't in any position to give up a single able-bodied man, not while there was still a chance—a diminishing one, fortunately—that the Germans might still be marching through downtown Bastogne and singing "Ach, Du Lieber Augustin."

Not only that, but escorting the German to the rear for interrogation would be a dangerous business, perhaps even foolhardy. It was hard to say who held the territory south of town. It might be Americans one minute and Germans the next.

The colonel glared at the clerk. "Go find Lieutenant Mulholland. Tell him I need a couple of his snipers. I hear he has a couple of real crackerjacks. If they can't get the job done, I don't know who can."

CHAPTER TWELVE

BROCK SUMNER HAD MANAGED to find one of the few bottles of booze still available in the city, then claimed it by eminent domain.

The bottle had started out in the possession of a young soldier who'd had the good luck to find it in the ruins of a café. Brock had quickly relieved him of his burden upon spotting the soldier carrying the bottle.

"Gimme that," he'd said after approaching the other GI.

"Finders keepers," said the GI, who was already feeling the effects of the couple of pulls he had taken from the bottle. If he noticed Brock's tone, he didn't seem concerned about it. The booze seemed to have gone straight to his head.

But it was clear from Brock's body language, as well as the menacing presence of three or four of his rough-looking buddies, that the rule of finders keepers no longer applied. It had been supplanted by the law of the jungle. The jungle, in this case, being the bombed and blasted streets of Bastogne.

Brock squared his shoulders and stood directly in front of the GI, blocking his path. The GI's giddy smile faded. He was sobering up fast. Brock held out his hand for the bottle, and the GI acquiesced.

However, the GI lingered, seemingly uncertain as to what to do next.

Brock gave him a shove, and the smaller man stumbled back a few steps.

"Get lost before you get worse than that," Brock growled. "Maybe you can find yourself some milk and cookies."

Brock and his cronies laughed as the confused GI scurried away, processing the fact that he had just been the victim of a strong-arm robbery.

"You sure told him, Brock," said a soldier to his right. Everybody in the squad called him "Brock"—no nickname necessary. Deep down, he took pride in the fact that "Brock" had a certain ring to it, like one of those movie stars who always played a tough guy.

As for the squad itself, it was more like his personal gang than a military unit. The boys did what he said, no questions asked. Vern was more or less his right-hand man, with Walt "Boot" McCann a close second. Boot had gotten the nickname because a girl at a roadhouse bar had turned him down when he'd asked her to dance, saying he was ugly as a boot. His army buddies weren't about to let that one go.

"Damn straight, Vern," Brock replied. "No sense lettin' good liquor go to waste on that poor excuse for a soldier."

They made short work of the bottle even before they reached the impromptu hospital where one of his buddies from home had ended up.

His buddy's name was Charlie Knuth. Charlie had been a star athlete and popular guy in high school, one of those genuinely nice guys everybody liked, but more than that, he was one of the few people who had actually seemed to like Brock, somehow seeing past his bullying facade to a quality in him that was worthy of friendship. Maybe it was the fact that Brock was loyal to a fault.

They had played baseball together and even gone out on a couple of double dates, which usually ended up with Brock and his girl making out in the front seat, and Charlie and his date making out in the back seat.

They had kept in touch during the intervening years after high school, playing baseball or going out for a beer from time to time.

Then the war had come along, and like so many old friends, they had lost track of each other as young men from home headed in different directions, either to fight the Krauts or the Japs.

Whatever good qualities Charlie had seen and encouraged in Brock had not been improved by army life, and he had mostly reverted to his bullying ways.

Inside the hospital was nothing but confusion and misery. Wounded covered the floor in rows, bandaged and in various stages of suffering. Brock searched for his old friend but was soon distracted.

"Hello, beautiful," Brock said rudely to a young woman working as a nurse. He made no effort to hide the fact that he was ogling her from top to bottom, though the nurse was barely more than a teenager. "What are you doin' after the show?"

She hurried past, ignoring Brock, her arms loaded with bandages. Most of the American men were respectful and kind, grateful for her efforts, but she had learned that there were always exceptions to the rule.

As the light from a window she was passing caught her face, Brock could only stare, coming to the sudden realization that the nurse he'd just seen appeared to be a young Black woman. Light skinned, to be sure, but Black all the same. Someone of her race was a rare sight in Belgium.

He wondered what she was doing here. Back home in Florida, the Jim Crow laws ensured that there were separate hospitals for Blacks and whites. Separate schools and water fountains too. He was taken aback by the color of her skin, not to mention the fact that she had given him the brush-off.

"Uppity broad," he said to her retreating figure, with little care as to whether she overheard him. He turned to an orderly nearby. "Hey, bub."

"What is it?" The orderly wore a white armband and the haggard expression of someone who had seen too much grief and heartache in too little time.

"How come we're letting a Black girl look after our boys?"

"If any of them don't like it, they can join the corpses outside," replied the orderly, who hurried on, his demeanor suggesting he had no patience for fools such as the one he had just encountered.

Little did Brock and his cronies know that this was the young woman who would go down in history as the "Angel of Bastogne" for her tireless care of the wounded. Years ago, her mother had fled war in the Belgian Congo to begin a new life in this peaceful town—only for her daughter to find war on her doorstep here in Bastogne.

Being a nurse was dangerous work, not to mention exhausting. Just two days before, her friend and fellow nurse had been killed—along with several helpless American wounded—when a stray German bomb struck a house where the men were being cared for.

Instant death was a constant threat they all lived under. She could just as easily have been sheltering with her family in a cellar like so many civilians in Bastogne, but she had volunteered to do what she could for the men fighting the German invaders. Perhaps peace would return to Bastogne, but it seemed hard to believe with the occasional artillery bursts as a reminder.

Meanwhile, it was clear that no help would be coming from the orderly. Brock shook his head in disgust and kept going. Inside the dark reaches of the hospital, Brock asked around until he'd tracked down his old friend.

He found Charlie stretched out on blankets on the stone floor, which could not have been comfortable. Brock had seen his share of wounded, but he was still shocked by the sight of his old friend from home. Charlie Knuth had always been handsome and athletic, but now he looked emaciated, his good looks marred by ugly frostbitten patches. One side of his head was wrapped in bandages that looked suspiciously as if they had been strips torn from bedsheets, now hardened with dried blood. More bandages covered his torso. The skin of his hands was blistered and cracked from frostbite, revealing raw meat inside the cracks. Brock looked away, keeping his eyes on Charlie's, because they were the only part of him that seemed unscathed.

It turned out that Charlie was in a distressed state, but not only because of his wounds. After expressing his initial delight at setting eyes on a familiar face from home, he struggled up out of his blankets and grabbed hold of Brock with his blistered hands.

"You won't believe it, Brock. I just saw him in here. That goddamn Nazi!"

"Who?"

"The bastard who tried to kill me, that's who!"

Obviously distraught by his experiences, Brock's old hometown friend quickly shared an upsetting story of how his own unit had been captured and then gunned down somewhere on the road to Bastogne. He couldn't even say where, exactly, on the snowy road that the massacre had taken place. He just knew that he'd been the only survivor among the prisoners.

"It sounds to me like you're lucky to be alive."

"They shot me, but I faked being dead."

Brock listened with something close to disbelief. He had heard rumors about these sorts of things—the execution of prisoners—but it had always been a "I knew a guy who knew somebody who" type of situation. This time was different. Bastogne was still isolated, but they had heard about the Malmedy massacre perpetrated by Kampfgruppe Pieper. More than eighty Americans had been gunned down. There wasn't a GI who wasn't outraged about it.

In a separate incident, his buddy had seen another slaughter of POWs and still carried the wounds of the encounter. Maybe the Germans hadn't massacred as many as they had at Malmedy, but it was a massacre all the same. Already, in the aftermath of Malmedy, angry Americans had retaliated by refusing to take prisoners. All the rules of war seemed to have gone out the window where the Battle of the Bulge was concerned.

To make matters worse, Charlie had spotted the Nazi officer who'd been in charge, visiting wounded Germans in the hospital.

"What did they do with the son of a bitch?" Brock asked.

"When I told him, the surgeon raised hell about the German being a war criminal, and they hauled his ass off to HQ."

"Is that so? They should have taken him outside and shot that Kraut."

Knuth grabbed Sumner's sleeve. "He killed them all! Every last one of our guys! You've got to make sure justice is done, Brock. Promise me you'll do that."

"I'll see what I can do," Brock said. He clenched and unclenched his fists, as if aching to hit something. He couldn't think of anything worse than being a helpless prisoner and having the enemy gun you down. They were sons of bitches, every last one of them.

Deep down Brock recognized that he hadn't always been the best person, having used his brawn to bully people all his life. Just a few minutes ago he had stolen a bottle of booze from another GI. He knew that was wrong, but during a war, what was the point of doing what was right? Also, he knew that he was small potatoes compared to the likes of Adolf Hitler, the biggest damn bully the world had ever seen, along with all his Nazi minions.

Thinking about helpless Americans being gunned down by the Krauts made his blood boil.

"Promise me!" Charlie repeated. It was clear his strength was fading after his sudden desperate burst of anger. Brock's sleeve slipped from his grasp, and he suddenly faded back into his sweaty blanket, his eyes still bright in his hollow, frostbitten face.

Brock nodded down at him, his expression grim. "If there's any justice in this world, somebody has got to put that Nazi in the dirt," he agreed. "And the sooner, the better."

* * *

CORPORAL BROCK WAS a mixed bag as a soldier. On the one hand, he got the job done, and that job was fighting the enemy. Looking at his combat record, it would be hard to find a better soldier. He and the rest of his squad always seemed to be in the thick of it. Wherever they went, they gave the Germans hell.

However, he was the kind of soldier who was surly to officers and gave anyone who outranked him a hard time. Then again, he knew better than to cross the line, knowing when not to push his luck. There were plenty of tough officers and seasoned sergeants who would've chewed him up and spit him out. He either steered clear of these men or kept his mouth shut. He wasn't stupid, after all.

On the other hand, Brock could smell weakness like a shark

smelled blood in the water. When he smelled that weakness, he went in for the kill.

If he had been stronger of character, he might have made an excellent sergeant himself. But everybody in any position of leadership knew that Brock Sumner was trouble, a good man in a fight but unreliable when the bullets weren't flying.

He also wasn't one to make idle threats. He hadn't made hollow promises to his wounded friend from home just to make them both feel better.

Not long after leaving the hospital where he had seen Charlie, Brock was hanging around the kitchen area that was being set up to prepare hot grub, hoping for some coffee, talking to a couple of guys doing the same thing. It wasn't just coffee that Brock was after. He had found that the best way to learn anything in the army was to keep your ears open. A lot of guys ran their mouths to show off how much they knew and how important they were. Unless it was top secret, somebody gossiped about it eventually.

"All we want is some hot coffee," a soldier groused. "Is that too damn much to ask?"

"I hear they've got some Nazi officer that they captured in there. I'll bet they give him all the hot coffee that he wants."

Brock's ears pricked up. "You say they've got a German officer in there?"

"Sure they do. I heard he's locked up in the cellar at HQ. They're keeping him down there because it would be an awful shame if a bomb from his own side killed him."

"Sounds more like justice if you ask me," another soldier said.

Brock picked up his rifle, which had been leaning against the building, and started walking away.

"Hey, where you goin'? Don't you want that coffee?"

"I've got somewhere else to be," he said gruffly.

Suddenly Brock wasn't interested in hot beverages. He had bigger fish to fry. If the German officer really was being held at HQ, then Brock knew what he had to do.

CHAPTER THIRTEEN

Contrary to what the Americans may have wanted to believe, not all the residents of Bastogne were sympathetic to the Allies. A few had ties to Germany, either having been born there or having family there. Others favored the Nazi cause, having believed Hitler's poison. There were even a handful who, as in all wars, didn't take any side other than their own.

One such person was Benoit Dauvin, who had worked on the Belgian railroad before the war shut it down. Bastogne had once been a somewhat important rail hub until the railroad had been destroyed in WWI. The rails had been rebuilt, only to be destroyed once more in this more recent war.

Consequently, Dauvin had worked at nothing more than odd jobs since then. He had also served in the Great War. Between the wars, he had worked with many Germans in his railroad career and found them professional and efficient. He was not all that surprised by Germany's initial military successes.

Though he was past fifty, Dauvin had a young family to feed, due to having remarried later in life after his first wife died of a fever. He did not have enough money to buy food at the inflated wartime prices, but he did have information to trade. It helped that he leaned toward being a German sympathizer. When he spotted the German officer being escorted from the hospital, he had trailed along in hopes that this might be useful information.

Obviously, this was a prisoner of some importance. Dauvin had pieced together the story from townspeople he knew who helped at the hospital. He also spoke a little English and had managed to pick up a few things here and there from eavesdropping on the Americans, who tended to ignore a fiftysomething resident of the city they were defending. In their eyes, he was nearly invisible.

From scraps of fabric, one could sew a quilt, and that was exactly what Dauvin did with the scraps of information that he gathered. A few townspeople running errands for the Americans liked to gossip and inflate their own importance. Even a soldier on guard duty let slip a bit too much when trading a bottle of the local juniper-flavored Jenever liquor for packs of cigarettes. Dauvin would trade the cigarettes later for something to eat.

Through his wheeling and dealing, he soon had the name of the German officer and the reason the Americans took such an interest in him. He also learned of the plan to spirit the German out of Bastogne.

That night he made his way through the no-man's-land between Bastogne and the German lines. It was dangerous, to be sure, but hunger and the need to feed one's family was a great motivator.

The German that the spy reported to in this case was Hauptmann Messner. What Dauvin did not know was that since most of Messner's unit had been lost in the devastating fight in the clearing, he had been put to use as a kind of factotum, and this included interviewing the occasional German sympathizers who wandered in to exchange tips for food.

Messner found that he liked the independence and even the small amount of power that his new role provided. The information that he gathered gave him the ear of higher-ranking officers.

Soon enough, he would be back in the fight. Every German soldier in the Ardennes Forest would need to fight, if they hoped to win. Until he was reassigned to a combat role, Messner got a new perspective on the war.

He was surprised that a few old men and boys had even volunteered to fight alongside the Germans, but he had sent them away. Still, he had admired their spirit. As for men like this informant, he found them barely tolerable, like dogs hoping for a few table scraps.

Messner's eyes had widened at the news of the German officer being held prisoner by the Americans, especially when he heard the prisoner's name.

"That traitor?" Messner muttered upon hearing Bauer identified. "I thought he was dead!"

"No, sir. He is being moved." The informant quickly summed up the plan.

The informant was rewarded with a loaf of stale bread, some Landjäger, or dried sausages, and a few tins of rations. He put them all into a cloth sack and began his return journey to Bastogne. If he made it through no-man's-land once again, his family would eat for a few more days.

He'd been lucky to leave in one piece. With his back turned, he had not seen the German officer's hand go to the snap on the holster of his pistol. In Messner's mind, a rat was a rat, even one that had provided him with information. For all he knew, this rat would be turning around and providing the Americans with information about the Germans. A rat could not be trusted.

One less rat would be doing the world a favor. After all, what was the life of a rat even worth?

But he let his hand fall, thinking that the man might yet prove useful.

* * *

Messner debated what to do with the information. He had disliked Obersturmbannführer Bauer, whom he considered to be an officer who had lost his nerve to the point that he was actively undermining the German advance—at least the portion of the advance that he commanded.

The memory of how he had been in constant conflict with Bauer brought a fresh wave of bitterness to his mind. In Messner's imagination, Bauer had seemed to go out of his way to thwart Messner whenever he could, seeming to think that the younger officer was too bold. The shooting of the prisoners outside Bastogne had been one occasion when Messner had been a step ahead of the Obersturmbannführer.

Recalling the look of shock on Bauer's face at the sight of the dead prisoners, Messner smiled.

To hear that Bauer was still alive and being held by the Americans was quite surprising. He'd been sure that the Obersturmbannführer had died in the confusing last moments of the battle as he attempted to surrender. Then again, wasn't it enough that Bauer was now a prisoner of the Americans?

Perhaps not, Messner thought. Maybe it was what Bauer had wanted all along. He had seemed ready and willing to surrender the entire unit. It was nothing short of betrayal.

Messner might simply have passed along this intelligence about Bauer now being a prisoner, but he was sure that it would scarcely be noticed. What his superiors really wanted to know was how many US troops were in Bastogne, their readiness to fight, how many tanks had reached the city, how many more were expected—the rat had provided no useful information about that.

At most, the information that Bauer had been captured might be included in an official report. With American reinforcements beginning to reach Bastogne, there were bigger concerns than a single captured German officer. The fight was widening, and the German advance was in peril.

For all that anyone would care, Bauer might as well have been dead.

Who was to say that couldn't still happen?

A plan began to hatch in Messner's mind. He smiled again at the thought.

In the end he decided that he would go after Bauer himself. With any luck, this could be accomplished in a few hours. Messner wouldn't even be missed.

There was more than one way this could go. It remained possible that Bauer could be taken from the Americans and returned to Germany for proper treatment at the hands of the SS or Gestapo. In Messner's mind, there was no doubt that Bauer was nothing but a traitor.

But recapturing Bauer might prove difficult, and he might be able to talk his way out of any accusations that he had given up the fight too soon.

Better yet, Bauer would never make it anywhere but would simply become another body by the roadside.

Either way, Bauer would be quite surprised to see him again. It would be the last thing he would expect. Messner smiled coldly at the thought.

He could have lied to himself and called his plan one of military importance, an effort to prevent strategic information from falling into Allied hands. But if he was being honest with himself, the simple truth of the matter was that Messner wanted revenge.

Looking around, he spotted Obergefreiter Dietzel and Gettinger, and waved them over. Both men were never far away. After explaining what he wanted to do, he was pleased to see that both men seemed game. In fact, Dietzel wore a slight smile that suggested he was also imagining the look on Bauer's face when they caught up to him. If their Hauptmann believed that Bauer was a traitor, then they believed it too.

It was likely that Bauer and his escort would take the road toward where the Germans knew the Allied command to be located. This road was not far from Messner's current position. With any luck, Messner and his men would find them on that road and return within a few hours.

If his informant was correct, the Americans were being quite foolhardy. Much of the city remained surrounded. The patrol escorting Bauer would likely have to fight its way out.

The Americans must be desperate to spirit Bauer away, taking a huge chance in doing so.

Timing was everything, but if they could only get in position ahead of Bauer and his escorts, their odds would improve.

In fact, Messner planned to bring those odds closer to zero. To do so, they would need to hurry if they hoped to intercept Bauer and his escort.

* * *

Hauptmann Messner wasted no time commandeering a Kübelwagen for their use. "We need to get into position right away," he said, getting in the back with Dietzel, who kept his sniper rifle propped between his knees, the butt resting on the toe of his right boot to cushion it from the bumps in the road.

Gettinger took the wheel. The scent of gasoline lingered in the air as the Kübelwagen's engine roared to life, contrasting sharply with the fresh winter air. Along with the gasoline smell was the sharp, metallic scent of weapons and other gear, ready to be used at a moment's notice.

Messner clapped Gettinger on the shoulder and urged, *"Schnell, schnell."*

The tires of the Kübelwagen spun in the frozen slush, showering some nearby Soldaten with icy mud and evoking a few curses. But then the sturdy vehicle gained traction and shot down the road, carrying the soldiers on their mission of revenge.

Messner had chosen two of his most loyal and dependable men to accompany him. There were others he could have taken, but this might be the kind of mission that could not be talked about later. These two knew to keep their mouths shut.

He was glad to have Obergefreiter Gerhard Dietzel with him in particular. The man was a highly capable sniper, the unit's designated Jaeger—a word that translated as *hunter*. In Dietzel's case, it was a very apt description.

He had seen Dietzel at work—the way that he had managed to pick off the escaping POW before he got into the trees was just an example of his skill with a rifle. Messner had seen the man drop targets at distances that did not seem possible. One thing for certain, he was glad he had never been in the Jaeger's rifle sights.

Not for the first time, Messner could feel Dietzel's gaze on him, evaluating his every move, his every decision. That was Dietzel for you, always watching, always the observer. He had been trained well by the Wehrmacht's sniper school. Those skills had been put to use more times than Messner could count.

The sniper's reputation was well known among the soldiers, to the point that he had become something of a legend among the men, and his presence gave Messner confidence that their mission would be successful.

Dietzel never asked for much, but Messner thought it wise to throw his dog a bone now and then. He turned to Dietzel and said, "Obergefreiter, your precision and accuracy are unparalleled. You are a force to be reckoned with."

"I am only doing my duty, sir," Dietzel replied.

"With your help, we will make short work of this traitor and the Americans escorting him."

"You can count on me, Herr Hauptmann."

The man spoke with such simple certainty that it did not sound like bragging or boasting.

Messner glanced ahead at the driver's seat, where Gettinger had a tense grip on the wheel, his knuckles white. Driving in these conditions was far from easy. The road itself was bad enough, of course, without the added threat of attack at any moment. For all they knew, the woods ahead might be filled with Americans waiting to ambush them.

Gettinger's apparent driving skills aside, Messner was even more reassured about the man's overall abilities. Where Dietzel was like a surgical instrument, sharp and precise, Gettinger was more like something blunt, perhaps a hammer or a wooden club. But Messner had no complaints. Time and again, Gettinger had shown himself to be a man who carried out his orders without question—as long as those orders could be easily understood.

To reach the necessary road, they had needed to come at it from the southwest, passing down a number of farm lanes, working their way around Bastogne. Of course, it would have been faster and easier to drive right through the center of town, but that was impossible with the Americans stubbornly holding Bastogne. Messner's routing problems were simply a microcosm of what was faced by the entire German advance. At one point they even cut across a couple of fields where the ground was frozen enough not to get bogged down. The Kübelwagen barely made it. A heavy panzer wouldn't have had a prayer.

Progress was frustrating and slow, but Gettinger seemed up to the task with Messner navigating. They were all relieved to arrive at the actual road—without an enemy soldier in sight.

The Kübelwagen then raced down the icy road, the frigid air whistling past their ears. Messner shivered but reminded himself that riding in the open vehicle was superior to walking. Besides, they were well on their way to gaining some measure of revenge.

There was no time to waste. Based on what the informer had told him, it was likely that Bauer and his escorts had a head start. Messner would not allow the hated Obersturmbannführer to slip through his fingers.

As they continued down the road in the direction that the traitor and his American escorts were supposed to have taken, Messner could see that it was surrounded by dense woods. Again, the thought crossed his mind that the conditions were perfect for an ambush.

The stretch of road had been empty, but now a modest farmhouse loomed ahead. No smoke rose from the chimney, despite the cold, so it was apparent the house was empty. This came as no surprise; many of the civilians had fled the fighting. As they came closer, it was clear that the farmhouse had seen better days. One of the shutters hung askew and dangled in the breeze, threatening to come crashing down. Part of the whitewashed stucco facing had cracked off, perhaps the result of nearby shelling or a mortar blast. The field stone wall beneath gaped like an open wound. The rubble made a small pile near the front door, which stood wide open.

Messner might have written the house off as abandoned if it had not been for a furtive movement in the vicinity of the front door.

"Herr Hauptmann," Dietzel said quietly, his voice full of warning.

"Yes, I saw it too."

He tapped the driver's shoulder, signaling for Gettinger to slow down and then stop a couple hundred meters from the farmhouse. They needed to approach cautiously if the house was occupied, possibly by enemy soldiers.

With any luck, that might even be Bauer and his escort inside.

As soon as the Kübelwagen stopped, Dietzel slid out of the back seat with his sniper rifle in hand and disappeared into the trees for cover. Messner followed suit, his own weapon at the ready. Gettinger stayed behind with the Kübelwagen, his own rifle balanced across the hood, ready to provide covering fire if needed.

Snow crunched under their boots as they made their way through the woods toward their target. The cold air burned in Messner's lungs as he carefully stepped around twigs and branches, trying not to make any noise.

He was not very successful, as proved by the fact that the sniper glanced back at him once or twice, unable to hide his exasperation. Somehow Dietzel managed to move through the trees like smoke.

They reached a fallen log that provided good cover, a spot where they could keep an eye on the farmhouse up ahead. It looked quiet and peaceful enough, but Messner knew that looks could be deceiving. There was definitely someone inside. He pulled out his binoculars and glassed the house, but still didn't see anything useful.

The noise of the Kübelwagen approaching had certainly given them away and warned whoever was in the house. They would either be busy hiding or escaping out the back—or preparing to open fire. Which would it be?

Messner got his answer when an American GI appeared in the doorway, his rifle leveled, ready for business. He squeezed off a couple of shots in the direction of the Kübelwagen.

In one swift motion, Dietzel aimed and fired, the sound of the shot echoing through the woods. The GI fell onto the snowy ground in front of the farmhouse.

But there was at least one more soldier in there. There was a muzzle flash from one of the windows, then another. Bullets whistled uncomfortably close, telling them that the soldier inside must have spotted Dietzel's own muzzle flash from the gloom of the winter woods.

From the Kübelwagen, Gettinger shot back. The GI inside traded a few shots with him, then fired again at the woods, seemingly not sure where to focus his attention. Not for the first time, Messner was impressed by the rapid firing of the semiautomatic M1 rifle that the Americans used.

He was armed with an MP 40 submachine gun, which was not very effective at this range. Nonetheless, he emptied his magazine in the direction of the farmhouse. Silently, he urged Dietzel to shoot, but the sharpshooter would not be hurried. From behind the cover offered by the Kübelwagen, Gettinger also kept shooting.

Then Dietzel fired again, his bullet going in through the window and silencing the American soldier. It was an impressive shot, considering that the target hadn't been visible, hidden within the shadows of the farmhouse. But Dietzel's bullet had found him all the same.

Cautiously, they approached the house, weapons at the ready. Could these have been Bauer's escorts? The traitor might still be alive inside the farmhouse, considering that the Americans would not have armed him.

Dietzel nudged the fallen GI with the toe of his boot, and the man groaned. Though badly wounded, he was still alive.

Not for long. Messner approached and shot the man in the head with his pistol. The pool of blood widened and stained the snow.

They moved inside and found the second soldier, but it was clear that Dietzel's bullet had killed him outright.

Quickly, they searched the house. The place was small and the search didn't take long. There was no sign of Bauer and no tracks leading out the back door.

"Let's go," Messner said, disappointed that capturing Bauer hadn't been as easy as this. But he remained confident that their quarry was close. "They can't be too far ahead of us."

Gettinger got behind the wheel of the Kübelwagen again, Messner and Dietzel climbed into the back, and they roared off down the road once more.

CHAPTER FOURTEEN

Cole and Vaccaro were looking forward to some well-deserved rest. Their sniper mission during the night had left them exhausted, but at least now the soldiers and citizens of Bastogne were able to move more freely without fear of being picked off.

That freedom was well worth the price of a little sleep. In fact, the mission had gone so well that they were planning to bring the fight to the Germans once darkness returned by doing some sniping of their own. It was high time that the enemy had something to fear.

They curled up in the basement of the house where they had spent their first night upon arriving in Bastogne. It was cold, dark, musty, and smelled a bit too strongly of the men who had sheltered there, but Vaccaro summed it up best.

"This sure as hell beats a foxhole," he said.

Cole grunted in agreement, then rolled over and promptly fell asleep.

It felt like just minutes later that Lieutenant Mulholland was kicking their boots to wake them up.

"For pity's sake, Lieutenant," Vaccaro complained groggily. "We just went to sleep."

"No rest for the weary," Mulholland said. "We're wanted at HQ. Be sure to grab your gear because you won't be coming back here."

Hank heard them and asked, "What about me?"

"Not you, kid. Go back to sleep. Colonel Roberts specifically requested these two knuckleheads. Apparently they have some kind of reputation."

Leaving Hank behind, the three of them made their way to HQ, where they found Colonel Roberts waiting for them. His mood had not improved since receiving the communiqué earlier.

But he was not alone. In addition to the clerk who was busy typing away, there was also a young British officer. However, their attention was mainly drawn to a tall German officer standing by the fireplace, which continued its struggle to heat the room. Cole, Vaccaro, and Mulholland looked at the German with open curiosity.

At that moment an officer barged in with an urgent message for the colonel, who read the piece of paper thrust into his hands and swore.

Cole took that time to size up the German. The man stood tall and proud, his gaze fixed on the three soldiers before him. His uniform looked impeccable, the brass buttons of his jacket shining brightly in the dim light. The officer's cap was perched perfectly on his head, a stark contrast to the disheveled clerk, hunched over his typewriter in the corner.

His hands were bound together, a testament to the fact that he was clearly a prisoner. His winter coat was open, revealing a thick white scarf draped around his neck, the only touch of color in the drab room. The scarf gave the officer a dashing, stylish air compared to the Americans.

But the German clearly wasn't some aloof, cold fish. An amused smile played over his lips. For some reason the smile set Cole's teeth on edge more than the sight of the officer's uniform.

To his surprise, the German appeared to be sizing him up as well. He could almost feel the man's eyes moving over him. He was appraising Cole from his boots to the helmet emblazoned with the Confederate flag. His eyes lingered on the Springfield sniper rifle before coming to rest on Cole's face. The German's look of amusement was gone, replaced by hostility, as if the sight of the rifle led him to the realization of how many Soldaten that rifle had claimed.

Cole glared back, not about to be cowed by some Kraut officer, no matter how fancy he seemed. Neither man appeared ready to be the first to look away.

It was the German who finally shifted his gaze, mainly because the colonel had launched into another fit of swearing after reading this latest communication.

"Get on the horn and tell them to hold at all costs, dammit!" the colonel finally exclaimed. He swore a few more times with such vehemence that it was like a car emitting a series of loud backfires, finally stopping to glare at the German, as if this were all this enemy officer's fault.

Then again, it sort of was his fault—or, at least, it was definitely the fault of his fellow Germans that Americans were fighting and dying on this wintry battlefield.

The tension in the room was as palpable as the hissing of a gas leak, and it seemed as if the sparks popping from the fireplace like gunshots threatened to ignite the tense atmosphere into an inferno.

Cole and Vaccaro exchanged a look. What the hell had they found themselves in the middle of?

Mulholland chose that moment to clear his throat and announced, "Sir, here are the snipers I was telling you about."

"Thank you, Lieutenant." The colonel's eyes flicked from Vaccaro to Cole and stayed there. "You must be Cole."

Cole spoke up. "I reckon that's me, sir."

"You reckon?" The colonel gave him a hard look as he chewed on the stub of a cigar, his eyes finally coming to rest on the Confederate flag painted on Cole's helmet. "Last time I checked, soldier, this was the United States Army, not the Confederate States Army."

The colonel seemed to be expecting a reply, but Cole let it hang for a long moment before he responded, "Yes, sir."

"I've heard about you, Cole," the colonel continued, with a tone that indicated what he'd heard wasn't all good. "There's a rumor going around that you're a crack shot and some kind of modern Daniel Boone."

Cole didn't say anything.

The colonel grunted. "So you're a man of few words, huh? I like that in a soldier. Here's the thing. I need a couple of men who know their way around the woods well enough that they won't walk right into the Germans' arms. Rumors aside, Mulholland here says that you're both up to the task."

"If the lieutenant says so, sir."

"The German officer you see over there is Obersturmbannführer Bauer. What you need to do is get our *guest* here over to VIII Corps HQ at Neufchâteau. That's about seventeen miles southwest of Bastogne. They want to know what he knows. Just so you know who you're dealing with, this German piece-of-shit Obersturmbannführer is also a war criminal, having gunned down several of our boys in cold blood on the outskirts of Bastogne. Be that as it may, you will get him there in one piece. Is that understood?"

"Yes, sir."

"Good. You will also be taking Lieutenant Rupert with you." The colonel nodded in the direction of the British officer, who had been standing quietly nearby, looking like the student in class who was hoping that nobody called on him. "I'm sure the lieutenant can fill you in later on his interest in Colonel Blitzkrieg here. He is our official deputy liaison with Montgomery's boys, so don't lose him along the way. That prickly bastard Montgomery might stop talking to us if that happened."

Both Cole and Vaccaro couldn't avoid looking doubtfully in the British officer's direction. From his apple-cheeked complexion, he appeared to be embarrassed just to be standing there.

At this point, the colonel added, "Lieutenant Rupert, you'll be the ranking officer, but you would do well to listen to what these men have to say. My advice is that when they tell you to jump, then jump. They might not look like much, but I have it on good authority that they're your best chance of staying alive out there. Never forget that this is a war zone."

Rupert managed to turn even redder with embarrassment, until his face resembled a ripe strawberry, or possibly a beet.

For his own part, the German simply looked bemused by it all.

"When do we move out, sir?" Cole asked.

"The sooner, the better. Right now would be good."

"Right now?"

"I hope to hell your eyes work better than your ears, son. What part of 'right now' don't you understand? Dismissed!"

The colonel then issued curt orders to the German to go with them. The German gave a single nod, showing that he understood. Apparently the Kraut spoke English well enough.

Moments later Cole, Vaccaro, and Mulholland found themselves standing outside HQ in the slush and cold, their numbers having been increased by one German prisoner and a British officer. The presence of the German caused several stares, not to mention a few hard looks. Many of the men on this street held a grudge against the Germans. They had lost friends to the enemy, after all. Others felt that the German attack through the Ardennes had been a dirty trick. The attitude seemed to be that the only good German was a dead German.

But they were supposed to keep this German alive.

Cole shook his head. How the hell had they ended up with this assignment?

Lieutenant Rupert was called away by one of the HQ clerks, who was trying to find him a warm hat and something more suitable to the winter conditions than his kidskin dress gloves. Cole and Vaccaro would just have to make do with what they already had.

It turned out that the German had better winter gear than the Americans. He had been allowed to keep his haversack, from which he produced another scarf, woolen mittens, a warm coat with a hood, even goggles against blowing snow and ice. It was more proof that the Germans had been well prepared for this winter campaign. His hands remained bound in front of him. The footing was slippery, and the German moved slowly, struggling to keep his balance.

Cole prodded him with the butt of his rifle. "We might be stuck with you, but you sure as hell ain't gonna slow us down," he said.

The German didn't respond other than to pick up the pace.

"This is a hell of a mess," Vaccaro said. "How did we end up having to babysit this Kraut."

"Just lucky, I reckon."

"What else is new?"

As it turned out, their mission nearly ended before it even got started. They had not gone far when several soldiers approached, making a beeline for them.

"What do you suppose they want?" Vaccaro muttered.

"Nothin' good," Cole replied. Instinctively, he tightened his grip on his rifle.

He was soon proved right. The biggest soldier in the group, apparently the ringleader, squared off in front of them, blocking their way.

"Where are you going with that Kraut?" he demanded.

"We have orders to move him," Cole replied.

"We saw you come out of HQ," the soldier said. "Where the hell else would you take him?"

"Like I said, we've got orders." Cole didn't elaborate.

"Listen, you probably don't know this Kraut is responsible for murdering some of our guys."

"So I heard. What about it?"

Seeing that Cole was going to operate by the book, the soldier changed tactics and adopted a friendly, reasonable tone. "Hey, I don't want to get off on the wrong foot here. My guys call me Brock."

"Cole. This here is Vaccaro."

"OK, that wasn't so hard, was it? Making proper introductions and all. We're all on the same side here, Cole. You can see that, right?"

"What's your point, Brock?"

"My point is that it sounds to me as if you and your buddy drew the short end of the stick and got stuck hauling this Kraut piece of crap to wherever he's supposed to go. My guess is you're supposed to take him to Corps HQ. That's a long way off, and it's a shit show out there, believe me. You look like you've already seen your share of that show. Why don't you save yourselves some trouble and hand him over to me."

"What are you gonna do with him?"

Brock's friendly tone lapsed and he grew angry. "Don't worry about it."

"I'd rather that you told me. Who knows, I might even like what you've got planned."

"Listen, buddy. Hand the Kraut over to me. Nobody is going to ask questions. Just say that the German got lost in the mail."

"Does he look like a postcard to you?"

"Aw, for the love of Pete." Brock had run out of patience. He stepped forward, rifle aimed at the prisoner's head. "Why don't you say something? Huh? You damn Kraut. I'm sure you can speak some English. Go ahead and say something."

But the German officer remained silent, his expression unchanged. It was as if talking to Brock wasn't worth the effort.

"We know you killed our boys back there," Brock said, trying a different tactic. "Didn't you?"

Still no response.

Frustrated, Brock reversed his rifle and prepared to hit the prisoner square in the face with the rifle butt. "Say something!" he shouted.

Cole stepped between them before Brock could strike. "That's enough," Cole said sternly. "You know what, I think I figured out what you're gonna do with him."

"It's easier if you don't know, buddy. But let's just say this Kraut is going to die trying to escape. We might rough him up a little first, for what he did to our guys, but never mind about that. Think of all the trouble you're going to save yourselves from going through, considering that you've got a snowball's chance in hell of getting from Bastogne to Neufchâteau in one piece."

"I don't think so." Cole shifted his rifle ever so slightly, the muzzle not quite pointing at Brock, but the message was clear. "Now get the hell out of our way."

Slowly, Brock lowered the butt of his rifle, making it clear that he had thought better of clubbing the prisoner. "All right, if that's the way you're gonna be about it."

"I reckon it is."

Brock and the other soldiers with him didn't move. Neither did Cole and Vaccaro. They had reached a tense impasse.

That was when the British liaison officer showed up again, hastily pulling on a wool hat and mittens. "What's going on here?" he asked.

"These boys don't seem to agree that the German prisoner should be allowed to leave Bastogne," Cole drawled, his eyes not straying from Brock's face.

"Is that so?" Rupert said. "Well, we have our orders. Step aside, soldier."

It was not a commanding voice, but an officer was an officer, British or American.

Besides, Cole backed him up. He said to Brock, "Best do what the lieutenant says and get the hell out of the way."

Reluctantly, Brock and his men moved aside.

"This isn't over," Brock said. "When I get through with you, you'll wish you'd done this the easy way."

"Anytime you want to try me, you go right ahead," Cole replied.

Cole kept an easy grip on his rifle, half expecting Brock and his group to try something. He didn't think there would be any shooting, not on the streets of Bastogne, but the best way to avoid trouble would be to make it seem like he'd be willing to shoot first.

However, Brock and his men slowly faded into the background. Cole could feel their stares boring into him.

"One thing for sure, hillbilly. You make friends wherever you go," Vaccaro said.

"You know me, city boy. Friendly as a porcupine."

Vaccaro stifled a guffaw. "Maybe a porcupine with rabies."

"I believe those men intended to cause us trouble," Lieutenant Rupert said.

"You'd be right about that, sir," Vaccaro said.

Cole glanced at the German officer. In the gray light, his face no longer wore its bemused expression. To his credit, the German did not appear frightened, but thoughtful. He seemed to know very well that he had just dodged a bullet. A literal one, in this case.

Looking back over his shoulder, Cole could see Brock and his crew still watching them in the distance. Cole had the sneaking suspicion that they might not have seen the last of Brock and his crew. As if the Germans weren't enough, now they might have to worry about vigilantes from their own side.

In a way, Cole understood how they felt. Had the shoe been on the other foot, he might also have wanted revenge on the German officer and wouldn't have cared who got in his way. But a job was a job, and orders were orders. More than that, he didn't like being threatened. *Nobody tells me what to do.* Nothing stuck in his craw worse than that.

He had met men like Brock before, men used to getting their own way, in and out of the military. Most were bullies and loudmouths that he had dealt with in his own way. Just ask the bully who had enjoyed picking on weaker men during boot camp. Cole had sent him to the infirmary for an extended stay. The man had been bigger, more like Brock's size, but he had been no match for the can of beans that Cole had swung inside a sock.

Back home in the mountains, a man made his own justice. Cole certainly hadn't shared it with anyone, but as a boy of fourteen, he had hunted down and shot the rival moonshiner who had killed his father. It had been a fair fight, a running duel through the woods and peaks and valleys against a dangerous opponent who was half-crazy and a crack shot. What Cole had done was prompted by more than revenge; with his pa gone, that moonshiner had reckoned that he could have his pick of Cole's sisters or maybe even push the family off their land.

That moonshiner had reckoned wrong.

Dead wrong.

Cole doubted that Brock was half the man that wily old moonshiner had been. That moonshiner had underestimated Cole. If Brock thought that he could push Cole around, he would be making the same mistake.

CHAPTER FIFTEEN

THE COLONEL ORDERED up a jeep for them. Transportation down the cold and snowy road would be welcome, but they would hardly be traveling in luxury.

A corporal from the motor pool delivered the jeep with some explanation. Well, it was really a disclaimer. He hopped out and approached them with a bowlegged swagger, wearing his grease-stained khakis like a badge of honor.

"If it was just you two and the prisoner, Colonel Roberts said he wouldn't have bothered," the corporal admitted. "But he had to make an effort to accommodate that British liaison. Heaven forbid that we should make a British officer walk anywhere. You'd almost think they were still sore about losing the Revolutionary War."

Cole glanced over at Lieutenant Rupert but had a hard time imagining him as a redcoat with a powdered wig, possibly carrying a Brown Bess musket. Then again, who knew—maybe one of his ancestors had tangled with one of Cole's people way back then. They were both on the same side now, at least.

He took a second look at the British lieutenant. Rupert wore a newer uniform and hadn't been living rough like the GIs, so that with his fresh-scrubbed face he barely managed to look older than a teenager. He had grown a thin mustache in the style of Clark Gable, as if to make himself look older. However, the mustache was so sparse that it more closely resembled the tines of a rake than a thick brush, so that it only managed to highlight his youth.

"Once the gas runs out, you're on your own," the corporal said cheerfully, as if that thought pleased him. "That's if the engine doesn't up and quit first. Or the brakes give out. I'd say it's a coin toss which one happens first. Nobody is going to miss this bucket of bolts, that's for sure."

"Gee, thanks," Vaccaro said.

The corporal strode off, whistling tunelessly.

Vaccaro got behind the wheel and started it up. The jeep ran about as well as the motor pool corporal whistled. Cole eyed it doubtfully. The strong scent of gasoline filled the air as the jeep's motor rumbled and sputtered, racing one minute and then threatening to die the next. A pool of black oil steadily expanded across the snow beneath the vehicle. A few bullet holes pockmarked the sides.

Though the average jeep was truly basic transportation, this one wasn't much more than a motor and four wheels held together with wire and rusty bolts. It had already been beat to pieces by untold miles of European back roads. Between the bullet holes and the rust, the thing had more spots than a leopard. Gasoline remained in short supply, but somehow a full tank had been procured for the jeep.

Though battered, the jeep beat walking. Within minutes of the vehicle's arrival, they were on their way. Cole wanted to cover as many miles as they could before dark—and hopefully put some distance between themselves and the fighting around Bastogne.

Their jeep threaded its way through the outskirts of Bastogne, with Vaccaro at the wheel. Cole rode shotgun, an old term from stagecoach days when it was the job of the armed man sitting beside the driver to defend the stagecoach against highwaymen. Cole obliged by keeping his rifle at the ready. The German and the British officer sat in the back seat. Everyone was squeezed in tight, and it promised to be a long, cold, uncomfortable ride in the open air.

Several times Vaccaro had to slow down and steer around the wreckage of mangled trucks or the burned-out remains of a tank. Fresh snow dusted the blackened metal skeletons as well as the bodies nearby, as if nature itself was trying to hide the ugly charnel house horrors left by men at war. Under their blanket of snow, it was hard to tell whether the dead were German, Americans, or civilians caught in the cross fire. For the dead, it no longer mattered whose side they had been on.

The road was rough, worsened by the winter conditions and cratered by shell holes. Deep ruts seemed to want to reach out and grab the tires, so that Vaccaro had to slow down and maneuver carefully. Even on the good stretches of road, the jeep loaded with four men struggled to reach speeds of more than forty miles per hour. The motor struggled and wheezed in protest. In the open air, that much speed felt as reckless as being in a race car.

Cole still appreciated the fact that they didn't have to walk, although it was anybody's guess if the gas in the tank would be enough to get them to their destination. There was also the nagging thought of how much oil the jeep was leaking.

Vaccaro broke his concentration long enough to pat the dashboard and say, "Hang in there, Betsy. You can do this."

As it turned out, running out of gas or engine troubles would be the least of their worries.

Just a few miles out of Bastogne, a mortar shell came screaming in. It was hard to say who had fired at them, and it really didn't matter. Any vehicle moving on the road might be considered fair game by either side.

"Holy hell!" Vaccaro shouted, his natural inclination being to jerk the wheel to one side, away from the sound of the incoming round.

His reaction kept them from continuing in the straight line that would have carried them right into the mortar shell, which burst off to their left. Hot metal flashed overhead, but they weren't hit.

However, Vaccaro had steered the jeep directly into a deep rut, one so deep that it was practically a trench. The forward motion of the jeep came to an abrupt halt as the front tires disappeared into the rut. The force of the jolt sent Cole, Rupert, and the German flying out of the vehicle.

Cole managed to grab the German by the back of his coat collar and shoved him toward a roadside ditch that offered some cover as another mortar shell rained down. Cole threw Bauer in the ditch and landed on top of him. The last thing he wanted was for the man to run away.

Fortunately, the barrage halted. Cole picked himself up out of the ditch and dragged the German after him.

"Everybody all right?" he asked, looking around.

Nobody had been hit. Lucky for them, the snow and mud had softened their landing when they had been thrown clear of the jeep. Vaccaro wasn't as lucky, slamming his head against the steering wheel with such force that he came away with a bloody nose.

"Dammit, I think it might be broken," he said, pressing a handkerchief to his face.

"It's better than a fat chunk of shrapnel in your face," Cole said.

"If you say so." He dabbed at his nose again. "Hurts like hell in this cold."

"I thought you said you were a good driver."

"Normally when I'm driving, people aren't shooting at me."

"There is that," Cole agreed. He didn't say it to Vaccaro, but Cole had never actually driven a vehicle. Growing up, the Cole family had been too poor to own so much as a rusty old Ford. Or a mule. If they wanted to get anywhere, they walked. In the mountains, all that they ever needed were their own two feet.

Vaccaro's bloody nose was no picnic, but as it turned out, the jeep got the worst of it. The four of them pushed it out of the hole that had caught the front wheels, but the force of the impact had shredded one of the tires, bent the steering rod, and bashed in the radiator. Considering the nearly indestructible nature of the average jeep, the amount of damage was testament to the force with which they had hit that hole.

Vaccaro was the most mechanically inclined of the bunch and was soon crawling under the jeep to get a better look at the damage.

"Think we can fix it?" Rupert wondered.

"Sure, if we had the tools, the parts, and maybe three days," Vaccaro replied. "A heated garage would be nice while we're at it."

"Looks like we're walking from here on out," Cole announced.

Having gathered a few supplies from the jeep, Cole led their small group away from the abandoned vehicle. He looked around to see how everyone was doing as they set out.

It was one hell of a motley crew, he decided—two half-frozen snipers, a wet-nosed British officer, and a German prisoner. The only thing that would make them more ridiculous would be if the German was leading a dancing bear.

The young British officer sported bright-pink cheeks as a result of the cold. His uniform was a little too clean, indicating that he was not a combat officer. His winter gear mainly consisted of a wool overcoat that looked warm enough but would have been more appropriate on a fashionable city street than the snowy woods of the Ardennes. He wore tall leather riding boots that didn't look comfortable for walking, but they would keep the snow out.

He'd been carrying only a sidearm, but Cole had insisted that the Brit be given an M1 carbine.

"I don't believe I've ever used one of these," he said, looking it over.

Cole showed him how to load the weapon and operate it. Rupert caught on quickly. Cole finished the lesson by adding, "The most important thing is not to shoot me or Vaccaro. You can shoot all the Germans you want, including this one we've got with us."

Rupert nodded. It would be understandable if he saw his situation as having been thrown to the wolves. Nonetheless, he maintained a cheery can-do attitude. He didn't complain. Cole couldn't decide if that cheerfulness made him like Rupert or hate him—the jury was still out on that one.

The prisoner still had his hands bound in front of him, although in an act of mercy, one of the clerks at HQ had tugged mittens over his bare hands to ward off frostbite. His vaguely amused expression had returned. It was as if the German realized that he should have already been dead by now, so he could watch the events that unfolded with detachment. Through his silence, it seemed as if this German officer was determined to remain stoic until the very end.

Cole felt a twinge of admiration for the man's resolve. He had expected their captive to bellyache or come up with some story that they had the wrong guy, but instead he seemed to accept his fate with quiet dignity. He hadn't even seemed afraid when Brock and his crew had threatened him. Cole gave him points for that, even if he was a no-good murdering Kraut.

As for Vaccaro, he also appeared resigned to his fate, his head down, a cigarette hanging from his mouth. Of course, Vaccaro also carried a scoped Springfield, but he had it slung over one shoulder as if confident they wouldn't run into any trouble this close to the city.

Cole wasn't so sure that they wouldn't have need of their weapons sooner rather than later. He kept his own rifle ready and would remind Vaccaro to do the same when the time came.

"How long do you think it's gonna take us to get there?" Vaccaro wondered.

"Tomorrow at most—if we don't run into any trouble," Cole said, adding, "Which we will."

"You are a regular ray of sunshine."

Cole smirked. "I ain't gonna sugarcoat it. This won't be easy."

"Hillbilly, when you of all people say something isn't going to be easy, it makes me nervous."

"Well, don't go sweating bullets about it."

"Yeah?"

"Yeah. I'd rather you were dodging bullets instead."

"If this is going to take us two days, it means we'll have to stay overnight somewhere. I hope there's a decent hotel along the way."

"I don't know about that. Hell, we'll be lucky if we can find a foxhole."

"It's damn cold, so the last place I want to sleep is a foxhole." Vaccaro glanced over at the German and lowered his voice. "If we have to camp out, what are we going to do about him?"

"I dunno," Cole admitted. "Hog-tie him if we have to."

"He won't like that."

"I don't really give a damn what he likes or doesn't like."

Vaccaro had raised a good point that nobody had thought through. Handling prisoners, especially important ones, was not usually in Cole's line of work. This was all-new territory.

Maybe Brock was right, Cole thought. They should have taken him up on his offer to take the Kraut off their hands. Nobody could have put up much of a stink if they claimed that the Kraut had run off. However, Cole had instinctively disliked Brock. The man couldn't be trusted. There was no way he would have handed the prisoner off to him.

Orders were orders, and Cole intended to follow them.

Bauer had overheard their conversation. "Excuse me," he said. "If I may?"

Up until now he had been silent, and Cole had forgotten that the man spoke English. When he did speak, it was with the careful annunciation of the educated class. It didn't make Cole like him any better—just the opposite.

"What the hell do you want?" Cole barked at him.

"There is no need to tie me up at night," he said. "I give you my word not to attempt an escape."

"The word of a murdering Nazi ain't worth much in my book."

"I am merely trying to save you some trouble and save me some discomfort. For that matter, I would appreciate it if you cut my hands free. It would make walking easier."

"I don't think so, Herr Barnstormer."

"Obersturmbannführer," Bauer said, correcting him.

"Yeah, like I said, Barnstormer."

Bauer gave him a blank look but didn't correct him this time.

Now on foot, they had no choice but to keep moving. Even that rattletrap jeep would have been better than slogging through the snow, mud, and slush up this road. There were a few tire tracks and tank treads, along with boot prints, to show that the road had been used recently—fresh enough that the snow hadn't covered the tracks.

"What do you think, Cole?" Vaccaro asked. "Our guys or their guys?"

Cole and Bauer replied at the same time, "Both."

Cole glanced over at Bauer, who arched an eyebrow at him. *That damn Kraut is probably hoping that some of his fellow Germans will come along and rescue him.* Cole had to admit that the odds were pretty good of that happening. The whole damn countryside had to be crawling with Krauts.

"Some of those are Studebaker treads," Cole explained for Vaccaro's benefit. "Some of the boots have hobnails, which means they're German." He might have added that the hobnailed boots seemed old-fashioned, but they actually provided better traction in the snow and mud. The rubber-soled US boots performed better on paved roads—and were that much quieter.

They kept going, with Cole keeping a wary eye on the surroundings trees. The trunks loomed dark and menacing on both sides of the road as the pitch grew steeper and they began to climb through the hilly country. The men were quiet except for the sound of their labored breathing. Halfway up, they paused for breath. Bauer was a little older and heavier than the Brit and the two Americans and seemed to be having the most trouble climbing the hill.

Again, it was Bauer who broke the silence. He nodded toward Vaccaro, who had stepped to the side of the road to relieve himself. "That is another reason why you may wish to free my hands."

Cole caught on to what he was saying and glared at him. "You gotta be kidding me. I sure as hell ain't gonna hold your schnitzel while you take a leak."

Bauer shrugged and offered what appeared to be an apologetic smile. "That makes two of us. There are some things you would prefer that I do on my own."

Cole thought about it. As much as he didn't want to cut the German's bonds, he wanted to help him take a leak even less. "All right, hold out your hands."

Cole drew his big bowie knife, the razor-sharp edge flashing even in the dull winter light. Bauer's eyes widened at the sight of it.

"I have never seen such a knife," he said.

"An old friend of mine from back home made it," Cole said, surprising himself by the proud tone he heard in his own voice. Most GIs carried the combat knives that they had been issued. While the standard-issue blade was an excellent knife, the blade that Hollis Bailey had forged for him was in a class by itself.

Bauer grunted in approval, although he eyed the blade warily. He did as he was told and held out his hands.

Cole started toward him, then stopped. He pointed the blade at

Bauer as he spoke. "Listen up, Herr Barnstormer. If this is some trick and you try to run, or you try to fight us, I'll use this blade to cut your heart out."

The German nodded. "Fair enough."

Cole cut him free. The blade was so sharp that it sliced through the strands as soon as it touched the rope.

Bauer stood rubbing his wrists. The tightly wound rope had left deep red gouges. Whoever had tied him up back at HQ hadn't been taking any chances. Cole stood tensely, waiting to see if Bauer tried anything.

"Thank you," the German said. "What was your name again?"

"Never mind that," Cole snapped. "Let's get one thing clear. I ain't your friend, Herr Barnstormer. I just didn't want to hold your dick while you took a piss. Now go on and take a leak."

Bauer moved beside Vaccaro and was soon sending his own stream into the snow. He even uttered a sigh of relief.

At least he hadn't lied about having to take a leak, Cole thought.

He returned the knife to its sheath and slid the rifle off his shoulder, watching up and down the road. It was only a matter of time before they ran into someone else. The question was, Would they be friendly or not? Cole stayed alert, hoping that if they encountered Germans, they would have time to get off the road before being seen.

They were taking a big chance by staying on the road. But they didn't have much choice, other than striking out through the woods, where the snow lay heavily among the trees. He didn't like that prospect, not if they wanted to make good time. They would just have to stay on the road and keep alert.

Bauer had buttoned himself back up and rejoined the group on the road. He still wore the heavy mittens, which Cole took to be a good sign. If Bauer planned on making a grab for one of their weapons, or otherwise make a run for it, he probably wouldn't have the clumsy mittens on.

"I won't tie you back up," Cole said. "But like I said, if you make a run for it, you're a dead man. Now let's all get moving. We need to cover as much ground as possible while there's still daylight."

CHAPTER SIXTEEN

COLE LED the way up the road, all his senses tense as a fiddle string, rifle at the ready. Even his nose sniffed the air for any whiff of German. They hadn't gone far before he heard the steady whine of an approaching engine, undercut by the clanking of steel treads.

Tanks.

More than one, and moving fast.

"Get off the road!" he said urgently, waving the others toward the trees. He pointed his rifle squarely at the German. He didn't want the prisoner getting any ideas about using that moment to escape. "Don't get any ideas, Herr Barnstormer. If you try to make a run for it, I'll put a big fat slug right through your back."

The look on the German's face indicated that he'd processed that mental image. He nodded curtly at Cole and followed Vaccaro and Rupert into the trees with the rifle aimed squarely at him.

It was hard to say whether the tanks were German or American and Cole, wasn't going to wait around to find out. The area was still hotly contested, with both sides probing and fighting in the countryside beyond Bastogne. It came down to the fact that the Americans were trying to send reinforcements and the Germans were trying to stop them. Cole didn't want to get caught in the middle of that meat grinder. He just wanted to deliver the Kraut like he'd been ordered and get back in one piece.

There was also the possibility that a tank patrol from either side would shoot first and ask questions later if they spotted men on the road. The tank commander would be worried about an ambush—a handful of men on the road more than likely meant snipers, mines, bazookas, or Panzerfaust. Mighty as a tank was, a lucky grenade throw could mean a tank tread getting knocked out. Out here on the front lines, repair was impossible, and the tank would need to be abandoned.

Whether the tanks were German or American, it wouldn't matter to Cole and his squad—the tankers wouldn't be taking any chances, which meant they would get machine-gunned all the same.

Vaccaro and Rupert took cover behind a fallen tree, their rifles over the log, trained on the road. The Kraut was down in the hole where the tree roots had ripped out of the ground. Cole slid in next to him. The snow was several inches deep here, kept from melting in this shady spot, the cold amplified by the shadows.

He kept his rifle ready but drew his knife. Silently, he cursed himself for not tying the German up again. If the tanks proved to be German, there was nothing to stop him from shouting a warning to his comrades or making a run for it.

"Make one peep and I'll slide my bowie knife between your ribs, easy like," Cole warned.

"Those tanks will be expecting an ambush," Bauer said. "It does not matter if they are German or American. The smartest thing to do is to be quiet and let them pass."

Cole nodded, glad that he and Bauer were on the same page regarding self-preservation.

Time stretched on and Cole had the nagging thought that they were once again falling behind schedule. What the hell was taking those tanks so long to go by? It sounded as if they had stopped. They seemed to be moving cautiously. The sound of engines grew louder before the tanks finally came into sight up the road. He was trying to tell from the engine noises whose tanks they were, but the echo off the hills distorted the sound.

Cole and Bauer were out of sight in the depression left by the windfall, gazing out from between the twisted tree roots at the rim of the hole. Wisely, Vaccaro and Rupert had their heads down behind the tree trunk. He was counting on Vaccaro to prevent the young British officer from doing something stupid, like deciding to take on the tanks and enemy soldiers single-handedly. Rupert didn't seem like the heroic type, but now would be a terrible time for him to get any notions that he was Prince Valiant.

Cole's heart sank when he saw that the approaching tanks were German panzers. This close, the things looked massive. Their 88 mm guns appeared big as tree trunks. The tanks carried machine guns as well, looking beastly and sinister.

There were three tanks, surrounded by a knot of supporting infantry. The soldiers were busy scanning the woods along the road for any sign of trouble. Wearing their white winter camouflage, some with white scarves over their faces, the German soldiers appeared inhuman or almost otherworldly, like wraiths moving through the woods. The businesslike dark stocks of their weapons stood out in sharp contrast. A few carried Panzerfaust to help the tanks deal with any US armor they encountered.

The name "stormtrooper" seemed apt as the wind blew and snow swirled around the foot soldiers. In this world of white, they were no longer men; it was as if they had been reduced to killing machines.

The harsh reality of the situation was that if it came down to a fight, Cole's group was outnumbered and seriously outgunned. But they had to stay put. If they tried to make a run for it now, they would be seen and chopped into mincemeat.

He took his eye off the scope long enough to glance over at Bauer, who watched the German troops on the road intently, calculation evident in his eyes as if weighing his chances of escape.

"Don't get any ideas," Cole whispered.

"Be quiet," Bauer snapped. "They will shoot us both."

That had sounded an awful lot like an order, which rankled Cole. The German officer seemed to have forgotten just who was in charge here.

Who the hell did this Kraut think he was? Cole debated going ahead and sticking that knife between Bauer's ribs just to shut him up for good.

But this was not the time for that. Reluctantly, he had to admit that Bauer was right about the need to keep quiet. The tanks would pass no more than fifty feet away from their hiding place at the side of the road. This was a time to hide rather than fight.

He looked over at Vaccaro, who seemed to be doing his best to sink into the snowy ground behind the log. Vaccaro caught his eye with an expression that seemed to say, *How the hell did we get into this mess?*

Cole felt the same way. He wished that they had retreated deeper into the forest. Better yet, not to have left Bastogne in the first place. They would just have to lie low until the Germans went past.

Vaccaro didn't give any indication that he was planning anything stupid. Cole still gave him a shake of his head to encourage that line of thinking.

Cole returned his eye to the rifle scope and scanned the approaching column. As soon as he did so, he felt Bauer go tense beside him. Obviously the man did not like the idea of watching idly while an American shot his comrades.

"Don't get riled," Cole whispered. "I'm just keeping an eye on your friends there."

He sensed Bauer relax ever so slightly.

Cole moved the reticle from one target to the next, but held his fire. The men weren't far away to begin with, and they sprang much closer through the scope to the point where he could see the details of their faces. These were not old men or boys rushed into uniform. They had the look of battle-hardened troops.

His sights settled on the lead tank. It would be so easy to pick off the tank commander, who stood exposed in the hatch. Cole's finger itched on the trigger, resisting the urge.

One comforting thought was that the panzers were so close that their 88s might be useless at such close range. But the Germans wouldn't need those big guns. Machine guns were mounted on the panzers, not to mention the detachment of infantrymen, several of them armed with Schmeisser machine pistols hanging from leather slings over their shoulders. At this range, their automatic weapons would be more than effective.

If we so much as sneeze, we're goners, Cole thought.

Again, he took his eye off the scope long enough to glance at Bauer. The man appeared to be holding his breath.

One thing Cole didn't see were any German snipers, which wasn't surprising. Who needed a scalpel when you were moving through the woods carrying a sledgehammer?

Once again he let the scope linger on the commander standing in the hatch of the lead tank. The man was gazing intently at the road ahead, not in the least aware that he'd be dead if Cole so much as twitched his finger.

The Germans seemed to be taking forever to go past. Seconds stretched into what felt like minutes. The cold from the frozen ground and snow had already seeped into Cole's elbows, cramping them, but he ignored the discomfort.

The panzers made an awful racket. In the quiet of the winter forest, that noise carried for a long distance.

Dimly, Cole became aware of more tank sounds. Were they coming from the opposite direction? Maybe it was just his ears playing tricks on him. With all the shooting and battles that he'd been through, it was a wonder that he wasn't completely deaf. The surrounding hills might be echoing the tank noises.

Bauer grabbed his arm to get his attention. "Down!" he urged. He turned toward Vaccaro and Rupert and repeated the command as loudly as he dared, adding a hand gesture for emphasis. In Vaccaro's case, the order wasn't necessary, because he held the log he was hiding behind in a lover's embrace. Foolishly, Rupert was still peering over the log. He held the carbine, the small rifle looking like a toy compared to what they were up against. At Bauer's urging, he ducked down.

Once again Cole felt annoyed that their prisoner thought that he could issue orders. But the reason for Bauer's urgency soon became clear.

It turned out that the sound of more tanks approaching wasn't simply in Cole's imagination. He knew something was up when he saw the Germans spring into action.

The commander of the lead tank shouted an order, and the infantrymen scattered, some running for the shelter of the trees and others staying on the road but dropping to one knee, using the panzers for cover. A couple of men unlimbered the unwieldy Panzerfaust and aimed them up the road at whatever was coming at the Germans.

Next, the tanks did their best to spread out, although there wasn't much room for that on the narrow forest track. The lead tank managed to race ahead, and the second nosed into the trees at the side of the road. The third tank stayed right where it was, swiveled its gun, and fired.

The blast made the ground shake, but that was nothing compared to the impact. Looking up the road, Cole was astonished to see the round from the panzer strike an American tank that had come into view around the bend. The round punched right through the armor, nearly dead center.

At first nothing happened, and Cole thought that maybe his eyes were playing tricks on him or that the shell was a dud. Then the tank seemed to hop up off the ground, followed by an explosion that sent flame and smoke shooting from every gap and chink in the armor. Seconds later, flames engulfed the tank. Nobody came crawling out of the inferno.

Cole was horrified at the destruction of his own side's tank, thinking that the poor bastards on the tank crew never had a chance, yet some part of him still admired the good shooting on the part of the panzer crew. Clearly they knew their business.

A second Sherman tank appeared around the bend, and this one seemed intent on kicking ass and taking names later, unperturbed by the fate of the tank that had been destroyed, firing as it advanced. This tank had supplemented its own armor with several medium-size tree trunks lashed across its front, the logs so green that some had branches with pine needles waving in the wind and crusted snow between the logs, like chinking in a log cabin. Cole didn't know how effective the logs would be against a direct hit, but they'd be better than nothing. The Shermans didn't have a good reputation for withstanding direct hits from the heavier German guns. The fate of the first tank had made that abundantly clear.

One shot from the Sherman struck one of the panzers but didn't penetrate its armor. Instead, the round bounced off the armor plating with an earsplitting *karoom* and detonated among the trees.

The Sherman kept advancing toward the three panzers. To Cole's way of thinking, it was nothing short of a suicide mission. Incredibly, the commander in the first German tank still stood in the hatch, almost resembling a soldier charging on horseback. He wasn't sure whether the German was brave or foolhardy. Then the panzer skidded to a halt and lowered its barrel, taking aim at the Sherman.

It was practically point-blank range. There was no way that the panzer could miss, even if the gunner had been blind in one eye and couldn't see straight in the other.

Cole made a split decision to do what he could to help the Sherman tank. He was well aware that a rifle was a puny weapon against a tank. Still, he had to try. He lined up the crosshairs on the commander standing in the hatch.

He felt Bauer jolt his shoulder, spoiling his aim.

"Do that again and I'll shoot you," Cole snarled.

"Wait," the German said. "There is another way."

To Cole's astonishment, the German stood up and started waving to get the attention of the tank commander.

Cole reached up and tugged at Bauer with such force that the man's officer's hat fell off into the snow. "Get down, you stupid Kraut!"

But Bauer ignored him and kept waving to get the attention of the Germans on the road.

His tactics worked a bit too well. The tank commander shouted something and pointed. The panzer's massive gun swiveled in their direction to face this new threat. If that wasn't bad enough, some of the soldiers on the road directed their fire at them, and bullets tore through the trees.

Now that the attention was momentarily off them, the Sherman tank crew seemed to realize that it might be better to live to fight another day. Like an indignant banty rooster, the Sherman reversed direction and retreated. It did still get off a couple of shots, one of which struck one of the panzers, enveloping it in a cloud of detonating high explosives. The tank survived, but certainly its crew would have been left with ringing ears and a headache.

Cole rolled out from his hiding place. Keeping low, he ran, yelling "Go! Go!" to the others.

He ran deeper into the snowy woods, aware of Vaccaro and Rupert crashing through the trees on his left. He wasn't sure where Bauer had gone. Cole really didn't give a damn about him anymore.

Back on the road, the panzer fired with a sound like the sky ripping open. The shell struck somewhere ahead of Cole, ripping open the ground and scattering clods of dark earth across the white snow. Cole ran through while some of the clods were still raining down.

Bullets still tore through the trees around them, but the firing was more sporadic and higher overhead. He was sure that the Germans had lost sight of them. It wasn't long before the firing stopped altogether, and thankfully the panzer didn't take another shot at them.

Cole kept running. He didn't stop until he emerged on a snow-covered lane that cut through the forest. He looked in both directions, but there wasn't so much as a footprint. The snow lay undisturbed.

No, that wasn't quite true, he realized. He spotted the telltale triangular pattern of rabbit tracks and the single-file trail left by a fox that was going after that rabbit. These forest creatures were going about their business, following the endless cycle of hunter and hunted, oblivious to the fact that there was a war on.

But there was no sign of any two-legged critters. No Germans. No panzers. Even the trees around them were still and quiet except for the taller bare branches clacking together in the winter wind. Nobody had been this way in some time.

Away from the sound of the fighting on the road, the lane felt secluded and peaceful. The tree branches above the lane wove together overhead to form a sort of tunnel through the forest, inviting them to follow it.

Cole bent over and caught his breath, panting. Vaccaro and Rupert came up beside him, doing the same.

"Damn, that was close," Vaccaro said. "Was that German trying to get us killed?"

"He didn't want me shooting that panzer commander, that's what."

"You were going to shoot at them?" Vaccaro asked, sounding incredulous. "That might have been worse than waving at them. Still, I don't know what the hell Herr Barnstormer was thinking."

Rupert interrupted them. "Here's our German, chaps. You can ask him yourself."

Bauer emerged from the trees, his hands raised to indicate that he was still their prisoner. Like them, he was panting and badly winded. One coat sleeve was torn where he'd caught it on a branch.

Cole stepped forward and hit Bauer in the chest with the butt of his rifle, knocking him down. With the German sitting in the snow, breathing heavily, Cole pointed the rifle at him. "Try anything like that again and I'll shoot you. Hell, I ought to just shoot you now."

Cole let the muzzle linger no more than a couple of feet from the Kraut's head, finger on the trigger. He narrowed his eyes.

Their orders were to get the Kraut to HQ, but Cole felt like the incident on the road had left those orders null and void.

What was one more dead German?

Lieutenant Rupert cleared his throat, seemingly reluctant to speak up. "Erm, Private Cole, may I remind you of your duty?"

Cole's finger tightened on the trigger.

"Private Cole—"

Still, Cole ignored him.

"Hold on there, Cole," Vaccaro said quietly. "Maybe you don't have to shoot him. Not yet, anyhow."

Cole kept the rifle pointed at the German for another half a minute. If the British officer hadn't been present, he decided that maybe he would have pulled the trigger. He'd had enough of this Kraut, who had risked all their lives just to keep Cole from shooting that tank commander.

Also, the Kraut was supposed to be responsible for shooting those prisoners outside Bastogne. Maybe he deserved to die right here, right now, in these snowy woods.

But orders were orders. Lieutenant Rupert would have had no choice but to report that Cole had intentionally shot the prisoner.

Rupert didn't seem like the type who would make up a story about the prisoner trying to escape. Though young, he definitely had a stiff pole up his ass in addition to the famous British stiff upper lip.

"You don't seem scared," Cole said.

"I am fairly certain that I am already a dead man," Bauer said, sounding resigned to his fate. "Die now, die later, what is the difference? Any soldier knows that."

Cole lowered the rifle.

Bauer looked down at the snow, nodding as if in silent thanks, or possibly surprise.

"You lucky son of a bitch," Vaccaro said, looking down at him. "You get to live another day. Well, maybe not a whole day. Another hour, anyhow. Possibly just on a minute-by-minute basis. We'll see how it goes."

Vaccaro turned away and lit a cigarette, the burst of smoke expanding in the cold, heavy air.

Cole didn't smoke, but fumes seemed to be coming off him anyhow.

"Hold out your hands, please," Rupert said to the German.

Bauer did as he was told, and the lieutenant bound his wrists together with a length of cord, though it wasn't nearly as tight as Cole would have made it. Still, the rough cordage bit into his wrists. Then the lieutenant stepped away and lit his own cigarette. He was smoking a Craven A, a brand of cigarette issued to British troops and named after the late Earl of Craven. Generally speaking, the British cigarettes were considered inferior to Lucky Strikes, but Rupert was a loyal Brit and not one eager to admit that anything American was superior.

Nobody offered Bauer a cigarette. Having his hands tied again made it harder for Bauer to get up, but nobody moved to help the German. He struggled slowly to his feet, his movements stiff and heavy with exhaustion from the race through the trees, underlining the fact that he was a good dozen years older than the others. Not such a young man anymore. He had lost his officer's hat somewhere and his face was crisscrossed with scratches from the tree branches he had run through escaping the hail of gunfire.

"This way," Cole said, his voice brittle as an icicle.

He started up the lane, his footsteps carving a path through the untrammeled snow.

Silently, the others fell into step behind him.

CHAPTER SEVENTEEN

THEY FOLLOWED the snowy lane for nearly a mile without encountering anything other than snowy trees, heckled all the way by curious, hardy birds such as grackles and cardinals. A few jays scolded them. Cole took it as a good sign that the birds seemed to be going about their business unperturbed except by the passage of their own party. They seemed to be alone, without any sign of the enemy, but Cole kept all his senses on high alert. He didn't want any surprises. The lane was far too narrow to accommodate a tank, but that wasn't to say there might not be an enemy patrol or scouting party to worry about.

He looked back at the group trailing in his footsteps. He was glad to see that Vaccaro also had his eyes open, scanning the woods. Then came Bauer. Lieutenant Rupert brought up the rear. Although the road was covered in snow, an icy layer somewhere under the white blanket caused their feet to slip at random.

With a satisfied grunt, Cole noted that the German struggled to keep his balance with his hands tied. Cole found it gratifying that the German wasn't having an easy time of it. He figured it was the next best thing to shooting him.

But Cole's satisfaction didn't last long. Having dodged several bullets, both those fired from the road and the one waiting in the chamber of Cole's rifle, an amused smirk returned to Bauer's face, as if this excursion was nothing more than a joke. Cole felt infuriated all over again.

Another snow flurry passed through, the cold flakes sending chilly shivers down their necks and exposed faces.

These winter days were short. Already, the dreary afternoon was turning darker as the light faded. The sun wasn't out, leaving the depths of the forest in shadow. The shadows were disconcerting, as they sometimes took on a life of their own in the imagination, turning into crouching Germans. Cole's eyes detected movement, and he swung the rifle that way but saw it was only a fox moving between the pools of gloom in the woods.

"What is it?" Vaccaro asked anxiously.

"Nothin'," Cole replied. "Just a fox is all, out looking for his supper."

"I hope he finds something better than C rations," Vaccaro grumped. He walked a few more steps quietly, casting nervous glances at the forest. "They say these woods used to be full of wolves, but it's been a while."

"It's Krauts I'm worried about, not wolves," Cole remarked. "Gonna be dark soon. I reckon we'd best find a place to spend the night."

"Shouldn't we keep going?" Lieutenant Rupert wondered. "If we push on, perhaps we can reach headquarters before nightfall."

Cole hacked up something and spat into the snow, then shook his head. "If we'd been able to use the jeep longer, maybe we would've been all right. But in case you ain't noticed, Lieutenant, we're not on the main road anymore. We don't really know where this is gonna take us."

Rupert pulled up short. "Do you mean to say that we're lost?"

"No, we ain't lost. Sir."

Cole never felt lost in the woods, but it helped to have the sun or even the stars to show the way rather than rely on dead reckoning and instinct. As it turned out, he had other tools as well.

Cole patted his pocket and took out a compass to show the British officer. A quick compass reading verified that they were still moving in the right direction. Normally Cole might have used the sun to navigate, but the heavy cloud cover hid it from view.

"As long as this lane is going the same way we are, it won't hurt to follow it," Cole explained. "Leastways, we don't have any panzers or Krauts to worry about."

Rupert didn't look happy, but he agreed with Cole's assessment. "I suppose you're right. But it sounds as if we may have to camp in the woods tonight."

Cole and Vaccaro had taken their rucksacks from the jeep, but neither Rupert nor the German had so much as a blanket. In hindsight, it hadn't been good planning.

Vaccaro seemed to read his mind. With a grin, he said quietly to Cole, "I'll snuggle up to the Brit if we need to share blankets. You can have the German."

"Like hell I will. He can freeze to death first, for all I care," Cole muttered. To the others, he said, "Let's go a little farther while we still have daylight and see what we come across."

They continued up the lane, their footsteps written in the virgin snow. The shadows deepened in the surrounding woods. If they didn't come across shelter soon, they really would have to make a rough camp for the night. Without a moon or stars, they wouldn't be able to find their way in the dark.

Their efforts to continue up the lane were soon rewarded. The lane led to two stone pillars, beyond which they could see a large manor house in the distance. Set in a clearing in the forest, the two-story stone structure featured thick walls and a heavy front door, giving it aspects of a fortress. Shutters covered the windows on the lower floor, but several of the upper windows were uncovered, as if someone in the house was keeping watch.

Cole studied the landscape carefully, but there was no sign of movement other than ravens flapping through the dismal sky. No smoke rose from the massive, rectangular chimneys at either end of the house. The fresh snow surrounding the old château stretched smooth as a white tablecloth.

"What do you think?" Vaccaro asked, sliding in next to Cole. Both men kept their weapons ready.

"Looks empty."

"Beats sleeping in the woods."

He would have been glad to find a barn or a woodcutter's shack, something that offered simple shelter, but this old château was something else altogether. "I reckon it does. There might even be feather beds."

"Should we just go up and knock on the front door?" Vaccaro wondered.

Bauer spoke up. "Use the side door," he said. "It will likely open into the kitchen. Besides, the front door will be locked and barred from the inside."

Cole made a point of ignoring the German, but he seemed to speak with knowledge of the subject. Cole looked over the massive house one more time for any sign that it was occupied. The empty, dark windows stared back at him. He had been planning to approach the front door, but he reluctantly admitted that Bauer had a good point. The front door looked thick as a fortress gate. Their best option might be the smaller side door.

"The rest of you stay here while I check it out," Cole ordered. He turned to Vaccaro. "Cover me."

Cautiously, Cole left the cover of the trees and approached the house across the open ground. He moved at a trot, keeping low, half expecting to hear the crack of a rifle shot. But there was only the whisper of the wind and the crunch of his feet through the snow. Even the birds had settled down now that night was coming on.

He reached the side door and lifted the latch. To his disappointment, it appeared to be locked tight. Like the front door, this side entrance was built of thick boards, more rustic than the boards used for the grand entrance. There was no way to batter this thing down.

Now what?

He heard feet moving through the snow behind him and turned to find Bauer there.

"Locked," Cole said.

"There is no keyhole," Bauer said, studying the door. "That means it must be locked from the inside."

"You mean someone is home, after all."

"Perhaps," Bauer said.

"Maybe if we knock real nice they'll let us in."

"I have another idea. Let's try the window."

Bauer moved to the window a few feet away, swept some snow off the deep sill, then raised the sash. "If you untie me, I could crawl through the window."

"Fat chance," Cole said.

"Shall I hold your rifle?"

"No, but you can hold the window."

Cole slung his rifle and shimmied through the window while Bauer supported the sash. Bauer had been right that this was the kitchen. He smelled old woodsmoke, along with the lingering aroma of bread and stew and roasting meat that permeated the brick walls. The ashes in the cooking hearth were stone cold.

Even in the kitchen, the house vibrated in a way that indicated emptiness. He relaxed a little. Maybe this wouldn't be such a bad place to spend the night after all. It sure as hell beat sleeping in the woods.

He moved to the door and lifted the latch, reluctantly admitting that Bauer was right—there was no key, so the door had been latched from the inside. It seemed likely that whoever had closed the door had never left.

On the other side of the door, Bauer knocked as if worried that Cole had forgotten he was out there.

That Kraut is awfully pushy, Cole thought.

He yanked the door open. Bauer was waiting on the stoop.

"Well?" the German asked. It came out as *Vell.*

"Nobody home."

"Good." Bauer pushed inside the kitchen and stomped his boots as if to warm them, although it was not noticeably warmer indoors. Instead, the kitchen felt cold and abandoned. "Better call the others."

"Don't you go giving orders," Cole growled. "You're still a prisoner, in case you ain't noticed."

Bauer nodded. "I have not forgotten. But under the circumstances, we might do best to work together."

"My mama always said, don't dance with the devil."

"Is that what I am, the devil?" The trace of a smirk had returned to

Bauer's lips, and Cole fought the urge to smash him in the face with the butt of his rifle.

"Close to it," Cole replied, then stepped through the door to wave Vaccaro and Rupert toward the house.

Inside the kitchen, the German was inspecting everything and using his two bound hands to open drawers. If there was still anything here to eat, he seemed intent on finding it. Despite all the good old smells, the kitchen cabinets and drawers were bare.

The kitchen was old-fashioned and lined with shelves rather than cabinets, the wood worn and dark from having absorbed who knew how many years of smoke, oil, and spills.

"Hmm," said Bauer, having reached the wood-fired range. It was a massive thing that seemed big as an aircraft engine. His hand rested on a cast-iron kettle. "Not warm, but not completely cold either. Whoever was here must have left recently."

"We didn't see any tracks coming or going."

"There is the mystery," Bauer said. "Someone may be hiding in the house."

They moved on from the kitchen, entering an expansive dining room with tall ceilings. Once painted a bright cheerful yellow, the color had faded on the damp plaster walls. The gray light did not improve the brightness. They could see an outline on the floor where a carpet had once been, but where there were now only scuffed floorboards in need of refinishing. The dining room table lacked a tablecloth, revealing scars from years of use. Hinting at past glories, a chandelier hung above the table. Rupert tried the light switch, but there was no power.

Cole moved through the dining room into what had once been a grand living room. Tall windows faced the forest and hills beyond, but they were covered by the exterior shutters. Heavy old drapes the color of dried rose petals had been pulled shut across the windows.

A huge fireplace dominated the space. It was not quite tall enough for Cole to stand up in, but it was close. The fireplace was surrounded by marble tiles. A mirror in a gilt frame hung over the fireplace. It was the only attempt at decoration. Although there were nails in the walls, any pictures must have been taken down by the owners and put into storage.

"Lieutenant, I guess this must remind you of your manor house back home," Vaccaro said.

"Hardly. I have to say that this place is a bit more posh than I'm used to," Lieutenant Rupert said. "You Yanks must think us Brits are all aristocrats. My father's a village doctor, not the Duke of York."

"I'm definitely not a duke, but this will do nicely," Vaccaro announced, flopping down on an antique sofa trimmed with carved wood. The upholstery had been covered with a canvas cloth, like a drop cloth, apparently to protect it.

"You think so, huh?" Cole found the grandeur of the room, however faded and apparently unlived in, to be overwhelming. "We best go have a look-see upstairs before it gets dark, just to make sure this place really is empty."

Vaccaro got to his feet. "I'll do it."

Cole snorted. "When did you ever volunteer for anything?"

"Ever since I wondered if there was anything valuable upstairs, that's when."

"See if you can find some extra blankets. And take Rupert with you." Cole caught himself. "Uh, Lieutenant Rupert. Sir. If you wouldn't mind—"

"Come along, Vaccaro," the lieutenant said, and the two men went in search of the staircase, leaving Cole alone with the German.

There were two candles inside glass globes on the mantel, so Cole lit them to dispel the gathering darkness. By candlelight, the room was transformed, its shabbiness forgotten, the soft glow creating an atmosphere of old-world elegance.

Then he got to work building a fire. He went back to the kitchen and rounded up the kindling that he had seen there. A small stack of logs stood beside the fire, evidently more for show, but Cole decided that there was no time like the present to put them to use. He set to work building a fire lay in the big fireplace, looking forward to some warmth after a long, cold day outdoors. They could also use the fire to heat their rations.

Quietly, Bauer watched him work for a minute, then spoke up. "Do you think that building a fire is wise? We may attract unwanted attention."

"It will be dark soon. Nobody will see the smoke. And the way those windows are covered up, the light won't show."

Bauer nodded, conceding the point. He sat down in one of the elegant chairs and made himself at home.

"I would help you, but you see . . ." The German raised his bound hands. "Also, at some point, we have the problem again with relieving myself."

"Shut up," Cole said. He was enjoying building the fire lay, and the German was ruining the moment.

Overhead, the ceiling creaked as Vaccaro and Rupert passed through the empty rooms. A few minutes later, they came marching into the living room just as Cole had managed to get the flames to lick at the wood in the fireplace. He squatted on his boot heels and watched the fire with satisfaction.

He couldn't help but think of growing up in the mountains, where building a fire was one of the first skills that a boy learned. In the Cole family's cabin, it had been the only form of warmth. In the woods, the ability to build a fire on a cold night could make the difference between life and death.

"Nothing," Vaccaro reported. He was carrying an armload of bedding and tossed it down on a sofa. "Looks to me like the whole place has been cleared out."

"Good to know," Cole replied. "Now let's divvy out those rations and heat up some supper."

"Home sweet home," Vaccaro agreed.

Beyond the shuttered windows, the night closed in around the château.

CHAPTER EIGHTEEN

Wanting to get a start before darkness fell, Brock led the others down the road leading out of Bastogne.

The soldiers' boots squished through the slush and mud with a sense of purpose and urgency. The clink and rattle of their equipment was the only other sound they made, mingling with the distant noise of combat that included the rattle of small-arms fire and the thump of artillery.

Somewhere in the distance, they could hear a woman wailing. Having heard similar sounds in dozens of towns since landing at Normandy months ago, they ignored it. Tears were simply part of the background noise of war. Their attention remained on the present. When they spoke, their voices were hushed, their words clipped.

"You got ammo?" Brock asked.

"Enough," Corporal McCann replied.

"Everybody got dry socks?"

"Yeah."

Bullets and dry socks. That was all a GI needed. Well, maybe that and a C ration or two.

In the confusion of the ongoing battle for the town, nobody questioned them about where they were going. Considering that their uniforms and gear appeared worn out and battle-scarred, showing the marks of countless past missions and endless muddy miles, they had the look of battle-hardened troops who knew what they were doing.

Because they sure as hell did.

They were on the road to revenge.

Brock knew that the actual road they followed was the same one taken by the group escorting the captured German officer to HQ.

Brock was determined that the German would never make it that far.

In fact, he had watched the German and his escorts leave the city, keeping to the shadows cast by a shattered building. His eyes had narrowed, watching them go, and it gave him a feeling of power to know that the little group of Boy Scouts led by that righteous hillbilly had no idea what was coming for them.

He thrilled at the feeling, similar to the sense of power he'd always gotten from being a bully.

Spying on them from a distance, Brock had seen the hillbilly soldier who seemed so intent on doing his duty. The soldier carried a sniper rifle and looked as if he knew how to use it. He had to admit, that sniper worried him a little.

The hillbilly reminded him of a quiet boy who lived on a farm at the end of a long dirt road back home. In school, Brock had habitually teased the boy about his dusty, worn boots. The boy had ignored him until one day Brock had made the mistake of calling the boy's little sister a name.

Though smaller than Brock, that farm boy had been tough as barbed wire and had ended up nearly kicking in Brock's ribs with those dusty boots. On that day, the high school bully had learned the hard way that there were some people in this world that you didn't mess with. He had steered clear of the farm boy and his sister after that.

This hillbilly sniper had that same look in his eyes.

Something to think about.

Brock also hadn't missed the fact that the German was the tallest of the bunch, his back held ramrod straight like he was on dress parade rather than marching off to a prison camp. Thinking about that German, Brock clenched and unclenched his fist.

Next to him, Vern noticed and said, "Relax, Brock. That Kraut will get what's coming to him before too long."

"That Kraut bastard ought to be begging for mercy, not walking with his head held high," Brock muttered.

"That's for sure," Vern agreed. "We'll sure as hell make him pay for what they did to those guys."

"Yeah," Brock agreed. "That Kraut thinks he's got nothin' to worry about, but he's wrong."

"Let's see how smug he is when he's behind barbed wire," one of the other soldiers said.

Brock rounded on the man, his voice almost a snarl. "Hey, numbnuts, I guess you haven't been listening. A POW camp is too good for that Kraut. He's not going to see any barbed wire unless I wrap it around his neck."

"Whatever you say, Brock."

"Damn right. Whatever I say."

Among the men in the squad, Vern and Boot were the ones Brock was closest to. They hadn't known any of the guys who had been gunned down by the Germans outside Bastogne, but like Brock, they felt a healthy sense of indignation about it.

Those two would do whatever he said and would back him up when push came to shove or if the others balked. The rest of the squad would fall in line if they knew what was good for them. In the end, he had opted to take just Vern and Boot with him.

His plan was to let the escort get a mile or two out of Bastogne, beyond any prying eyes, then overtake them. Maybe they would have the good sense not to put up a fight. If they did, well, that was too bad for them. Maybe that hillbilly wasn't as tough as he looked.

"C'mon," he said to the others, pushing off the wall. He tossed away the stub of his cigarette. "Keep your eyes open once we get out of Bastogne. There are still plenty of Krauts out there."

"What are we gonna do when we catch up to those guys?" Vern wanted to know.

"We're gonna ask them real nice to turn that Kraut bastard over to us, that's what. They should have done that in the first place."

"OK, but what if they don't want to?" Vern pressed. "Then what?"

"Then we either take the Kraut from them or shoot him right there."

"I dunno, Brock. That hillbilly guy looked like he meant business. You really think he'll go along with that?"

"If he doesn't, then too bad for him," Brock said.

Boot lowered his voice. "I don't want to shoot our own guys to get even with that German. What sense would that make?"

"Look, nobody is gonna get shot, except that Kraut. Anyhow, don't be a granny about it," Brock said, quickening his pace. "Now hurry it up. I want to catch up to those guys before it gets dark."

To Brock's satisfaction, Vern finally shut up. Boot didn't seem worried about asking any questions and seemed content to do whatever Brock told him to. Neither said another word, but just went along. It was what followers always did.

Away from town, it was quickly apparent that they were on their own. They passed a couple of outpost positions, but otherwise they were soon in a kind of no-man's-land.

The wind swept across the barren snow-covered fields and chilled them, tugging at the scarves and scraps of cloth that they had wrapped around their necks and faces. The wind always found a way in, often carrying crystals of ice or wet snow with it.

This winter weather had been relentless. Everyone said it favored the Germans because it was keeping the American planes grounded, but Brock wasn't so sure. The Krauts had to be just as cold and miserable as everyone else in this mess.

Then again, Brock didn't mind the cold. He scarcely noticed it. The thought of revenge warmed him. However, the empty landscape made him feel jumpy, especially as the shadows in the distant wooded hills grew longer.

"Hurry it up," he said to the others. "The sooner we get this over with and get back to Bastogne, the better."

As it turned out, it wasn't going to be that easy. Up ahead, he could hear the sound of firing—not just small arms but also heavier stuff. If he didn't know better, it sounded as if they were headed right toward a battle.

"You hear that?" Vern asked.

"Doesn't matter," he said. "This is the way that Kraut and his babysitters went, so it's where we're going too."

"Sounds like tanks."

"Don't worry, we'll get off the road if we hear anything heavy coming our way," Brock said.

* * *

UNKNOWN TO BROCK and his squad, they weren't the only ones on the trail of the German and his escort detail. After the skirmish with the American soldiers at the farmhouse, Hauptmann Messner and the Kübelwagen with the two other Germans had continued down the road.

"Keep your eyes open," Messner warned, shouting to be heard over the roar of the straining motor and the wind in their ears.

His words weren't really necessary. Gettinger kept his eyes squarely on the road ahead, dodging any obstacles, while keeping his foot planted as firmly on the gas as he dared.

As for Dietzel, his gaze roamed the roadside on both sides, his grip tight on his sniper rifle. If there was any more trouble ahead, he would be sure to be the first to see it.

Messner had his pistol along with an MP 40 submachine gun—dubbed a Schmeisser by American troops—that he had picked up from the unit armorer before leaving on their quest. Officers didn't normally carry combat weapons, but Messner had decided that the more firepower they had, the better, considering that there were just three of them.

The shadows across the woods and fields were growing longer. Messner did not relish the thought of trying to navigate the road in the dark. The sooner that they caught up with their quarry, the better.

Suddenly Dietzel called out a warning. "Tank!" he shouted, making the distinction that it was not one of their own.

Messner squinted down the shadowy road but couldn't see a thing. He decided that the Jaeger must have the eyes of an eagle and the ears of a wolfhound.

No matter—if an American tank spotted them, the Kübelwagen

might be reduced to a hunk of burning metal in an instant, and all three of them along with it.

He tapped Gettinger on the shoulder to get his attention, then pointed at a copse of trees at a bend in the road. "Quick, get into those woods!"

Gettinger did as he was told, steering the Kübelwagen off the road. There was just enough space between the trunks to get the vehicle between the trees. He started to come to a stop, but Messner swatted his shoulder and pointed deeper into the woods. "Hop, hop, hop!"

The side of the sturdy car was badly scraped and battered as Gettinger pushed deeper into the trees. Finally, the trees grew thicker and they could go no farther.

"Turn off the engine," Messner ordered. "Get out and find some cover. If the Ami tank does see the Kübelwagen and opens fire, we will have a better chance on foot."

Dietzel had already been getting out before the Kübelwagen even came to a complete stop. He hurried several yards away and got behind a fallen log, his rifle pointed toward the road. Messner and Gettinger got behind trees nearby.

Now they could hear the tank coming, its engine a steady roar, the tank treads clanking up the snowy road. A whiff of exhaust drifted their way. Gettinger raised his own submachine gun, but Messner pushed it back down.

"Hold your fire," he said. "Let them go past us."

Through the trees, they caught a glimpse of the tank moving along the road. Several logs had been lashed across the front and sides of the Sherman to thicken its armor. It almost looked as if the forest had come alive and was on the move. Some of the tree trunks were newly scarred and shattered, as if the tank had recently been in a fight for its life.

They all held their breath, not so much for fear that the tank crew could hear them, but to keep telltale clouds of their frozen breath from hanging in the air and giving them away.

Messner could see the tank commander standing in the hatch. Dietzel kept his rifle trained on the man but didn't fire. If the tank commander had paid any attention at all to the tire tracks veering into the forest, he must have dismissed them as nothing more than a vehicle skidding off the snowy road. Besides, there was already a confusion of tire tracks and ruts. The tank did not slow down to investigate.

The main gun pointed up the road, but Messner knew well enough that the Sherman tank was also equipped with deadly machine guns. How much protection would the trees offer if those machine guns opened fire?

More worrisome for the Germans was the fact that the tank was being followed by a squad of infantry. They carried rifles, machine guns, and a couple of bazookas. Some of the men wore bloody bandages as if they had been wounded in a recent fight. Looking more closely, Messner spotted a GI with a heavily bandaged leg riding on the Sherman tank itself.

If any of the Ami soldiers had looked into the woods, they might have seen the Kübelwagen. That might have aroused their curiosity. But they plodded on, heads down, clearly exhausted, happy to let the tank lead the way.

"Keep going," Messner urged under his breath.

Slowly, the sound of the tank engine faded. There had been no warning shouts from the infantry squad. They were in the clear.

At least for now.

However, they had lost precious daylight. Even in the last several minutes, the woods around them seemed to have grown darker.

Messner nodded at the two men. Gettinger wore a look of relief plain on his face, while Dietzel appeared disappointed that he hadn't been able to shoot anyone.

Then Messner looked at the Kübelwagen. Gettinger had driven it until it was nearly wedged between the tree trunks. To the man's credit, it was quite a feat of driving that he had navigated this far into the woods. However, there was no hope of turning it around. Messner was reluctant to give up their means of transportation, so they would have to back out.

"Dietzel, keep an eye on the road," Messner ordered. "Gettinger, follow my directions. I will help you reverse the Kübelwagen."

Painstakingly, that was just what they did. Once again, tree trunks scraped patches of paint off the Kübelwagen. By the time they reached the road again, they had lost even more daylight. The temperature had also dropped, which wasn't such a bad thing, because the slushy spots in the road had begun to freeze over, giving them a more solid surface for driving.

"Get in," he said to Dietzel.

The sniper shouldered his rifle and climbed into the back seat next to the Hauptmann. Soon they were on their way again.

CHAPTER NINETEEN

AT THE WHEEL of the Kübelwagen, Gettinger steered carefully, picking his path through the rutted road, which seemed to alternate between frozen ridges that jolted them down to their bones and slushy mud puddles that threatened to bog them down. He rarely shifted out of second gear, although on a few straightaways the engine revved high enough that he shifted into third gear. It wasn't long before he downshifted again. At any rate, the Kübelwagen wasn't exactly a vehicle built for speed.

"Can't you drive any faster?" Messner complained. The shadows in the woods grew deeper by the minute. Messner had hoped that they might have come across their quarry by now.

"The road is a mess, Herr Hauptmann," Gettinger responded.

"Here, trade places with me. I will show you how it is done."

Messner took the wheel, but after a few satisfying bursts of speed, he realized that Gettinger was correct. From the passenger seat, the slippery nature of the slush and mud had been less obvious. In places, Messner swore as he fought to keep control of the Kübelwagen. The ruts threatened to wrench the wheel out of his grip. Some of the puddles were so deep that they would be hard to drive out of again.

He took his eyes off the road long enough to glance over at

Gettinger, but the man remained stone-faced. He knew better than to gloat over the fact that the Hauptmann wasn't doing any better driving the vehicle.

As for Dietzel, all his attention was reserved for the shadowy woods on either side of the road. He kept his rifle at the ready.

Messner drove them around a bend in the road and came to a spot where there had clearly been a skirmish. The still-smoldering remains of an American tank partially blocked the road. A little farther on were the smashed remains of a Kübelwagen. A handful of dead bodies—some American, some German—were scattered alongside the road.

Messner couldn't know for certain, but he suspected that this was where the American squad they had hidden from had likely fought. There was no sign of where the German forces had gone. They had either struck out cross-country to unite with the forces encircling Bastogne, or they had turned around and gone in the other direction.

He pulled the Kübelwagen to the side of the road and killed the engine.

"We must check the bodies and make certain that Bauer was not killed here," he said. "We know that he is traveling this road."

He and Gettinger did that while Dietzel kept watching, walking along the skirmish site in the process. A wooded hill came down sharply toward the road on one side, and on the other, an open space created a wide place in the road. A low stone wall that was little more than a long pile of snow-covered rocks bordered the open space and the woods. Dietzel seemed to be studying the space intently, then began crossing it, moving toward the woods on the other side.

Messner checked the dead Germans, two of them just teenagers, while the other dead man looked to be in his sixties. They wore the insignia of the Volksgrenadier. He knew that Germany was scraping the bottom of the barrel for manpower, but boys and old men? He shook his head, because these Volksgrenadier would be no match for battle-hardened American forces.

Another German body had been smashed to jelly by a passing tank. Even now, having seen his share of war, Messner hadn't gotten used to such a sight. What should have been on the inside of the soldier was now on the outside, his body smashed into a patty like so much raw sausage. He looked away, hoping that the man had already been dead when the tank rolled over him. He knew for sure that it wasn't Bauer, because the dead man wasn't wearing an officer's uniform.

"He is not here, Herr Hauptmann," Gettinger reported. He had checked the dead Americans, but they did not seem to have been part of Bauer's escort.

Messner grunted. On the one hand, it would have been easier for them if Bauer had been among the dead. On the other, Messner would have felt shortchanged if he hadn't been the one to kill the Obersturmbannführer.

"Herr Hauptmann!" Dietzel shouted from the edge of the clearing. He was standing over something in the snow that Messner could not identify.

"What is it?"

"You had better have a look."

Messner started across the snowy clearing, Gettinger on his heels. Once he had moved closer, he could see that Dietzel had indeed found something interesting in the snow.

It was a German officer's hat, emblazoned with the insignia that was sometimes derided by enlisted men as "cabbage leaves" for its resemblance to that humble vegetable. In this case, it was the insignia of an Obersturmbannführer.

Bauer's rank.

Dietzel slung the rifle over his shoulder, then picked up the hat and studied it. "It belongs to Bauer," he announced, pointing out a name tag sewn into the liner.

"If he lost his hat, perhaps he is dead," Messner said.

"No blood," Dietzel said. "The tracks go off into the woods. Three Americans and one set of German boots. I see a few cartridges on the ground, but I suspect that they were trying to escape the fighting on the road."

Messner nodded, feeling some of his excitement return. Not only were they on the right track, but their quarry must be that much closer. "Gettinger, go fetch the Kübelwagen. The trees in this direction are just far enough apart for us to drive through."

Gettinger scratched his head and studied the woods doubtfully. "Herr Hauptmann—"

"What are you waiting for? *Hop, hop, hop!*"

"Yes, sir." He ran back through the snowy open space toward the Kübelwagen.

Dietzel tossed the hat back into the snow, almost as if in disgust at having handled the officer's hat. "We do not have much daylight left."

"Then we had better hurry," Messner said.

"Heading into the woods at this hour—"

"I don't care about that," Messner insisted. "We are going after him."

Gettinger pulled up long enough for them to get in, then started driving through the trees, trying to pick a route through the woods, keeping the tracks in sight the whole time. Who knew where they were going? There didn't seem to be anything out here but more trees. Perhaps Dietzel was correct and their quarry had only been fleeing the fighting with no real destination in mind.

Their chances of catching up to the men were much better with a vehicle, especially if they ever got clear of the trees. However, it was slow going, and the Kübelwagen picked up a few more dents as it careened off first one tree trunk, and then another.

Despite the cold, beads of sweat appeared on Gettinger's face as he wrestled with the wheel, throwing it first one way and then another to avoid the trunks that blocked their path. The tires rolled up and over rocks and fallen logs. Bouncing along in the Kübelwagen, the other two men held on for dear life. The journey down the frozen road now seemed like traveling on the Autobahn in comparison.

But the effort was worth it. A few minutes later, they emerged on a snow-covered lane. The lack of tire tracks or tank treads indicated that no vehicles had passed down the lane, but even in the fading light, they could clearly see four sets of footprints in the snow. It seemed likely that their quarry had come this way.

"Now we have him," Messner said with satisfaction.

"Those are German boots," Dietzel noted, nodding at one set of tracks in the snow. "The others look like they are American, or maybe British."

Messner squinted at the footprints, but they all looked roughly the same to him. "How did you get to be such a tracker, Dietzel?" he asked. He had seen the man's skill before, but it had never occurred to him to ask about it.

"I grew up hunting, sir. There is nothing on this earth that I cannot follow. Of course, the snow makes it easy, like reading words on a page."

"Then let us follow them. This is taking longer than I thought. The sooner that we catch up to the traitor, the sooner that we can get back."

But even with the relative speed offered by the Kübelwagen, it became evident that their quarry had more of a head start than they had realized.

It was full dark by the time they reached the end of the lane and the stone pillars leading to the château. The footprints clearly led to the grand old house. The temperature had dropped considerably, causing the snow to crunch under their tires.

"They must have taken shelter for the night in that house," Messner said.

"Better stop the engine," Dietzel said. "The noise will give us away."

Messner studied the château but could see no lights or any sign that it was occupied. "Maybe they kept going," he said.

Dietzel slipped away to see what he could find out from the tracks. In the quiet of the woods, the only sound was the ticking from the cooling engine. The Jaeger returned a few minutes later, arriving as quietly as he had gone.

"Their tracks lead right to the side door," Dietzel reported back from his scouting. "I think they are inside, but they are being careful to stay hidden. I don't see any lights."

Messner was losing some of his confidence that they now had their quarry trapped, realizing that the solid walls of the château made the old stone house into a sturdy fortress. "Should we rush it?" he wondered.

"I think we should wait for daylight," Dietzel said. His doubtful expression made it clear that he must have been thinking the same thing as the Hauptmann. "They could be a tough nut to crack if we rush them in the dark. However, they don't know we are here. We can take them by surprise and shoot them when they come out in the morning."

"It will be a cold night for us."

"Not as cold as the grave, Herr Hauptmann," Dietzel pointed out.

Hauptmann Messner could not argue with that. They would wait until morning to catch their quarry unawares as they left the château.

* * *

SLOGGING ALONG THE SLUSH-AND-SNOW-COVERED ROAD, Brock worried that their journey was starting to feel like a wild-goose chase because they hadn't yet caught up to the German prisoner or his escorts. Brock was surprised that they hadn't made better progress.

So far they had lucked out and not run into any other Krauts. They hadn't run into any Americans either. The general lack of anyone else around was starting to feel spooky.

But not for long. They soon encountered the tank and infantry squad coming from the other direction. This was the same lone Sherman tank that Messner and the Germans had hidden from in the woods, the lone survivor of the fight that had sent Cole and his group running for cover.

Again, the hits that the Sherman tank had taken were evident in its log-covered sides that showed the scarred fresh wood. Thick steel armor was preferred, but the makeshift armor provided by the logs had probably saved the tank on more than one occasion by deflecting the full force of a German shell.

"Let's ask these guys if they've seen that escort party," Brock said. "At least then we'll know that we're still headed in the right direction."

"You think they'll stop for us?" Boot asked. "They look like they're hell-bent on getting to Bastogne."

Boot needn't have worried about the tank not stopping for them. When the tank commander spotted them, he steered the Sherman closer to the middle of the road to block their path. The tank stopped short of pointing its gun at them, but the Sherman's machine gun was now trained on them.

Behind the tank, the infantry squad fanned out, keeping their weapons trained on Brock and his companions.

The engine turned off, leaving an ominous silence in the winter woods. Brock felt his insides give a little flip. He didn't like the looks of this at all.

"What gives?" he shouted, his voice sounding too loud in the sudden silence. "You fellas are pointing those guns at the wrong guys."

"Oh yeah, how can we be so sure of that?" the lieutenant in the tank hatch replied. "We hear there are German commandos dressed as our guys all over the place. They speak English. Three men headed the wrong way from Bastogne doesn't seem right to me."

Normally, as a battle-hardened enlisted man, Brock felt dismissive toward lieutenants, especially ones who rode around in tanks. However, this lieutenant seemed no-nonsense, like maybe he had been promoted up through the ranks. It didn't help that not only was Corporal Brock outranked, but he was seriously outgunned.

"We're supposed to link up with a squad escorting a German POW," Brock said, deciding that he would tell only half the story. "You haven't seen anybody like that, have you?"

"Mostly, the only Germans we've seen that haven't been dead have been shooting at us," the lieutenant said. "But we did see some of our guys apparently escorting a German officer back where we had a skirmish with the Krauts. They were in the distance, and they ran off instead of helping us fight, which makes the fact that you're looking for them even more suspicious. Like I said, how do we know *you're* not Germans?"

"C'mon, Lieutenant—"

"Better start talking before we start shooting."

"So ask us a few questions," Brock replied.

"That sounds like just the sort of thing a German agent would say." The lieutenant seemed to think it over. "OK, sing us some of 'Mairzy Doats.'"

Brock stared at him incredulously, wondering whether he had heard the lieutenant right. The song filled with seemingly nonsensical words had been a big hit when released in 1943. He knew the name of the song, all right, but couldn't remember any of the words.

"You mean that kids' song?"

"You heard me right. Start singing, if you know what's good for you."

Brock stared at Vern, who shrugged. Neither of them had a clue.

One or two of the soldiers in the infantry squad cocked their weapons.

It was Boot who saved them. Breaking the tense silence, he belted out a few lines of the song, tunelessly. It was a convincing performance, if painful on the ears. Boot was no singer.

Brock couldn't have known it, but similar scenes were being played out all over the sprawling battlefield, with even colonels and generals being quizzed by doubtful sentries. The mere rumor of German saboteurs had wreaked far more havoc than the saboteurs themselves.

"How's that, Lieutenant?" Brock wondered. "You maybe want us to dance too?"

"Naw, that's good enough for me," the lieutenant finally said. The song might have been childish, but the lieutenant's threat had been real enough. However, he seemed more than satisfied by the rendition that Boot had offered. "Like I said, that squad you were looking for ran off into the woods. You can link up with us if you want to. We're headed to Bastogne."

"Thank you, sir. But I think we'd better keep looking."

"Suit yourself."

The tank engine roared back to life, and the Sherman started moving forward with a clank of treads. Still, the troops moving with the tank eyed Brock and his squad warily. Brock didn't relax until they were out of sight.

"You think that lieutenant was serious about shooting us?" Vern asked.

"He looked damn serious to me. How did he look to you?"

"Serious as a heart attack," Vern agreed.

"Staring into that tank's machine gun sure as hell almost *gave* me a heart attack," Brock admitted. "Boot, how the hell did you know that song?"

"Aw, my niece sang it nonstop the last time I was home on leave," he said. "She used to make me sing it with her."

Brock just shook his head. "Ain't it a wonder, boys. We've got all the ammo we need, but it was a damn kids' song that kept us from ending up as worm food."

It wasn't long after that when they reached the wreckage of the skirmish that the lieutenant and his tank had survived. They could see the smoking remains of another Sherman that hadn't been so lucky. Several bodies lay in the slush and snow, most of them German.

He looked over the bodies—at least the ones where the faces were still recognizable. He didn't see their German among them—or the hillbilly sniper either. He wasn't sure whether he was disappointed. To be honest, part of him was ready to give up the chase and turn around, promises be damned. It would be night soon, and he didn't relish the notion of sleeping out here in the woods, where there might be a German hiding behind every tree.

Brock recalled what the lieutenant had said about seeing some Americans accompanied by a German officer. Surely, those had to be the same men that he was looking for—they would be on this road. Apparently they had tried to avoid the skirmish that had taken place here. But where had they gone?

"Hey, Brock!" Vern called. "I found something."

Brock hurried over to where Vern stood by a low stone wall at the opposite end of a wide place in the road.

"What is it?"

"Looks like a Kraut officer's hat to me," he replied, kicking at the hat in question.

"It's got to be our Kraut," Brock said.

Vern nodded toward the trees, where four sets of tracks disappeared into the growing darkness of the woods. Curiously, there was also a set of tire tracks headed in that direction. "It looks like they went this way."

"Then what are we waiting for? Let's go."

CHAPTER TWENTY

"WE'LL BED DOWN HERE for the night," Cole announced. He glanced at Rupert. "That is, if it's all right with you, Lieutenant."

"Carry on," Rupert said.

"All right, then," Cole said. "We'll keep the fire going, spread out some blankets. I'll take first watch tonight."

Vaccaro groaned. "C'mon, Cole. We're snug as a bug in a rug in this place. We don't really need to have guard duty."

"You never know who's out there," Cole said with finality.

Lieutenant Rupert weighed in, backing Cole up. "I agree with Private Cole," he said. "Better safe than sorry. For all we know, these woods could be crawling with Germans."

The truth was that Cole felt uneasy in these surroundings. It wasn't the empty old château that put him on edge, but the trappings of wealth. Although the château had seen better days and had an air of abandonment, everything from the soaring ceilings to the antique carved-wood furniture hinted at an opulence that was completely foreign to the likes of someone like Cole.

Vaccaro took pots from the kitchen and used them to heat up their rations, plus brew a pot of hot coffee. They were so tired that the coffee wouldn't keep anyone awake, but it would warm their bones.

As the food was dished out, Bauer lifted his still-bound hands toward Cole and raised his eyebrows.

"All right, but don't even think about trying anything," Cole said. He unsheathed his bowie knife and cut the cords binding Bauer's wrists. The German sighed with relief and massaged his wrists, into which the tight cords had cut a pattern of red lines.

"Thank you," he said.

Cole grunted as Vaccaro handed their prisoner a plate and a chipped mug of black coffee.

Bauer seemed right at home in this château. It was a realization that rankled Cole. He sat down near the German to keep an eye on him.

"I suppose you'll want us to put out a tablecloth for you and maybe a silver spoon," Cole said.

Bauer had tucked into the food with surprising vigor, showing how hungry he was. He took a long drink of coffee. "Mmm, American coffee. Not bad." Once he had eaten his fill, he returned his attention to Cole. "You seem to have the wrong impression of me, Private Cole. I do know about manor houses, but not because I lived in one.

"You see, my father's lungs were damaged by mustard gas during the Great War. The only work he could get was on the estate of an old baron whose son had been my father's commanding officer. His son did not survive the war, but the baron had a soft spot for army men that had served with his son. He created jobs for three men who had been injured in the war, doing what he could for them, though by then he could scarcely afford it with the inflation that Germany went through. I suppose he saw it as his duty. Our economy was ruined by the war. Even the rich suffered.

"My mother worked in his kitchen. When I was old enough, I helped my father or ran small errands for the baron. So you see, that is how I know about châteaus, from being the hired help."

"I didn't think that errand boys could become German officers," Cole replied.

Bauer smiled ruefully. "The Nazi Party promotes the equality of all good Germans, so that was a path upward, at least to a point. But they say that even Hitler gets stars in his eyes when he's around the old aristocracy."

"Too bad for you that you ain't the baron's kin."

"It just so happens that I was able to pass myself off as upper class due to a misunderstanding. There was some confusion about my connection with the baron. When people began introducing me as the baron's nephew, I did not correct them. That was enough to get me in the door, you see."

"You lied."

"Does a man ever lie about how much money he has to get a woman into bed? Does a fisherman use a lure to catch a fish? You might understand how an ambitious young man would not correct the mistaken assumption that he comes from the aristocracy to hide the fact that he was nothing more than an errand boy."

"If you say so." Cole understood what the German was saying about the fact that we might not always tell the truth, at least not exactly, when it was to our advantage, but he wasn't about to admit it.

"Everyone in Germany lies. It is how we have reached this point. We lie about where all the Jews have gone. We tell ourselves lies that we can still win the war. Der Führer is the biggest liar of them all."

"What about the Jews?" Cole asked with genuine curiosity. There were plenty of dark rumors about the fate of Europe's Jewish population. However, at this point in the war, the full extent of Nazi Germany's "Final Solution" still wasn't known.

Bauer just shook his head without answering Cole's question. "What I am saying is that there have been too many lies already."

"All right, now we're getting somewhere. You're finally telling the truth. How will I know that you're not lying to me in the future?"

Bauer sighed. "You won't, at least not if it means—how do you Americans say it?—*saving my bacon*. But at least you have been warned."

"Fair enough. Now answer me another question, Herr Barnstormer. Why did you surrender?"

"I was trying to save my men. The war is coming to an end. They have done enough." Bauer hesitated before adding, "Also, I surrendered because I am tired of the pointless loss of life. Isn't that reason enough?"

"Loss of life, huh? What about those American boys you murdered?"

Bauer shook his head. "My subordinate, Messner, took it upon himself to shoot the prisoners. He is a hardliner who would have been better off in the ranks of the SS. Of course, he was under my command, so the responsibility for his actions falls on me, but I did not condone it."

"Passing the buck, huh?"

"I cannot change what happened. That does not mean I am not sorry for it. Prisoners should be treated with respect."

"Easy to say when you're the prisoner."

"Well, there is that." Bauer smiled.

At least the Kraut bastard has a sense of humor, Cole thought.

With their meal finished, the men took time to relax before turning in. The only light came from the fireplace and the two candles that Cole had lit—despite the shutters covering the windows, more light than that might be tempting fate, considering that there could be enemy patrols in the woods or even Luftwaffe fighters passing overhead. No point in drawing curiosity to themselves unnecessarily. The warmth from the leaping flames in the fireplace had dispelled the cold and damp so that the room was actually pleasant. In fact, these were the most comfortable surroundings that he and Vaccaro had experienced in days, if not weeks.

Rupert pulled a chair close to the fireplace to take advantage of the warmth and light, then took out a small book and began reading it. Clearly he was instantly engaged by the words on the page. Watching him, Cole realized how envious he was of the ability people had to get lost in a book—pulled out of themselves for a while. To someone without that ability, it seemed like an incredible gift. He vowed that someday, after the war, he would put his pride aside and find someone to teach him how to read.

Vaccaro lounged on a sofa and smoked a cigarette. That city boy always preferred the sound of his own voice to anyone else's, much less words on a page, but for now he seemed content to smoke and contemplate.

The German was doing the same. Cole debated tying him back up

—he didn't want that Kraut bastard sneaking into the kitchen, finding a knife, and cutting all their throats in the night. But for now he thought it was safe enough to give the man his freedom.

Cole had given up cigarettes because they cut his wind. Instead of smoking, he began cleaning his sniper rifle, although it had not seen much use that day. Still, the winter weather and dampness took their toll. He field-stripped the rifle and ran an oily patch through the bore, noting with satisfaction that it came out clean. He then gave the bolt and action, plus the exterior surfaces of the rifle, a once-over with an oily rag to ward off any rust.

Maybe guns are what I have instead of books, he thought.

Looking up, he noticed the German watching him.

"You look as if you have cleaned that rifle many times," Bauer remarked.

"You don't know the half of it, Herr Barnstormer," Vaccaro said, picking up on Cole's nickname for the German. "Cole here has got the cleanest rifle in the whole damn army this side of boot camp."

"The cleanest rifle? Of that I have no doubt," Bauer said. "It is a good soldier who takes proper care of his weapon."

Cole ignored them. He swung the barrel toward the firelight and peered through it, admiring the elegant twists of the rifling. The dancing flames reflected on the bright metal. He thought about the power those simple twists gave a rifle. Looking through the barrel was like gazing into a whirlpool—or a tornado.

"Cole is also the best shot in the whole damn army," Vaccaro said, bragging now. "He's not just a pretty face."

"How many Germans have you shot with that rifle?" Bauer asked matter-of-factly.

"He stopped counting at twenty, or was it thirty? I don't remember exactly," Vaccaro said. "But it's a lot more than that."

"Is that right? You stopped counting? But why? German snipers are expected to report their kills," Bauer said.

Finally, Cole spoke up. "It ain't a game," he said. "There ain't no score. If I shoot some Kraut bastard before he shoots me, I reckon that's good enough."

"So many," Bauer said. The shadows cast on his face by the firelight made him appear suddenly older, and sad. "So many dead."

Cole reassembled his rifle, satisfied that it was clean. In the morning, he would put it to work again. He leaned it against a sofa, within easy reach.

He now felt relaxed and not a little sleepy. Since he had volunteered himself to keep the first watch, he looked over toward Rupert, who was closest to the fireplace, and asked, "Lieutenant, you got any coffee left in that pot?"

Rupert put down his book and reached over to give the coffeepot a shake. He had just opened his mouth to respond, but before any words came out, they all heard a distinct creak.

It sounded like there was somebody upstairs.

* * *

THEY ALL HELD their breath for the span of several heartbeats.

"Did you hear that?" Vaccaro whispered.

"Yeah, we heard it," Cole replied, reaching for the rifle that he had just put down.

"Steady on," Lieutenant Rupert said quietly. "Old houses make noises in the night. They settle and whatnot. Heating and contracting and all that."

"Perhaps it is a ghost," Bauer suggested, eyebrows raised, clearly amused that the others were so unnerved.

After a minute went by without another sound, Vaccaro said, "I guess it's nothin'. Like the lieutenant said, it's an old house."

They had all just begun to relax when the sound came again, this time in a different spot.

Creak. *Crack.*

Maybe Rupert was right and old houses made noise, but this noise reminded Cole of nothing so much as a stealthy footstep.

"Dammit, city boy. I thought you and the lieutenant checked upstairs," Cole said.

"We did check upstairs," Vaccaro said. "There wasn't nobody nohow."

"There is an attic," Lieutenant Rupert said, looking as white as a sheet. Out of all of them, Bauer's comment about ghosts had seemed to unnerve him. "We didn't go into it."

"Why the hell not? Sir."

"We searched upstairs and there was nothing," he said, suddenly sounding like a flustered schoolboy who was explaining his actions to an irate headmaster. "It seemed pointless to search the attic as well. I stuck my head up the attic stairs, and I'm pretty sure there's nothing up there but dusty furniture."

"Well, we're sure as hell gonna go take a look in the attic right now," Cole announced.

Vaccaro and Rupert rounded up their weapons. Cole looked over at their prisoner, who was still lounging in an armchair, having made no effort to stir himself.

"You too, Herr Barnstormer."

"The Geneva Convention states that I do not have to exorcise ghosts."

"Very funny. But I ain't leavin' you here alone, not without tying you up again, and I ain't got time for that. You're coming with us."

Reluctantly, the German did as he was told and joined them as they headed for the stairs.

Without electricity, the house was pitch black away from the firelit room. They navigated by flashlights, which cast odd, elongated shadows on the walls. Cole went up the stairs first, rifle at the ready, with Bauer behind him. Then came Lieutenant Rupert, with Vaccaro bringing up the rear.

"Search the bedrooms again," Cole whispered.

They went from room to room, cautiously at first, but then with more confidence as it became clear that nobody was there. Then again, there was no doubt that they had heard those creaking noises that had sounded an awful lot like footsteps.

"Nobody here, just like I said," Vaccaro said with a certain amount of righteous smugness. "Must just be the house settling."

"But you didn't go in the attic," Cole pointed out. "That's where we're headed next."

He nodded at the door in the hallway that led to the attic. He then nodded at Vaccaro, indicating that he should open it. Cole stood to one side and put his rifle to his shoulder, ready for anything.

The door creaked open. The steps were steeper here, bare wood, more utilitarian. He could understand why Rupert had decided that searching the attic wasn't worth it.

Then again, they had heard something.

"Follow me and hold the flashlight, Lieutenant," he whispered. "Vaccaro, you stay here with Herr Barnstormer."

Cole let the muzzle lead the way up the steep attic stairs, the nervous Lieutenant Rupert so close that he was practically stepping on Cole's heels.

One didn't grow up in the mountains without developing a healthy respect for haints and ghosts—there were all sorts of things that couldn't be explained in this world. Maybe the house really was haunted by the ghost of old Baron So-and-So or whoever had lived here. Maybe—

Something moved at the corner of his vision.

He swung his rifle in that direction just as the flashlight beam got there.

Two faces looked back at him. They were pale, all right, but they weren't spectral.

And they were female.

"Hold it!" he shouted.

Immediately, the older of the two women began spouting angry French at him. He could recognize the language, if not the meaning. She did not seem frightened, but indignant.

She also held an ancient double-barreled shotgun, which she pointed meaningfully in Cole's direction.

"No fusil!" he shouted at her.

This was about the limits of his French, but the woman seemed to understand. She pointed the shotgun elsewhere, but didn't let go of it.

The pair had been hiding behind furniture. There was an abundance of it up here, much of it dusty, just as Lieutenant Rupert had predicted. He could also see bedding on the floor, a jug of water, and what appeared to be an old-fashioned chamber pot. Clearly, the two women were sheltering up here.

Cole waggled the rifle at them, indicating that they should come closer. Rupert played the flashlight over their faces, lingering a bit longer on the face of the younger woman.

Cole pegged them instantly as mother and daughter. The resemblance was clear. The mother was probably in her late forties or early fifties, tall and portly, but regal as a middle-aged Queen Victoria. The daughter was in her late teens or maybe early twenties, gently curved in all the places where her mother was rounded. Even in the harsh battery-powered light in the dusty attic, her good looks drew the attention of the men. She wasn't pin-up pretty but something more elegant. Oddly, her face was covered in dark smudges, as if it had been rubbed with soot, but that was not enough to hide her obvious attractiveness.

Cole decided that these were not the household servants. No, these were the ladies of the manor.

The mother was still cackling French like an angry hen. Cole had no idea what she was saying and didn't much care. Again, he waggled the muzzle at them, indicating that they should go downstairs.

When they still didn't move, Lieutenant Rupert surprised everyone by making the request in French. It sounded halting to Cole's ears, but apparently it was understandable to the two women.

They got the message and started for the stairs. As the mother went past, Cole grabbed the shotgun out of her hands.

This got her started on a fresh tirade. It was clear that having been forced to come out of the shadows, the woman of the house was now as riled as an angry hen by the intruders in her home.

I reckon I would've preferred a ghost, Cole decided.

CHAPTER TWENTY-ONE

RETURNING to the second-floor hallway from the attic, they got things organized and headed down to what Bauer called the drawing room, which had become their headquarters. This time, Cole brought up the rear so that he could shoot anyone who tried to make a run for it—Bauer in particular.

He wasn't all that worried about the two women. They still needed to figure out what was going on with them, but Cole didn't see them as a real danger or threat.

In a few minutes, he would find out that he might have been wrong about that.

Downstairs, the warmth of the fireplace was welcome after prowling through the cold rooms above, not to mention the light from the flames themselves. There had been something unnerving about the search through the empty upstairs rooms and then coming across the two women in the attic. It was one thing to face the enemy, quite another to confront the possibility of ghosts and spooks, and something altogether different to find flesh-and-blood occupants.

The warm glow of the fireplace cast a welcoming light in the otherwise dark and cold room. The flickering flames danced on the walls, providing a sense of comfort and safety. The burning logs crackled and popped, sounding vaguely to Cole's ears like distant gunfire in the otherwise quiet room.

The quiet did not last for long—there was a storm brewing in the form of the indignant lady of the house, who did not seem to like the feeling that she was now a prisoner in her own home, even if she was theoretically on the same side as the soldiers.

* * *

SHE HAD HELD her tongue in the attic, but within moments of arriving downstairs, the scowling woman lit into them with a torrent of words that Cole couldn't understand, but considering that her eyes blazed with anger, the woman's meaning was clear enough.

Cole and Vaccaro had a limited understanding of French. Like most GIs, they could pick out a word here and there after having been in France since D-Day. They had already discovered that Rupert spoke French and were surprised that Bauer was also able to communicate in that language. Adding to the mix, the girl spoke English with a heavy accent that made her even more endearing.

Based on his own experience with the French Resistance fighter Jolie Molyneaux, Cole knew that a girl could make the weather forecast sound like a love poem if she said it in a French accent.

Under different circumstances—perhaps an R & R dance arranged with some local girls in attendance—the three younger men would have been vying for her attention. But they now watched one another warily.

The daughter translated for everyone's benefit. "My mother wishes to know, what is the meaning of this?" she said politely. Meanwhile, her mother was gesturing angrily at Cole and the others. "She says, 'How dare you come into our home like this!'"

Because he was ostensibly in charge, Lieutenant Rupert turned to face her, doing his best to look official. "Madame," he began calmly. "We apologize for any inconvenience we may have caused."

"Inconvenience?" Through her daughter the woman made it plain that she scoffed at the lieutenant's words. "This is an outrage! You have no right to invade our home!"

"We are just passing through," Rupert explained. "We'll be out of your house soon enough. Until then, I fear that we must ask you to remain in this room with us."

Upon hearing what the lieutenant had to say, the woman's face flushed red with indignation. Another stream of angry words followed.

"My mother says that she will not be held prisoner in her own home by a group of—" The daughter bit back the final word.

"Yes?" Lieutenant Rupert asked, a slight smile playing over his lips.

"Ruffians!" the girl finally exclaimed, reddening.

Cole reckoned that they had been called worse.

"Please assure your mother that we mean you no harm," Rupert said to her. "We are simply trying to do our duty and protect your country."

Again, the daughter translated, but it was plain to see that she was not satisfied.

"Mother says that she does not care about your duty!" the girl said. "She says that you have no right to treat us like this."

"Miss, please inform your mother that we shall leave as soon as we can tomorrow morning. In fact, you might remind her that you're better off having us here rather than the Germans."

Once her daughter had translated these last words, all the fight drained out of the woman. Her indignation faded as the truth of Rupert's statement sank in. She seemed to take in the tired and weary soldiers as if seeing them for the first time.

More words followed, but the matriarch's tone had changed. She took command of the drawing room. Through her daughter, she began issuing orders like a general—there was no other way to describe it. She made it clear that this was *her* house and that the soldiers were interlopers or possibly guests (albeit socially inferior ones) who had wandered in out of the night, which indeed they had. Consequently, she had no qualms about putting them to work.

She pointed at the pile of wood, and then at the fire, indicating that it needed more logs piled upon it. Rupert was quick to do her bidding, and fresh logs sent crackling sparks up the chimney, and the warming flames rose higher. She oversaw the shifting of furniture to accommodate everyone in a rough half circle around the warm fire.

Although French rushed from her lips, most of the commanding was accomplished by waving her hands at everyone in a manner that needed no translation.

Bauer seemed amused by the communication gap between the two Americans and their put-upon hostess.

"I have always found it curious that most of you Americans speak only English," Bauer noted. "I don't know if that is arrogance or your famous Yankee practicality."

"Don't go callin' me a Yankee," Cole warned. "That's a downright insult where I'm from. Anyhow, there ain't much need to speak French or German back home in Gashey's Creek."

Bauer cocked his head. "From what I hear, you barely speak English."

Cole bristled at that remark. "Keep it up, Herr Barnstormer. The only one you'll be talkin' to shortly is Saint Peter at the pearly gates."

Bauer shook his head, the familiar amused smile flashing. "I mean only that at times you are barely understandable to my ears because you have such a strong accent. Is that why your friend here calls you a hillbilly?"

"I'm a hillbilly and proud of it."

Cole felt himself getting angry again at Bauer, but the heat faded when he saw that the German was giving him that wry grin of his—not a superior smile, but an impish one. Cole relaxed, realizing that the German was needling him. Busting his chops—and he had walked right into it like a blind mule into the side of a barn.

Cole shook his head. Reluctantly, he had to admit that Bauer had a sense of humor that matched his own. German or not, Bauer seemed to appreciate sarcasm and shared the same dark sense of humor as your typical GI. Maybe that style of humor was universal to soldiers everywhere, regardless of which side they were on.

The lady of the manor couldn't seem to sit still, rushing around to light more candles. The daughter disappeared into the kitchen and returned with some cheese, a loaf of bread that had somehow escaped their search, a small knife, and a carving board. She also had a dampened cloth that she used to clean the dark smudges from her face.

It was later explained that the dirty marks came from the mother rubbing the daughter's face with the burned end of a wine cork. It was a strategy to make her less attractive to the male soldiers who had invaded their home.

This tactic had been around as long as there had been pretty daughters and invading armies. The girl didn't have a mirror, so the mother took the cloth and dabbed at a few spots that her daughter had missed.

Although she had been pretty enough to start with, the girl's freshly scrubbed face now looked radiant in the firelight and candlelight, bringing a flush to her cheeks. One person who noticed the transformation was definitely Lieutenant Rupert, who stared as if transfixed. The girl saw him staring and blushed.

The mother then produced a bottle of brandy from a cleverly disguised cupboard to one side of the fireplace and poured them all a drink—even the German officer, although she supplied his brandy in a mismatched glass with an extra measure of frosty attitude. It was clear that she was no fan of the German, but having gotten over her initial dismay at having their hiding place discovered, she appeared delighted to have encountered two American soldiers and a British officer. In her view, they were the good guys.

Cole picked up on one word that she kept repeating, "Libérateurs! Libérateurs!"

Cole hoped she wasn't just being polite on account of them being the ones with the guns.

Finally, she settled into a massive upholstered armchair, looked around like a queen holding court, and began to tell their story. Around the fire, the story of Château Jouret and the family who lived there began to unfold. Lieutenant Rupert and the girl took turns translating whenever she paused.

"We have been waiting a long time for the Americans to arrive," she said through her daughter. "It is so exciting to see what you look like! We have tried to keep the house looking empty to avoid attracting attention. If there is a fire in the chimney, there is someone home, and where there is someone home, there is food, and where there is food, you will have foragers. When I glanced out the window, we saw the German officer's uniform and feared the worst and fled with my daughter to the attic."

She explained that they had taken a chance and come downstairs for blankets and a jug of water they had left in one of the bedrooms. That foray had turned out to be a mistake because the creaky floor had given them away.

Her name was Madame Jouret. She had been a widow since before the war. The house had been in her husband's family for many years. She had a son who had gone off to join the fighting back in 1941, opposing the flow of the Nazi tide that had seemed unstoppable then, and had not been heard from again. After so many years, it was assumed that he was dead, one of the legions of young men who had stood up to the Germans and whose fate might never really be known, other than that he had been swallowed up by the war.

Rupert turned to the girl. "Your mother says that you are Carolina. It is very nice to meet you, Miss Carolina."

"Lena," the girl announced.

He took her hand in greeting, Lena took his, and to the onlookers, it was as if Lieutenant Rupert and Lena had wrapped themselves in a bubble to become the only two people in the room, or possibly the universe. Cole didn't believe in love at first sight, or love in general, but the lieutenant and the girl sure seemed to.

Seeing what was going on, Cole and Vaccaro exchanged a look. "The girls always go for the officers," Vaccaro muttered. "That's the way of the world. But at least there's brandy."

"Amen to that," Cole said, raising his glass in a toast to Vaccaro. He'd had a sufficient amount of the strong brandy so that he could feel its warmth down to his toes, which he hadn't been sure would ever feel warm again.

He felt relaxed enough that he took off his boots and set them by the fire to dry, just like he'd done as a boy back home—but not so close to the heat that the leather would crack. Gratefully, he wiggled his toes and warmed them in the heat cast by the fireplace.

Cole glanced at Bauer, who, from his expression, also had not failed to notice the chemistry between Rupert and the girl. Cole might have expected another one of Bauer's cynical smirks but was surprised to see that the German's expression was wistful, as if remembering someone or something—perhaps even a German girl he had once looked at in much the same way. Or perhaps he was thinking of the many young German men who were now in the dirt, or frozen corpses buried face down in the snow, never to know love again.

Madame Jouret continued to hold court, but it was getting hard for the men to keep their eyes open. It had been a long day in the cold, compounded by several preceding days in bitter temperatures, plus biting wind and snow. He felt the sleepy tug of the brandy. Cole didn't do much to stifle a yawn.

The fire began to die down, and they had burned through much of the wood from the small pile stacked near the hearth. Lena offered to fetch more wood, and Lieutenant Rupert jumped up and volunteered to go with her. Cole recalled that there was a woodshed not far from the kitchen door.

The two disappeared and the minutes stretched on.

"I'll bet she found some wood, all right," Vaccaro said, smiling knowingly. "The lieutenant is probably giving her all the wood she wants right about now."

The mother began to look anxious and stood up as if to go after them.

Bauer said something gently to her in French and she sat back down, poured herself more brandy, and seemed to wrap herself in dignity as if putting on a shawl.

"What was that all about?" Cole wondered.

"I reminded her that love is life," the German explained. "I have seen so many young men dead before their time in this war. Young women as well. Why not let the lieutenant and the girl have a few minutes to themselves?"

Another five minutes went by before the couple returned, carrying armloads of wood. Both looked rather flushed, Cole thought.

"I reckon someone's been dancin' the blanket hornpipe," Cole said quietly to Vaccaro.

"You and your hillbilly sayings. Back home we call it playing hide the sausage."

"Whatever you call it, they were doing it, though they really weren't gone that long. Lieutenant Rupert must be quick as a jackrabbit."

"Rupert is a lucky bastard," Vaccaro said.

"No argument from me."

More logs were put on the fire, and Rupert expertly banked the coals for the night. Not long after that, the women left to go upstairs to bed. First, Madame Jouret took a few of the coals and put them into an old-fashioned bed warmer to help heat the cold bed upstairs. Not even Cole had seen anything like that in years.

Finally, Madame Jouret asked for her shotgun back. Cole thought it over and then agreed. He supposed that the lady of the house had a right to feel as if she could defend herself.

Once the women had gone, Cole told Bauer to hold out his hands.

The German sighed. "Are you really going to tie me up again?"

"I don't want you to steal my rifle and shoot me during the night," Cole said. "Or hit me over the head with a chunk of firewood."

"Do you really think I would shoot you?"

"I would sure as hell shoot *you* if I had to. Now put out your hands," Cole ordered. "Or I can hog-tie you if you prefer."

Bauer did as he was told, and Cole once again tied him up. If the German thought this business of being tied up was getting old, then so did Cole. He was tired of feeling like a nursemaid to their prisoner. He hoped that they would be able to drop Herr Barnstormer at HQ tomorrow and be done with him. The German would be someone else's problem.

Once Bauer was secured again, Cole felt like that was one less threat to worry about and had a change of heart about keeping watch. After the women had been discovered hiding upstairs, it seemed unlikely that the château itself would hold any additional surprises. After barring the kitchen door—which she hadn't had time to do earlier before fleeing to the attic—Madame Jouret had assured him that the house was locked up tight.

Cole had no reason to doubt her. After all, the heavy shutters over the downstairs windows transformed the place into a fortress. They would awaken in plenty of time if someone tried to get in, because there was no way to do that quietly.

Cole gave a final glance around the room. Vaccaro was already snoring, thanks to the brandy. He'd had a lot more to drink than Cole.

The German had stretched out on a sofa, his boots hanging off one end, put his bound hands under him for a pillow, and now appeared to be asleep.

Only Lieutenant Rupert still seemed to be awake, tossing and turning on the floor—most likely thinking about that girl upstairs.

The fire crackled gently in the hearth, red embers glowing. He mused that if this was as bad as the war got, it wouldn't be half-bad.

Cole wrapped himself in his blanket and closed his eyes.

* * *

COLE SLEPT DEEPLY, unfettered by dreams. He awoke to gray morning light filtering between the cracks in the shutters and through the gaps in the thick drapes. It wasn't anything close to sunshine, but instead the gloom of another dreary winter day. That was all there seemed to be in Europe, one gray day after another.

He was just starting to wonder whether they would ever see the sunshine again. The winter was beginning to seem endless, and summer felt like some dim memory. He longed for a crisp winter day with the sun bright on the new-fallen snow and not a breath of wind.

Like most country people, Cole tended to be an early riser, up before dawn, but he had slept late in the relative luxury of the château drawing room. He was just as exhausted as anyone.

He sensed that something had awakened him, so he looked around the room. In the dim light, he saw that Bauer and Lieutenant Rupert were still slumbering, but not Vaccaro, which was something of a surprise.

The city boy was already up, grasping his rifle as he peered anxiously through a gap in the shutters.

"What the hell are you doing up?" Cole muttered.

Seeing that Cole was awake, Vaccaro whispered, "Country boy, we've got a problem."

"Just one? That ain't hardly worth mentioning."

"Yeah, but it's a big one."

"What's that?"

"We've got company."

"The way you're sayin' that makes me think it ain't the Rockettes."

"It's sure as hell not. Better take a look."

Cole roused himself, crawling out from under the warm blankets. The fire had died out during the night, leaving the room cold. The morning air also held a lingering mustiness from the house, like an old book that has spent too long on a dusty shelf. That slight whiff of dampness added to the overall feeling of being surrounded by gloom.

He joined Vaccaro at the window.

"I got up to take a leak and decided to peek outside to see how the day was shaping up before I grabbed a few more winks," Vaccaro explained. "That's when I saw them."

Cole looked. He spotted a group of men huddled at the edge of the forest, watching the house. It was still somewhat dark under the trees, so he retrieved his rifle to get a better look at them through the scope. He studied the soldiers, confirming what he already suspected.

Germans. A trio of them.

Something about them made it seem as if the Krauts had been out there awhile, maybe all night. They looked cold, stamping their feet, their breath making clouds in the morning air. Then he realized that the Kübelwagen was dusted in snow. He couldn't see any tracks in the snowy ground either. *Dammit, how long have they been out there?*

Cole and Vaccaro exchanged worried glances. "We should wake the others," Vaccaro whispered, his fingers tightening around his rifle. "Maybe we can all still get out of here without attracting attention."

Cole shook his head, his gaze still on the Germans. "It's too late for that. They're close enough that they'll see us if we leave."

"So what do we do?" Vaccaro demanded, his voice low as he scanned the room, as if searching for any weapons they could use against the Krauts. But they had no mortars, no machine guns, just their rifles.

"We wait and see," Cole replied, no hint of doubt in his voice. "We've been lucky so far. Maybe we'll be lucky again."

Cole watched the Germans through the crack, reassured that they couldn't see him. The Krauts were watching the house as if determining what to do next. Maybe they were trying to decide whether the house was occupied by friend or foe.

He was glad to see that they hadn't approached the house yet, and with any luck it was just a small patrol passing through and they would move on. The fact that they hadn't done so yet made him a little nervous.

Move on now, he wanted to tell them. *Ain't nothin' to see here.*

"Those Krauts are gonna be disappointed if they think I'm about to invite them in for breakfast," Cole said. "We'd best wake up the others."

CHAPTER TWENTY-TWO

Outside the ancient house, Hauptmann Messner and the two other Germans had grown impatient. They had been up since before the bitter winter dawn, waiting for their quarry to show itself.

The plan was a simple one—to catch Bauer and his escort as soon as they left the shelter of the château. They would take them by surprise and eliminate Bauer once and for all—and his American escorts along with him.

But the gray light grew and there was still no sign of any activity.

Dietzel had already scouted around the house as soon as there was sufficient light, putting Messner's fears to rest that their quarry had somehow given them the slip. More snow had fallen during the night, partially covering the four sets of tracks that led to the house. There were no fresh tracks in the snow, which meant that no one had fled the château.

"Why don't they come out?"

"Maybe they have seen us."

Messner had to admit that once again Dietzel was likely correct. When they had stopped the Kübelwagen last night, they had not realized in the dark that it was within view of the house. That had been an unfortunate oversight. On the positive side, they could easily bring the machine gun mounted on the back of the vehicle to bear on the château or front lawn, as needed.

Perhaps they had lost the element of surprise, but no matter. Bauer and his escort couldn't hide from them forever.

"They will have to come out sooner or later," Messner said.

"Or they could fight," Dietzel pointed out.

Messner thought about that. "In that case, perhaps the time has come to offer them a deal—their lives for Bauer's. I doubt that the Americans will be willing to die for their German prisoner."

* * *

From inside the château, Cole kept watching the Germans, wondering what they were up to and what they were waiting for. He ran through a few mental scenarios, none of them promising.

The Germans were too far away to tell much about them, but they appeared to be Wehrmacht troops wearing winter-white camouflage. Their Kübelwagen carried a mounted machine gun, giving the Germans a distinct advantage in firepower. Through the scope, he was surprised to notice that one of the Germans was also studying the château through the scope on his own rifle.

So, a sniper then.

He felt a quiver of interest run through him like an electric current. He wouldn't have admitted it out loud, but deep down, the thought of matching wits and bullets with another sniper excited him.

"What do you think?" Vaccaro asked.

"Doesn't look good," Cole said. "They must have spotted the smoke rising from the chimney, or maybe they saw the tracks we made in the snow, leading right to the house. They figure that somebody is in here. They just don't know who."

"You don't suppose the ladies of the house sold us out, do you?" Vaccaro wondered. "Maybe last night was just an act and they're actually German collaborators—or selling us out for some sausages or something."

Cole hadn't considered that possibility, but he quickly dismissed it.

"Madame Jouret wasn't too keen on our German friend here. That wasn't any act."

"You'll think differently if she comes down the stairs this morning and shoots us in the back with that antique shotgun of hers."

"I don't buy it," Cole said. "Plus that girl had the hots for Rupert. That wasn't any act either."

Vaccaro grinned. "Yeah, I'm surprised Rupert didn't sneak upstairs last night to give that girl the business, but there he is, sleeping innocent as a baby."

"Don't forget Mama standing guard with her shotgun. He probably didn't like his chances."

Vaccaro nodded. "All right, so they're not collaborators. I thought that was a long shot, anyhow. As for the Krauts out there, maybe they'll just keep going and leave us the hell alone."

"When have you ever known the Krauts not to be thorough? If they suspect that there are Americans in here, they're not just going to ignore us. Hell, we wouldn't either. You can see them out there, sizing the place up."

"Maybe poke your rifle out there and pick them off," Vaccaro suggested.

Cole shook his head. "I wouldn't be able to get them all before they scattered and got into those trees. Besides, that's small for a patrol, and there might be more Krauts out there that we can't see. Also, one of them is a sniper."

"Are you afraid he'll shoot back?"

"What I'm saying is, shooting at them might just piss them off if I don't get them all. Maybe you're right and they really will just keep going. I sure as hell hope so."

Cole woke up Bauer and Lieutenant Rupert, informing them of the situation. Rupert peered through the gap in the drapes and immediately looked worried, but Bauer just shrugged and wondered whether he could get some coffee. "Perhaps the ladies of the house have some hidden away?" he suggested.

"You just sit tight and stay out of the way," Cole told him. The German's hands were still bound. "Lieutenant, why don't you go upstairs and look out the back windows to see if there are more Krauts around the back of the house. Better tell Madame Jouret and your new girlfriend not to go outside."

"She's not—"

Cole didn't wait to hear Rupert deny his romantic interests. "Go on, Lieutenant. The last thing we need is for one of the ladies to open the back door because they don't know what's going on and let those Germans waltz on in. That would be one hell of a mess that we don't need right now."

Rupert ran upstairs, then shortly reported back. "I don't see anyone," he reported. "Just those soldiers out front."

"All right, that much is good news."

From his position by the window, Vaccaro said, "One of the Krauts is headed for the house."

"All right, let's shoot him."

"Hold on. You won't believe this, but he's waving a white flag. What the hell do you think he wants?"

Cole had been about to break the window glass with the muzzle of the rifle to get a good shot at the German. Reluctantly, he took his finger off the trigger. Outlined against the snow, the approaching German soldier made a perfect target. He was either a brave bastard or a fool. "Let's see what he's got to say."

"I've got a bad feeling about this," Vaccaro said.

Before leaving the room, Cole suggested that Lieutenant Rupert take out his pistol and cover Bauer. "Herr Barnstormer, sit your ass down on that sofa. Lieutenant, shoot him if he tries anything."

Out in the great hall, Vaccaro asked, "Shouldn't we send Rupert out to negotiate? He is an officer, after all."

"You don't send the hen to talk to the hawk," Cole pointed out. "You send the meanest rooster you've got. You want the hawk to think twice about swooping down on the henhouse."

Vaccaro had to yank on the front door to get it to open a crack. He peered through. "Here he comes. He looks like a mean bastard. It's not too late to shoot him."

"Might as well hear what he's got to say."

"How's your German?"

"If he doesn't speak English, we'll get the girl. I think she can *Sprechen Sie Deutsch*."

Outside, the German was walking right up to the massive front door. Built of thick oak, it hadn't been used for some time and wasn't easy to open, having swollen in the winter damp so that it was stuck in the doorframe. Cole opened it just enough to stick his head out, keeping the rest of his body behind the thick door.

He found himself face-to-face with another German officer. This one had a grimy rag tied to a stick. He said something to them in German, and he seemed angry about it. Seeing that Cole hadn't understood a word, he switched to English. Though heavily accented, Cole could understand the words well enough.

"I am Hauptmann Messner," he declared. "I wish you to release Obersturmbannführer Bauer to us."

"How the hell do you know we've got Bauer?" Cole had the fleeting thought that maybe Vaccaro was right and the two women really were collaborators. How else could the Germans possibly know about Bauer?

"We have been tracking him," the German said. "Give him to us and there will be no need for bloodshed."

"What do you want with him?"

"He is a traitor. Give him to us and we will let you go."

"Can't do that."

"You do not seem to understand your situation," the German said.

"My situation?" Cole snorted. He didn't like the looks of this German officer. Hell, he didn't like the looks of *any* German officer. "The way I see it, there's just three of you, and we are holed up behind these nice thick walls. We ain't givin' him up. So come and get him if you want to. But you'd better bring a rifle next time instead of a rag tied to a little stick."

The German frowned. He didn't have a good answer for that. He muttered a curse, then dropped the stick with the rag tied to it into the snow.

Too late, Cole realized that dropping the flag of truce was some sort of signal.

In the next instant, a rifle fired from the tree line and a bullet struck the door an inch from Cole's head. The bullet would have hit him if he hadn't tilted his head down to look at the flag the German had dropped.

Behind him, Vaccaro slammed the door shut just as another bullet hit. The wood was too thick for the bullets to punch through, the dense grain of the ancient oak making it nearly as good as armor plating.

Cole ran to a window, and through the shutters he saw the officer hightailing it back to cover. He was out of sight before there was a chance for Cole to bring his rifle into play.

"Well now, don't that beat all," Cole said, lowering his rifle. "It's gonna be an interesting day around here."

"Dammit, that was close," Vaccaro said.

"That Kraut sniper almost got me," Cole agreed.

"You can't trust these damn Krauts. Next time one of them wants to talk, let's just shoot him."

"I ain't gonna argue with that."

"What the hell do those Krauts want with our prisoner?" Vaccaro wondered.

"To hell if I know. Let's go ask him."

* * *

ONCE DARKNESS FELL, Brock and his squad had made camp. It was a cold camp, without any fire that might attract the attention of the enemy. Consequently, the trio had shivered through the night. There was grumbling from Vern and Boot, but they knew better than to complain too much to Brock.

They feared the Germans who might be creeping up on them, and frostbite was a constant threat. But their healthy fear of Brock outweighed both. They knew that when Brock set his mind on doing something, then you had better get out of the way or follow along.

He'd been just as cold as anyone. Zeal only did so much to keep you warm, and his own determination to track down the German had started to wane in the cold, dark, wee hours of the morning.

When the gray light of morning finally arrived, Brock had been just about ready to call it quits, get everyone turned around, and head back to Bastogne empty-handed without their quarry.

That was when they heard two gunshots, not very far away, somewhere toward the end of the lane that they had been traveling before darkness had rolled in.

It was the first sign that they weren't the only ones out there.

He'd been afraid that the trail had gone cold, but here was a spark, at least.

And in Brock's experience, where there was smoke, there was fire.

"C'mon," he said to the others. "On your feet. Let's go see what that shooting is all about."

As they started to get up, it was clear that Boot was having trouble.

"What the hell is wrong with you?" he demanded.

"It's my toes, Brock," Boot explained. "I can't feel them at all. It might be frostbite."

"Dammit, how many times have I warned you and everybody else in the squad to make sure you were wearing dry socks."

"Never mind dry socks," Vern spoke up. "Cold as it was, we're lucky that we didn't freeze to death."

"I don't want to hear your crap," Brock growled, prompting Vern to clam up. "All right, Boot, let me have a look at those feet."

Boot's fingers were so stiff that Brock had to help him unlace his boots. His socks were stiff, too, either with grime or partially frozen. They finally peeled off to reveal his toes.

It wasn't a pretty sight. The toes were dark, the skin resembling bruised fruit.

Watching over Brock's shoulder, Vern winced and looked away. Brock forced himself not to react.

"You'll be all right," he said, trying for a positive note. "You just need to get up and moving, is all. Get the blood flowing, you know."

"I guess you're right, Brock," Boot replied, although the words were emitted through shivering lips.

We're all cold, Brock thought. *Too damn cold.*

He told himself that it was all going to be worth it to get some justice, not just for his old pal Charlie Knuth, but for all the poor bastards that the German officer had ordered gunned down in the woods outside Bastogne. For once in his life, Brock felt like he had to do something right.

He straightened up and wriggled his own toes, grateful that he could feel them. The morning was grim and unforgiving, the sky a dull shade of gray, as if it were reflecting the miserable circumstances they found themselves in. The barren trees and snowy ground added to the gloomy atmosphere. He realized that their voices sounded strained and tense in the frosty air, their words clipped and urgent as they communicated with each other.

Brock trudged forward, feeling the biting cold and dampness seep into his bones. He knew that it was always coldest in the early hours of the morning, and he told himself that they would warm up soon enough.

He glanced over at Boot, who managed to hobble along. He decided that it was one hell of a nickname for a lame guy. Boot was going to lose his toes, sure as the sun came up in the morning. They would get the German and then get Boot back to Bastogne, where the docs could get a look at him.

His shoulders slumped under the weight of his rifle and gear as he led the others forward. They passed between two stone pillars and found themselves looking at a massive stone château.

The tracks they had been following led right to the château.

It irritated him that the German prisoner and his escort had apparently spent the night there, where they'd been warm and dry. *Probably sleeping in a bunch of damn feather beds.*

He studied the old house. The château was an impressive place, rising like a solid wall of stone from the clearing surrounded by forest. He considered the kind of money the people who owned that place must have and whistled softly to himself. Somebody was definitely the lord of the manor. So far the war hadn't seemed to touch this remote château.

The war had left so many towns and villages a wreck. Growing up in Florida, he had once seen the aftermath of a hurricane that had swept in from the sea and turned entire towns into scattered piles of sticks and rubble. He and his friends had driven around, amazed at the debris. The surrounding Belgian countryside reminded him of that same destruction, although in this case it was war that had swept in rather than a storm.

There was no doubt that the local people were suffering, especially now that the Germans were on the rampage, but there were occasional reminders, such as this massive stone house, that Europe was the land of princes and princesses.

Brock settled in to watch the house and plan his next move.

CHAPTER TWENTY-THREE

Cole and Vaccaro went to confront their prisoner, having made sure that the Germans outside weren't planning an immediate attack, considering that their meeting under a flag of truce had not gone well.

"What did the Germans want?" Lieutenant Rupert asked. "I heard shooting."

"It turns out they wanted to negotiate," Cole said. "It didn't go well."

The commotion had also roused Madame Jouret and her daughter, who had come down the stairs half-dressed. The sight of the thickset Madame Jouret in her dressing gown, her hair disheveled, was a sight that the young soldiers would gladly have been spared. However, the appearance of her daughter certainly drew the eyes of the young men. Her dressing gown had been worn thin with use, probably a necessity of wartime and reduced circumstances. The worn gown did little to hide the shape of her body and left little to the imagination.

Gallantly, Rupert moved to drape a blanket around the girl's shoulders to keep off the morning chill in the room—and perhaps to protect her from the other male eyes.

Cole had to give him points for that act of thoughtfulness.

Evidently the girl did as well, her sleepy face breaking into a shy, grateful smile.

Vaccaro started to explain what had just taken place during the parlay with the Krauts, keeping his eyes on their German prisoner.

"The funniest thing just happened," Vaccaro said. "That Kraut officer asked for you by name. He wanted to invite you outside, and I'm pretty sure it wasn't for a picnic. What do you think, Cole?"

"Not unless the picnic involved Herr Barnstormer getting used for target practice."

Vaccaro nodded. "Definitely not a picnic. In fact, that Kraut officer said something about you being a traitor. He wanted to make a trade. He said that he and the other Krauts would let us go if we handed you over to them."

"Then they tried to shoot us," Cole pointed out. "Don't forget that part."

Vaccaro nodded. "Oh yeah, they tried to shoot us when we declined his kind offer."

"Never trust a Kraut," Cole said.

Cole decided to let Vaccaro ask the questions, since he was the talkative one. Instead, he stood off to one side, looking through the gap in the shutters to keep one eye out for any move by the Krauts who had disappeared into the woods. He kept his other eye on Bauer with his rifle pointed in the German's direction. He wanted to send a not-very-subtle message.

"We ain't foolin' around, so start talking," he said.

Bauer raised his eyebrows in surprise. "Talking?"

Vaccaro was now focused on Bauer. "You know what? Cole and I are real curious. How the hell would some Krauts out here in the middle of the damn forest know who you were and that you happened to be in this château?"

From his position by the window, Cole commented, "It just gets more tangled than a bag of snakes, don't it?"

Vaccaro looked meaningfully at the two ladies of the house. "Of course, it's just possible that not everyone in this room is who they claim to be. Just maybe some people here are friendlier toward the Germans than they pretend to be."

The girl understood what Vaccaro was hinting at. Her eyes widened. She looked at her mother and translated. The mother then launched into an indignant rant that implied she would never have anything to do with the Germans. She began shaking her finger angrily at Bauer, as if it was all his fault.

Vaccaro held up his hands like a referee. "All right, all right. You know we had to ask. But now that that's out of the way, I think we can focus on one particular person in this room."

He looked meaningfully at Bauer. "We're waiting."

"Did this officer have a name?" Bauer asked.

"Messerschmitt, or something like that."

"Ah. You have met Hauptmann Messner."

"Friend of yours?"

Instead of answering directly, Bauer replied, "You should give me up. Perhaps it is not too late, despite them shooting at you. I will talk to them. Maybe they will agree to leave you alone."

"Herr Barnstormer, I hate to tell you this, but the whole reason we're out here is because of you," Cole said. "We ain't giving you up. You're our prisoner, and our orders are to get you to headquarters, which is just what we're gonna do. Hell, I'd just as soon shoot you myself first than turn you over to your own side."

Bauer's amused smile had returned, despite the fact that Cole had just threatened him. "You always seem so eager to shoot people."

"You don't know the half of it. Some days I shoot two or three people before breakfast. Then again, maybe I'm just eager to shoot *you*. Don't worry, I'd make it quick compared to your friends out there. You won't feel a thing, I can promise you. I've had some practice shooting Krauts like you."

"Of that I have no doubt." A look of sadness rather than fear crossed Bauer's face.

"So what does Messner want with you?" Cole asked.

"He believes that I am a traitor for surrendering my unit outside Bastogne. He would have preferred that we fight to the last man."

"I take it that *he* didn't surrender."

"No, he and a handful of others managed to escape. I would imagine those men are with him now."

"How many?"

"Possibly just two or three men if we are lucky. Perhaps more if we are not."

"They have a sniper," Cole said. "He damn near took my head off. He'd pick us off if we tried to get away from the château right now."

"A sniper? That must be Obergefreiter Dietzel. He is a Jaeger. This is what you would call a scout and sniper."

"Is he any good?"

"One of the best."

"I was afraid you might say that."

Lieutenant Rupert spoke up. "Our best course of action may be to wait until dark and then slip away. We'll be safe enough here. This place is practically a fortress."

"From your lips to God's ears," Vaccaro said, then added, "Sir."

The plan sounded easy enough. Of course, they would have to keep a lookout for any funny business that Hauptmann Messner and his men tried, but they had food, a warm fireplace, and the company of young Mademoiselle Jouret to help them pass the day.

"I say we sit by the fire and let those Krauts shiver their keisters off out in the woods. Lieutenant?"

"I agree." The confidence of the two GIs was evidently contagious, because Rupert smiled. "Perhaps we can rustle up a spot of breakfast and a pot of tea."

Vaccaro and Cole exchanged a look. They both thought tea tasted like boiled socks. "If it's all the same, we'd rather have coffee, Lieutenant."

Bauer didn't have anything to say, not that anyone had asked him. He seemed lost in thought, and his hands remained tied.

It sounded like a good plan. They would try to wait out the Germans.

* * *

BUT THE GERMANS had other ideas. Hauptmann Messner did not plan to pass the day quietly. He was disappointed that the Americans had not seen reason by turning Bauer over to them.

He might even have let them live. Now that wasn't going to happen. If they were so determined to protect their prisoner, then they could die doing it.

"You missed that American, Dietzel," the Hauptmann complained, referring to the fact that the Jaeger's bullet had struck the door instead of the soldier.

"He moved," Dietzel said. He shrugged nonchalantly. "Do not worry. I will not miss again."

"See that you don't."

Climbing aboard the Kübelwagen, Messner turned the machine gun in the direction of the château and fired a short burst. Bullets hammered the heavy front door and tore chunks out of the château's stone walls. He focused on the windows and fired another short burst, watching with satisfaction as bullets splintered the shutters. Bits of stone and wood rained down and scattered across the snow.

The Americans had made a mistake if they thought they were going to have an easy time of it.

* * *

BROCK WAS STILL WATCHING the house, figuring out what to do next, when he heard a machine gun open fire.

"Get down," he hissed, although Boot and Vern were already pressed into the snow.

"Who's doing the shooting?" Vern whispered.

"Got to be Krauts. Who the hell else would be out here?"

No bullets pierced the air over their heads, so they hadn't been seen. "If they're not shooting at us, then who the hell are they shooting at?"

"Let's find out," Brock said.

He and the others crept forward through the trees, toward the sound of the firing. Soon he spotted a German Kübelwagen. It was Krauts, all right. The Germans appeared to be firing at the château.

Maybe the smart thing to do would have been to crawl way, but that wasn't in Brock's nature. Instead, he opened fire. Taken by surprise, the Germans quickly recovered and turned their guns in the direction of the Americans. The Krauts knew their business, that was for sure. Their machine gun chewed up the trees, sending bits of bark flying.

"Take cover!" Brock cried, and he and the two others threw themselves to the snow-covered forest floor.

Brock got down as low as he could, willing himself to sink into the snow. A stray bullet whined inches from his ear, making his spine crawl. He was afraid to move a muscle for fear of making himself even more of a target. He was dimly aware of snow sifting through a gap between his coat and trousers, icy against his belly, as if the winter cold was gnawing at his bare skin.

Frozen in place, he wondered what to do next.

Brock had been trained to fight Krauts, however and wherever he saw them, but he realized that now wasn't the time or the place for fighting. Besides, they were here to get one particular Kraut—who all signs indicated was in the nearby château.

"Let's get the hell out of here," he whispered to Vern and Boot, forcing himself to move. His coat had pulled up so that the snow worked its way against his skin, but the cold was better than a bullet.

They belly-crawled through the forest, away from the sound of the German guns.

* * *

HUNKERED DOWN IN THE CHÂTEAU, Cole and the others heard gunfire coming from a different location from where they had last seen the Germans. Hidden in the trees, the Germans continued shooting, seeming to spray bullets in every direction as they defended themselves. For the moment, their fire was not directed at the château, but at wherever the gunfire in the woods was coming from.

"Uh-oh," Cole said. "Sounds like the applecart done been upset."

"Must be the cavalry," Vaccaro said. "Hopefully it's our guys out there."

Vaccaro was half-right. There were Americans out there, but they sure as hell weren't the cavalry.

The brief firefight in the forest ended and the Germans resumed firing at the château.

* * *

As Brock and his men retreated, putting more trees between themselves and the enemy, he saw that the Germans had returned their attention to the château, pouring fire at it. By now, there were a few answering shots from the château.

Not to be outdone, Brock opened fire briefly on the château, ordering his men to do the same. If the German prisoner was in that house, he wanted a piece of him.

* * *

Inside the château, Cole finally used the muzzle of his rifle to crack a pane of glass, enabling him to shoot through a gap in the heavy wooden shutters. The old glass had wavy distortions and was so brittle from the cold that it shattered readily into jagged shards that pattered to the drifted snow around the château's foundation.

Behind him, Madame Jouret made a *tsk* sound of dismay at the broken glass, but Cole ignored her. He had bigger fish to fry. Besides, several German bullets had already blown out the upstairs windows.

Through the rifle scope, he scanned the woods, hoping for a German target to present itself. But the Krauts were staying out of sight.

With his focus on where he thought the Germans were taking cover, he was caught by surprise when several shots peppered the wooden shutter.

Clearly that rifle fire was coming from the direction of what he assumed was the American side of the firefight that had taken place in the woods.

Though the wooden shutters of the old château were heavy enough, they were really no match for .30-06 rounds. Bits and pieces of wood went flying.

Cole ducked.

"Hey, knock it off!" he shouted, hoping that his voice carried on the cold air. "Y'all are shootin' at the wrong folks!"

To his relief, no more bullets hit the château. Friendly fire wasn't unheard of in the confusion of war. The firing in the woods where the Germans were hidden also came to a halt, bringing a tense silence to the morning.

Keeping low, Cole slid his rifle into place and waited for a target.

* * *

When he heard the shout from the château, Brock ordered his men to stop firing.

Good to know we got their attention.

Brock decided to take a chance and see if the escort detail would be willing to hand over their German prisoner, or maybe exchange him for help fighting the Germans in the woods. If nothing else, they had a common enemy.

Deciding that it was worth a try, he slowly stood up, certain that he was concealed from the Germans somewhere on his flank, but visible to the occupants of the château. He kept plenty of thick trees between himself and the German position.

After showing himself, he shouted to get the attention of the troops holed up inside the massive stone house.

"Anybody home?"

* * *

After hearing the shout, Cole watched as a lone GI appeared at the edge of the woods, keeping several large trees between himself and the German position. Cole studied him through the scope, thinking that something about the man looked familiar, and not in a good way, but he couldn't place his finger on it. What the hell did this guy want, and why had he been shooting at the house?

"Who the hell are you?" Cole hollered.

"If you've still got that German prisoner in there with you, send him out," the GI shouted.

Cole was taken aback. What was it about Bauer? Everybody wanted a piece of him. How did that GI know anything about their German prisoner, anyhow?

"What the hell are you talking about?"

"Don't you remember me? I remember you, hillbilly. The name's Brock. Corporal Brock. All we want is your prisoner. Send him out. There's no need for us to shoot at each other. We're on the same side, after all."

Then it dawned on Cole where he had seen the GI before. He realized that he was looking at the same man who had confronted him in Bastogne over Bauer.

He took a deep breath and shouted back, "Hell no! That ain't how it works."

"It's your funeral, hillbilly."

Brock ducked behind the tree, but not before firing a few shots at the house. Bullets pinged off the side of the château; stone chips and more bits of wood flew. Cole had no choice but to duck. Being shot at by his own side was a first.

Over his shoulder, Vaccaro wanted to know what was going on. "What the hell is happening out there? They're shooting at us. Are they our guys or not?"

"Yes and no," Cole said.

"What's that supposed to mean?"

"They want us to turn Herr Barnstormer over to them."

"What did you say?"

"That's why they're shootin' at us."

Vaccaro turned to look at Bauer. "You sure are popular."

Cole shook his head. He couldn't believe it, but both the Germans and the Americans wanted their prisoner.

As much as he disliked Bauer, Cole didn't plan on giving him up to anybody. Orders were orders.

If Cole was completely honest with himself, it also came down to the fact that he didn't like being told what to do. Not by some vigilantes from his own side, and definitely not by a bunch of Krauts.

Meanwhile, the shooting had started up again. Bullets peppered the château from two different directions, apparently from both the German and American forces.

They were stuck in the middle, attacked from two different directions, by two different groups.

Cole had never encountered anything like this yet, but it was a familiar story. *Three dogs, one bone.*

"Well now, don't this beat all," he muttered.

CHAPTER TWENTY-FOUR

"Think we can hold 'em off?" Vaccaro wondered.

"We can as long as we have daylight," Cole said. "Once it gets dark, we won't be able to see them come at us, so that's gonna be a problem."

Vaccaro lowered his voice. "Maybe it wouldn't be such a bad idea to hand Herr Barnstormer over to our guys and let them fight it out with the Germans while we slip away. It would sure be easier."

"Easy ain't the same as right," Cole said.

Vaccaro shook his head. "Hillbilly, let me ask you something. What does that German even matter to you?"

"It ain't about the German. It's about somebody thinking they can tell me what to do." After a moment he added, "Tell *us* what to do."

"Uh-huh. You have got to be the stubbornest bastard that I've ever met. But you know what? I kind of feel the same way about it."

"Then that makes two of us," Cole said.

"In that case, I'll ask again. How do you like our chances?"

"The house is solid, but it's a lot for us to cover. I'd feel a whole lot better if there were more than two of us who could shoot straight."

Cole looked over at Lieutenant Rupert, to see if the officer had any ideas to deal with the situation that they were in. Rupert looked pale as the snow outside. It was a reminder that the lieutenant wasn't a combat soldier. He was an intelligence liaison, whatever that meant, other than the fact that Rupert wouldn't amount to a hill of beans in a fight. He was holding a carbine, but without any real conviction, like someone who had picked something up at the store and hadn't made up their mind to buy it or put it back. He also carried a Webley revolver in a holster that looked as if it might be permanently snapped shut.

Considering that they were outnumbered and outgunned, Cole decided that Rupert needed a crash course in using that rifle.

"When was the last time you fired that weapon, Lieutenant?"

"I've never fired it, if truth be known," Rupert admitted.

"Come on over here a minute, and let me show you how it's done," Cole said.

He got Rupert positioned at the window, where he had a clear field of fire across the open lawn to the woods. The open space was covered with fresh snow, unmarked except by a few footprints that the German had left when he'd approached the door.

"Aim for that stone pillar yonder," Cole said, indicating the entrance pillars to the final approach to the château.

"Shouldn't I shoot at someone? It seems like I'm wasting a bullet."

"Don't worry about that. They won't know you're not shooting at them. You'll be making them keep their heads down."

Cole knelt behind Rupert and made a few adjustments. For starters, he repositioned the stock so that it fit better into the lieutenant's shoulder. He also showed Rupert how to let the full weight of the weapon rest on the windowsill, which made it easier to aim.

"Better?"

"I'd say so. Now what?"

"Aim for the middle of the pillar, just like you'd aim for the middle of your man. Don't try anything fancy. Let your breath out, then breathe in again and hold it. Now repeat after me, Lieutenant. Breathe, aim, fire."

"Breathe, aim, fire," Rupert whispered.

Cole sensed the rhythm of Rupert's breathing, then said, "Squeeze the trigger gently. Don't yank it. You want to kind of surprise yourself when the rifle goes off."

The rifle fired, breaking the silence of the winter landscape. Instantly the empty brass cartridge went spinning away, and the action fed another shell into the chamber. That was the beauty of a semiautomatic.

In the distance, a chip of stone flew from the pillar.

"I hit it," Lieutenant Rupert said with satisfaction.

"That's good," Cole said. "When it matters, you might hit your target and you might not. He could even get back up after you hit him. In that case, adjust your aim and fire again. Keep pulling that trigger until you run out of bullets or the son of a bitch is down for good."

Rupert nodded. Maybe it was Cole's imagination, but the young lieutenant looked less pale than before. He didn't have the heart to point out that the hard part of shooting at someone was that they were likely to be shooting back. Rupert would find that out soon enough.

He left Rupert keeping watch at the window.

Looking around, he was surprised to see both Madame Jouret and Lena brandishing shotguns. Both guns appeared to be antiques with fancy scrollwork and fine-grained wood stocks, the sort of shotguns that had likely cost a small fortune and were meant to impress, very different from the plain, sturdy Iver Johnson 12-gauge that Cole had grown up with.

However, he had to admit that the antique shotguns had likely been used for their share of hunting. Neither the daughter nor the lady of the house seemed to have any qualms about using them, and they handled the weapons with familiarity. They certainly looked more confident than the lieutenant did. Here in the Ardennes region, it made sense that women had their fair share of experience with hunting and shooting.

Cole nodded toward the hallway. Madame Jouret nodded back, and both she and her daughter positioned themselves there. From their post, they could use the shotguns to cover the front door and any other windows at the front of the house. If any of their attackers got past the door or through the heavy shutters covering the windows, they were going to be peppered by those shotguns. The walls were thick enough, but the windows were the weak points.

For good measure, he and Vaccaro shoved some of the heavier furniture against the windows. Madame Jouret's glass-fronted china cabinet might not stop the enemy from getting in, but it would sure as hell slow them down—and help keep their bullets out. Despite its delicate contents, the thing weighed as much as a locomotive.

Cole felt better now about their ability to defend the château. They had just doubled their numbers thanks to Rupert's shooting lesson and the ladies with their shotguns. He and Vaccaro could float as needed. Cole intended to head upstairs to see what damage he could do with his sniper rifle.

They should be OK as long as their attackers didn't bring up any heavy weapons, at least until nightfall. The fight could get a lot more challenging then.

This was the best they could do. The question was, Would it be enough?

He noticed Bauer watching him. There was no smirk or amused look on his face. Instead, he appeared deadly serious, every inch the experienced combat officer that he was.

The German officer held up his hands, which were still bound.

"Cut me loose," he said in a tone that rankled Cole, because it sounded very much like an order.

"Not a chance," Cole replied.

"The men out there are here because of me," he said quietly. "You must at least allow me a chance to defend myself—unless you prefer to rely on the two ladies and a *kinder leutnant?*"

Vaccaro had overheard and offered his two cents' worth. "He's got a point, hillbilly. We can at least give him Rupert's revolver."

Cole thought it over. After a moment's hesitation, he drew his big bowie knife, stepped closer to Bauer, and cut him free.

The German shook out his hands to restore circulation. The cords had left red, painful-looking indentations on his wrists.

"Don't make me regret this," Cole said, the look on his face and the knife in his hand making it clear how things would go if Bauer caused any trouble. Slowly, he sheathed the knife. "Lieutenant Rupert, give Herr Barnstormer your sidearm."

Bauer took the weapon and expertly flipped the cylinder open to make sure that it was loaded. He also accepted a handful of spare bullets from the lieutenant. It was a six-shot .38-caliber Webley revolver. The revolver would be useful only at close range, but they didn't have a lot of weapons to go around.

"Thank you," Bauer said.

"I've only got one rule for you," Cole replied. "You can't shoot any Americans. You can only shoot Germans. Otherwise, this might be kind of hard to explain later."

"You mean that I can only shoot Messner and his men?" Bauer offered a cold smile. "It will be my pleasure."

"What can you tell me about this Messner and the men with him? Do we need to be worried about them?"

"They are competent soldiers," Bauer said. "I am only guessing this, but it is likely that he has Obergefreiter Dietzel and Gettinger with him. These are men who have some personal loyalty to him. Perhaps they are inspired by him. He shows them some favoritism in return. Gettinger has no special talents other than obedience, but Dietzel is a Jaeger—the equivalent of what you might call a scout-sniper."

"Yeah, I reckon he's the son of a bitch who took a shot at me," Cole said.

"Lucky for us, he missed."

Cole snorted. He couldn't tell if Bauer meant that. "One more thing. You stick with me. Where I go, you go."

As it turned out, they had made their arrangements just in time. From the window, Lieutenant Rupert shouted, "Here they come!"

Cole turned and raced upstairs, taking the steps two at a time. Vaccaro followed and so did Bauer. He could hear both men pounding up the steps behind him.

Cole couldn't help thinking, *I hope to hell that Kraut doesn't shoot us both in the back.*

It had gone against Cole's better judgment to cut Bauer free and let him have the revolver, but in this situation he was willing to take a chance. They needed every fighter they could get.

The German machine gun opened up, once again hammering the walls and windows. A flurry of bullets stitched across the front door like an insane woodpecker, sending wood chips flying.

But the machine gun was only a distraction. The Germans that Rupert had seen were trying to take advantage of the hail of fire to get closer to the château. They came at the house from the left, one man running forward as the other covered him, then repeating the process for the other man.

The problem was that they had to cross the open ground, both making clear targets against the snow.

Cole went to an upstairs window where the glass had already been blown out by the machine-gun fire, the shards poking from the frame like jagged teeth. The German crouched beside him.

Cole put his rifle through the window and took aim. Through the scope, both Germans sprang closer. They were out in the open with nowhere to hide. With luck he would be able to shoot both men.

Then came another burst from the machine gun. The gunner must have spotted Cole in the window because several rounds came through and struck the wall behind them, ricocheting down the hall with an unnatural whine that made his spine crawl.

"Scheise!" Bauer shouted, throwing himself flat.

It wasn't an unreasonable reaction to being targeted by the machine gun. Cole found himself doing the same.

The gunner knew his business, firing in short, measured bursts. Finally, the firing stopped long enough that Cole dared to poke his head back up. The two Germans were out of sight, having managed to cross the open ground.

Now it was his turn to mutter *"Scheise."* He reckoned that it was as good a swear word as any.

Where had those two Krauts gone to?

He realized that meant that they must have reached the front of the house. Pressed against the wall, they would have been out of sight of the defenders.

The machine gun hadn't resumed firing, probably so the gunner wouldn't hit his own men.

"Where did they go?" Vaccaro shouted. "I can't see them."

His question was answered when they heard the deep BOOM of a shotgun downstairs. She and Lena were stationed at the front windows. Did this mean that the Germans were trying to get in?

There was another BOOM.

"Dammit, Vaccaro, go help 'em!" Cole shouted.

"You got it," Vaccaro replied, then flew down the stairs. Soon after, they heard a rifle shot, then another.

"Should we not help them?" Bauer wondered. He started to get up, but Cole pulled him back down. "Hold on, I've got another idea. You stay here."

Cole ran to one of the bedrooms. He immediately found what he was looking for—a handheld mirror sitting on a dresser. He didn't know if it belonged to Madame Jouret or Lena, not that it mattered.

What he really wanted was a grenade, but it hadn't seemed necessary to bring any on their escort mission.

He hustled back to the window where he had left Bauer. The German saw the mirror in Cole's hands and raised his eyebrows.

"You wanted a crack at these guys, so now is your chance," Cole said. "If I hold the mirror for you, think you can get a shot at them with that pistol?"

Bauer smiled with understanding. "That is very clever, hillbilly."

With his thumb, Bauer pulled back the hammer on the revolver, cocking the weapon.

"Now!"

Cole stuck the mirror out the window, trying to angle it so that Bauer could see the two Germans crouching out of sight at the front of the house.

"Tilt it down," Bauer said.

Cole obliged. A moment later, the German officer leaned out the window and took a shot. There was a curse and a yelp of pain from below.

However, the machine gunner was being watchful and must have spotted the movement at the window. A burst of fire shattered what was left of the glass. Bullets smacked into the back wall of the hallway as Bauer and Cole tried to melt into the floor. Lucky for them, the exterior walls of the château were thick enough to stop any stray bullets.

Downstairs, a shotgun boomed again.

That was soon followed by a whoop of triumph from Vaccaro. "They're running!"

Both Cole and Bauer looked out the window, weapons ready. They caught a glimpse of the two Germans headed for the trees, one of them limping badly. Apparently Bauer's bullets had done some damage.

With the pistol, Bauer was quicker than Cole and got off a couple of shots, although at this distance there would be little hope of hitting anything. Cole was just getting the scope lined up on the limping soldier when a burst from the machine gun hit the window. Cursing, he ducked, but he soon found himself covered with bits of glass and shredded wood.

The attack had been repulsed, but the Germans had gotten away.

"That damn machine gun," Cole said.

"There will not be much ammunition on the Kübelwagen," Bauer said. "They may not have enough for another attack."

"If we ain't dead first."

After brushing themselves off, Cole and Bauer went downstairs. They found Madame Jouret reloading her shotgun. The lady of the house seemed calm, cool, and collected, not at all shaken up by the attack as she slipped two fresh shells into place. Cole felt reassured.

"We ran them off," Vaccaro reported.

"They'll be back," Cole said.

CHAPTER TWENTY-FIVE

IN THE LULL that followed the assault on the château, more bread and cheese were produced by Madame Jouret, along with a bottle of red wine.

"I could get used to this kind of war," Vaccaro said. "You know, a war where we sleep on some cushions instead of the ground, there's a fireplace to keep warm, then decent food and some wine in between gun battles."

"Don't get too comfortable," Cole warned him. "The Krauts will be back. They may be more determined the next time around."

"What about the other Americans out there?"

"Who knows. I reckon that they decided to sit this one out. Maybe they wanted to see what happened, let us wipe each other out, and then swoop in to pick up the pieces."

"The pieces being our prisoner."

"Seems like it," Cole agreed.

They had gotten off easy during the attack. The only person to be wounded had been Lieutenant Rupert, who had rushed to help the women defend the front of the house. Seeing Lena being attacked had ignited a fury inside him that he didn't know he had.

A bullet had grazed his arm, but he didn't appear to mind, considering that Lena had insisted that he take his shirt off and was now bandaging his arm carefully. Like a typical Brit in a land where rain was more common than sunshine, his bare arms and chest looked milky white. However, judging by his well-toned muscles, he also appeared to keep himself quite fit, a fact that didn't seem to be lost on Lena.

"Was it really necessary for her to take his shirt off?" Vaccaro wondered. "I guess it's a good thing that he didn't get shot in the ass. You know that thing has got to be white as a lily."

"You're just jealous, is all," Cole said.

Bauer hadn't had much to say. Maybe he was having second thoughts about shooting at his own kind. It had been good shooting, all the same.

Cole decided to leave the German to his own thoughts. He used the time to double-check their defenses, finding a few more pieces of furniture that he and Vaccaro could pile in front of the downstairs windows.

"Now what?" Vaccaro wondered.

"Now we wait."

But as any soldier knew, waiting for the next attack was the hardest part.

* * *

BROCK HAD WATCHED in astonishment as the Germans attacked the château. What the hell were they thinking? To him, crossing that open ground had seemed like a suicide mission. They'd been lucky to have plenty of covering fire from the machine gun.

He still couldn't figure out why the Krauts were so determined to get inside the old mansion. It wasn't like he could saunter over and ask them.

With professional interest, he watched the assault unfold.

"What should we do?" Vern wondered. "It doesn't seem right just to watch. Those are our guys in there."

"Let's see how far the Krauts get and then decide what to do."

Under the covering fire, two Germans were able to reach the house itself. If they'd had grenades, that might have been the end of the fight.

The Germans would have been able to toss in a few grenades and take out the Americans inside.

But the defenders had been able to return fire from an upstairs window, evidently wounding one of the attackers. The Krauts had then beat a hasty retreat back to the woods, where they still seemed to be licking their wounds.

"Damn, I was kind of hoping that they would crack open that nut for us," Brock said.

"Should we try?"

"Not yet. Let's see if the Germans make another go of it."

"They will," Vern said. "You know how the Germans are. Stubborn."

"Yeah," Brock agreed. "When they do attack again, we'll come at the château from another direction."

* * *

ANOTHER HOUR WENT by before the Germans tried again. Inside the château, their first warning was the sound of a vehicle engine on the cold air. The forest was very quiet, so a revving engine was quite noticeable.

Vaccaro was upstairs as a lookout, peering out one of the windows at the front of the house.

"What the hell are they up to?" Vaccaro shouted.

Cole raced up the stairs, Bauer right behind him.

They heard the racing engine, the sound of grinding gears, and then the Kübelwagen came flying out of the woods, headed directly toward the house.

This time, the Germans threw caution to the wind. All three were riding on the Kübelwagen. One man at the wheel, one riding shotgun, and another hanging on for dear life as he swung the machine gun toward the château.

Cole tried to get off a shot, but the machine gunner was faster, sweeping the front of the château with a burst from the gun. More stone chips flew, along with splinters from the wood shutters. The splinters threatened to be just as deadly as the bullets. Again, a couple of rounds found their way inside the house itself.

He and the others had no choice but to duck and cover. When they looked again, the passenger and driver of the Kübelwagen were already out, scrambling to reach the foundation of the house, where it would be harder to pick them off.

Against the backdrop of gloomy gray snow, Cole glimpsed a bright flash of burning flame. One of the men rushing toward the house appeared to be carrying something that was on fire.

Cole caught only a glimpse before he had to duck down again because the machine gunner was still with the stopped vehicle, firing away.

Downstairs, something exploded with a deep *whumpf* that shook them to the bone.

The explosion seemed to suck the air out of the house.

What the hell?

Cole put two and two together, realizing what the flaming object had been.

Lacking grenades, the Germans had made a Molotov cocktail. They must have drained some of the fuel out of the Kübelwagen to do so.

Clever Krauts, Cole thought.

***

"Get ready, boys," Brock said. "We're gonna go in the back door, so to speak."

There wasn't an actual door, just the side door for the kitchen made of stout wood, but there were ground-floor windows.

With Brock leading the way, they used the woods for cover to skirt the open ground and reach the back of the house.

Brock was betting on the defenders being occupied with beating off the German attack on the front of the house. From that direction, there were several shots, then the dull sound of an explosion. Not a grenade, he thought, but something else. The acrid smell of burning gasoline roiled skyward, and he wondered whether the Germans' Kübelwagen had somehow blown up.

Right now that didn't concern him. He sprinted hard across the open ground to the back of the château. For a big man, Brock could move quickly. The snow did slow him down, however. Vern and Boot came charging after him.

They knew the drill. They had all done this before, fighting from house to house in towns they had passed through since D-Day.

Brock reached the base of the château's back wall and crouched there, panting and regretting every damn cigarette he'd ever smoked. The other two men spread out along the wall, keeping their heads below the windows.

Again, he wished for a grenade. But they would just have to make do.

Brock stood up and used the butt of the carbine to smash the shutter. He then poked the muzzle at the window, shattering glass.

Careful to keep his head down, he squeezed off three quick shots into the window. There was no target. His goal was to make anybody inside the château duck and cover.

When nobody shot back, Brock was pleased by the thought that the defenders must all be at the front of the house. The Krauts had created the perfect diversion.

Brock used the butt of his carbine once again to knock away more of the shutter and the shards of broken glass jutting from the window sash.

With an effort, he was able to lever himself up so he was hanging half-in and half-out of the window. There was still a lot of broken glass around, and he cursed as a shard cut the bottom of his forearm.

But he was almost inside. He stuck his head up and looked around.

He was surprised to find himself locking eyes with a young woman.

Who happened to be holding a double-barreled shotgun.

Brock's gaze went from the young woman's face to the twin muzzles.

Her eyes narrowed, squinting down the barrel. His own eyes widened.

He just had time to tumble back out the window as one of those muzzles unleashed a stab of flame and lead shot. The snow wasn't as deep here in the lee of the foundation, and Brock felt the breath get knocked out of him as he landed on the frozen ground.

He gasped for breath, wondering whether he'd been hit.

Nearby, Vern stood up and fired through the window.

The shotgun roared again, and Vern cursed as a pellet stung the side of his neck. It wasn't fatal, but it bled freely, leaving bright drops of red on the trampled snow around the base of the house.

More shots came from within. Not a shotgun this time, but the rapid-fire crack of a rifle. The girl wasn't alone. One of the soldiers must have joined her in defending the house.

Brock had to admit that there was no way they were getting into the château if someone inside was covering the rear windows. Without grenades or a machine gun, they didn't have the firepower. They had lost the element of surprise.

Like an exclamation mark on that thought, another shotgun blast followed. Boot had been taking a peek through the shutters and ducked down hastily—but his reaction wasn't quick enough. He now had a nasty red gash on his cheek, either from a shotgun pellet or a flying splinter—or maybe a little of both.

Vern was already doing the smart thing and running back toward the trees. Brock couldn't blame him. He struggled to his knees. All three had gotten a little beat up in the attack.

"Let's get the hell out of here," Brock shouted.

* * *

AT THE FRONT of the house, the Germans were having more success.

Out on the front lawn, the machine gunner on the Kübelwagen was still firing short bursts, forcing the defenders to keep their heads down.

Cole had guessed correctly that the explosion had been caused not by a hand grenade, but by a Molotov cocktail that the Germans had crafted out of an empty schnapps bottle that they filled with gasoline siphoned from the Kübelwagen. A burning rag served as the wick.

It had been Messner who had thrown the bomb, waiting to get as close to a window as possible, although he had nearly lost his nerve at the thought of the bomb going off early and covering him with flaming gasoline. He had managed to smash the Molotov cocktail against the window and fill the front hall with flames and roiling, thick smoke. Only the fact that the interior walls were also stone had prevented the fire from spreading throughout the entire house.

A second Molotov cocktail soon followed, this one thrown by Gettinger, exploding against the front door and wreathing it in flame. The fire licked at the wood, threatening to engulf it, blackening the stone facade, sending clouds of acrid black smoke skyward. The occupants of the château had managed to keep a low profile by lighting fires only at night, but the smoke was now visible far and wide.

Messner fired shots into the smoke and flame, hoping to hit someone inside. Inadvertently, the flaming bombs had provided cover for the defenders. Near the burning front door, Gettinger also fired shots furiously.

But it was Dietzel behind the machine gun who was doing the real damage. Another burst hit the facade. If the Germans had been able to press the advantage with just a couple more men, the battle of the château would have been all but over.

Cole realized that he had to do something—and soon. He had positioned himself at an upstairs window alongside Bauer, but the leaping flames and smoke prevented them from repeating the tactics that had driven off the Germans last time.

"Go see if you can help downstairs," Cole ordered.

Bauer gave a curt nod and hurried away. In the last few hours, Cole had given up worrying about Bauer's loyalties. If the German had wanted to get the drop on his captors, Cole decided that he would have done it by now. He was fighting for survival like everybody else in the house.

He looked out the window to where the Kübelwagen crouched like a beast, spitting lead and fire at the château. Another burst made him duck down, but he had gotten a mental picture of his target.

One, two, three—

Cole popped up and fired a quick shot at the German behind the machine gun. It was hard to say if he had hit him, but the firing suddenly stopped. When he took a closer look, he saw that there was nobody manning the gun.

He smiled with satisfaction, but not for long. A shot came from beneath the Kübelwagen, striking near his head.

Too close.

But without the machine gun, the Germans had lost the advantage. He heard a shout, and the attack came to an end. This time the Germans were smart enough to use blind spots created by the far ends of the house to screen their movements as they slipped back into the woods.

The sniper under the Kübelwagen must have managed to scurry away while Cole had his own head down, because when he got back on the scope, there was nobody there. On the plus side, the Germans had left the Kübelwagen behind.

Cole heard a sound behind him and turned to see Bauer entering the room.

"They are gone for now," the German announced.

"For now," Cole agreed.

CHAPTER TWENTY-SIX

They had survived one attack from two different directions and had forced their attackers to retreat, licking their wounds. But they had a few wounds of their own. Rupert had been grazed by a bullet—nothing too serious, but painful all the same. Vaccaro had caught some glass in the face thanks to a bullet going through a window. Cole helped him pick out the glass. Vaccaro had insisted on inspecting the damage in a mirror.

"You think that's gonna leave a scar? I don't want it to spoil my good looks."

"No worries there," Cole said. It was well known that Vaccaro operated under the illusion that he bore some resemblance to the silent film star Rudolph Valentino. "Besides, you can tell all the girls back home that you got that scar in the war."

"Better than a medal," Vaccaro agreed.

The sun was getting lower. Under cover of darkness, it was likely that one side or the other would be back, and the defenders would no longer have the advantage of being able to pick them off as they crossed the open ground between the forest and the château. Once it got dark, things would get ugly.

They would hold out as long as they could, and then fight to the end. Try as he might, Cole couldn't come up with a better plan.

Cole had always wondered whether he would make it through this war. He just hadn't expected to be making his last stand in an old château, protecting the life of a German prisoner.

Out the windows, the unseen sun sank lower in the winter sky. The wooded hills seemed to march closer. The daylight faded like sand running through an hourglass. Soon enough, they would be out of time.

Cole would not have pegged Madame Jouret as a military strategist, but she seemed to grasp the situation as well as any of them. This house was like her Fort Sumter and Fort McHenry all rolled into one.

She set down her shotgun and approached Cole with her daughter in tow as an interpreter. She looked at Cole and said something in French, then looked expectantly at her daughter.

Reluctantly, Lena translated. She didn't seem to like the information that her mother was sharing. "My mother says it will be much worse for us once it gets dark."

"She ain't wrong about that."

Lena translated Cole's reply; then the two women looked at each other. They both seemed to have agreed already on a course of action, because this time Lena spoke without waiting for her mother. "She also says that there is a way out."

Cole wasn't sure what she was saying. The house was surrounded, watched from all sides by Germans and Americans waiting to pounce on them. "A way out?"

"I can show you."

Lena explained that there had not always been peace in the Ardennes, even before the current war. Great armies passed through, or sometimes local rivalries and conflicts escalated into bloodshed. There were even times when it was convenient to bring people in or out of the house unseen, whether it was a dalliance or a political alliance that was better kept from prying eyes.

They descended into the cellar. There were no electric lights down here, and nary a window, so that they had to rely on candles and flashlights. The dancing light revealed thick stone walls dripping with moisture, massive floor beams, some with the bark of ancient trees still clinging to them or hanging down in crumbling strips, and a dirt floor. The air smelled of dirt and damp, not to mention decaying wood. It was not an inviting place. Madame Jouret stopped in front of an ancient wooden cupboard that was dripping with cobwebs. With surprising ease, the cupboard was pushed out of the way to reveal a thick wooden door.

And beyond the door, a tunnel.

The dark tunnel was not inviting, to say the least.

Dirty spiderwebs ringed the entrance, and Cole noted a fat, pale spider that must have lived its whole life in darkness retreating into a crevice. Beyond the bit of light from their candles and flashlights, the tunnel looked black and pitiless as the muzzle of a cannon. The still air wafting from the tunnel depths smelled even more musty and earthy than the old cellar.

"This emerges in the woods, near a springhouse in the forest," Lena explained. "You must go now, while there is still time before the next attack on the house."

Madame Jouret poured forth more unintelligible words at a feverish pace and began pushing Lena toward the tunnel entrance. It became clear that Lena and her mother were arguing, but in the end, Lena appeared to relent. Her face had become a mask of twisted emotions, both tears and anger.

"What is it?" Lieutenant Rupert asked with concern.

"She says that I must go with you, as a guide. You will need to find your way through these woods to a road, and it will be difficult to do so on your own. I know these woods well."

As they prepared to leave, Madame Jouret made no effort to join them. Rupert noticed and asked, "What about your mother?"

"My mother will stay here. She says she is too old to flee through the forest. She will hide again in the attic, this time in a place where no one will find her. And if they do, they will not harm her. Or so she would like to believe."

"I wouldn't be so sure about that," he said.

Cole knew that Madame Jouret was gambling with her life if her hiding place was discovered. He decided that the Americans wouldn't hurt her. He trusted that even someone like Brock must have some basic morality, but then he thought about the Germans. All bets were off, considering that Messner and his men had already murdered American POWs. This Belgian lady would be the least of their worries.

More arguing between Lena and her mother ensued, but once again, Lena yielded. Madame Jouret was staying behind and would not be swayed. The rest of them would escape through the tunnel.

"She insists that there is no other way," said Lieutenant Rupert, who had been listening in.

"I've got to agree with the old lady on this one," Vaccaro said.

The others looked to Cole. There were two officers present—although the opinion of the German didn't really count—but they had all come to view Cole as their best hope to get out of this mess.

It looked to Cole as if they had two choices—either make a last stand in the château or plunge themselves into the gloomy tunnel.

"All right," he said. "Let's get out of here."

Cole was prepared to lead the way, but Lena slid ahead of him without hesitation. Vaccaro followed Cole, then Bauer, with Lieutenant Rupert bringing up the rear. Bauer still carried the lieutenant's Webley revolver, but Cole had long since stopped worrying about that. The German would have had plenty of opportunities to use it on his captors if he had chosen to do so. Instead, he had joined them in fighting for their lives.

Behind them, Madame Jouret pulled the door shut. They heard the cupboard sliding back into place. The darkness inside the tunnel was complete, but he could sense the damp walls and low ceiling. Cole couldn't avoid the sensation of moving through a long, narrow grave.

The girl did not seem intimidated by the darkness ahead. This was probably not Lena's first time using the tunnel. It occurred to Cole that this could be why they had seen no tracks in the snow leading to or from the château. Using a tunnel would have been a clever way to give the appearance that the château was abandoned by avoiding any footprints around it.

He had to admit, the two women of the house had been full of surprises.

"It's dark as the inside of a black alley cat in here," Vaccaro muttered. Although they had candles and flashlights, the intense darkness beyond the reach of their candles and flashlights seemed ready to snuff out their lights. "Do you think this actually comes out somewhere?"

"I sure as hell hope so," was all Cole could say. They had put their trust in Madame Jouret and Lena to get them out of the château. It wasn't that he didn't trust them—they had fought tooth and nail alongside them today—but Vaccaro was right that the tunnel was so dark that it seemed possible that it didn't lead anywhere but deeper into the darkness, maybe all the way to the center of the earth.

Cole had no choice but to follow the girl through the dark confines of the tunnel. The walls seemed to shrink in on them, and the ceiling grew lower so that he had to duck his head. Initially, near the doorway into the cellar, the tunnel walls had been lined with bricks, though they were damp and crumbling.

The deeper into the tunnel that they went, the more rudimentary its construction became. Soon the walls were only bare dirt, laced in places with tree roots. A few boards held the roof up; these boards were themselves shored up with posts they had to squeeze past without jostling for fear of bringing the roof down on their heads.

Vaccaro managed to bump into one of these posts, bringing a shower of dirt onto their heads. Then a few rocks fell, followed by the entire board, which glanced off his helmet with an audible clang.

"Watch where you're going, city boy," Cole grumped as a few small stones pinged off his helmet. "You'll bring the whole damn roof down on our heads."

They kept going, careful not to bump into anything. Nobody liked the thought of being buried alive.

Finally, Lena halted at the foot of a short ladder. Just beyond the ladder, the tunnel ended in a seeping dirt wall. It was quite damp here, with a few drops of water filtering down through the ceiling. Cole gulped in spite of himself—he couldn't wait to get out of this place.

"Give me some light, please," she said.

Cole shined the flashlight up to reveal a hatch of some kind hammered together out of heavy boards. The girl went up the ladder and pushed at the hatch. It appeared that the weight might be too much for her and that they were all trapped.

Slowly, a crack appeared at one edge. She paused to listen, her arms trembling with the effort of holding up the heavy hatch.

Cole wanted to help her, but there was no room on the ladder for more than one person. He did, however, draw his pistol, just in case somebody was waiting on the other side.

However, Lena seemed to have judged that the coast was clear. With a grunt, she shoved the hatch the rest of the way open. A square of gray dusky light appeared. Cold, fresh, winter air filled the stagnant tunnel, and Cole breathed deeply.

Lena went up the ladder and then beckoned for Cole and the others to follow.

He saw that the hatch opened into the interior of a stone-walled springhouse. He was familiar with springhouses from his own upbringing in the rural mountains, where folks didn't have electricity, much less an icebox. A springhouse provided cool storage for your milk and butter, maybe even fresh meat. He looked over and saw the shallow, stone-lined pool that would have held bottles of milk and cream in summer. This explained the water dripping into the tunnel below.

He had to hand it to the previous château residents who had built this tunnel. It was likely that it had come in handy more than once. There was no doubt that it had saved their lives tonight.

There wasn't enough space for them all inside the springhouse, so they stooped to go out the low door and found themselves looking back at the château some distance away through the trees. It seemed impossible that they had traversed this distance underground.

Silhouetted against the old stone walls of the château, he could see a figure at one of the lower windows. The sound of breaking glass reached them, followed by several quick shots.

"I reckon they'll be disappointed when they find out we ain't there," Cole said. "Then they'll surely come looking for us. We'd best get a move on."

"This way," the girl said, and slipped away through the trees like a nymph, so that even Cole had to hurry to keep up.

* * *

THE GERMANS HAD MANAGED to get inside the château. They had been disappointed to find it empty. Their search of the house had mostly been fruitless, although they had come across a half-empty decanter of brandy in the drawing room, along with clear signs that the group must have spent the night there.

"They have not disappeared into thin air," Messner announced. "Once it is daylight, we will search for them."

They camped out in the empty house, sleeping on the furniture and polishing off the brandy. The next morning Dietzel's skill as a Jaeger eventually rewarded them with being able to find their quarry's trail. They had been searching in larger and larger rings around the perimeter of the château, but so far had found nothing.

Where Bauer and his escort had gone was a mystery—until now.

"Over here!" Dietzel shouted.

The Jaeger stood by a stone springhouse with a low roof. Several sets of tracks in the snow led away from the springhouse, but none went toward it.

Messner confessed that he was mystified.

"A tunnel, Herr Hauptmann," Dietzel explained. "There is a hatch inside the springhouse. The tunnel must lead to the château."

"We searched that place high and low!"

Dietzel shrugged. "Old houses have their secrets. This one, at least, has been revealed to us."

Impatiently, Messner called Gettinger over. He had also been searching the snow for some clue as to where their quarry had gone. Gettinger was limping a bit, having been wounded in the first attack on the château the previous day.

"There is no time to lose," Messner said. "They must have given us the slip during the night, so they could have a head start of several hours."

Dietzel smiled and gestured toward the tracks with the muzzle of his sniper rifle. Clearly he was enjoying himself. "Let the hunt begin," he said.

Messner realized that for the Jaeger, perhaps this was simply a game. He was enjoying the thrill of the hunt. Messner himself had not lost sight of his desire for revenge. There might still be hope of catching up to Bauer.

Dietzel was studying the tracks. "It is interesting that they have added someone to their party," he said. "The shoes are different. Smaller. I would say that these are the footprints of a woman."

"What are they doing with a woman?" He realized that the house had not been unoccupied after all. At least it hadn't been when the Americans arrived.

"Perhaps she is their guide," Dietzel said, guessing the situation correctly. "No matter. We don't need a guide. We can follow these tracks easily enough."

"Good, because there is no time to lose. Let's go!" Messner ordered, and started off at a trot, following the tracks as easily as he might follow the road signs down a highway.

* * *

BROCK WATCHED the Germans from a distance. By now he had come to realize that they very likely wanted the same thing—the German prisoner. Nothing else about their pursuit of the same group made sense.

He wasn't sure why they wanted the German officer, but it clearly wasn't to play tiddlywinks. The way that they had attacked the château with a vengeance made it clear that they weren't all that interested in taking anyone alive—even one of their own.

If he was going to guess, it was that they also wanted the German officer dead.

This didn't mean that he was willing to team up with the Germans. They were Krauts, after all. The enemy.

Unseen, they watched the Germans from the cover of the surrounding trees.

"Should we shoot them?" Vern wanted to know.

Brock thought about it. "No, let's see what they turn up. Let them do the hard work, you know."

Their patience was rewarded a short time later when they heard a shout from the woods. You didn't need to speak German to understand the meaning of the tone. The Germans had found something, and they sounded excited about it.

"All right, let's go check it out."

First, they did a quick check of the château but found nothing of interest. Once some time had passed, they crept around and found the springhouse and tracks. They could see the footprints left by the escort patrol and the pursuing Germans.

All that they had to do now was follow the trail.

CHAPTER TWENTY-SEVEN

"How much time do you think we've got before they catch up to us?" Vaccaro asked, his voice tight with urgency.

Good question, Cole thought. One that he didn't have the answer to. What he did know was that every minute they could put between themselves and their pursuers could mean the difference between escape and death.

"I reckon we have a decent head start, and that's all I can say," Cole responded, glancing over his shoulder. "It really depends on how good of a tracker that German Jaeger is and how much luck we've got. I've got to say, I ain't feelin' all that lucky right now."

"In that case, we better get a move on," Vaccaro replied. Everyone in their group looked tired and worn out, their nerves on edge from their narrow escape through the tunnel, but they had no choice but to keep going. "Well, at least Madame Jouret sent that pretty daughter of hers along with us."

Cole rolled his eyes. "Yeah, like she would ever have anything to do with us."

Vaccaro chuckled. "Cheer up, hillbilly. If we survive this, I'll buy you a drink. Or maybe two. We'll deserve it."

The journey through the tunnel, up the ladder, through the springhouse, and out into the woods had warmed them up, but now the cold of the forest settled into their bones. Their breath blew out in vaporous clouds, and their feet crunched through the snow that lay undisturbed under the thick evergreen branches overhead.

Cole knew the trouble with the snow was that it would make it easier for the German Jaeger to follow them. He'd been half-kidding when he mentioned luck to Vaccaro, and now he wasn't so sure that their luck really hadn't run out. As for the Americans who were also after them, that was simply a wild card.

Then again, maybe the Germans and Americans in pursuit would run into each other and fight it out while Cole and the rest made their getaway, but that was probably too much to hope for.

Lena said something urgent in French that Cole took to mean "Hurry up," because Rupert looked back at them and waved them on. He swayed a bit as he walked, thrown off balance by his wounded arm, but to the British lieutenant's credit, he did not complain. Cole thought that maybe the young officer was made of sterner stuff than he had given him credit for. Then again, maybe Rupert just didn't want to look bad in front of Lena.

Cole never liked being told what to do, especially by this whipper-snapper of a Belgian girl, but in this case he knew she was right. Every minute that passed meant that their pursuers might be getting closer.

"Come on," he said to Vaccaro, then picked up the pace.

Cole had to admit that Lena really did seem to know her way through the forest, so that much was reassuring. There wasn't actually a trail to speak of, although every now and then they followed a deer path before veering once more into the woods, but she seemed to be moving with confidence toward some destination she had in mind.

It was likely that she had been exploring these woods since she was a little girl. Also, the way she had handled that shotgun during the attack on the château had convinced him that Lena was an experienced hunter. As far as he could tell, they were in good hands.

* * *

Cole was right to worry about the Germans, who at that moment were not more than a couple of miles behind them and moving fast. Dietzel was on their trail, following the tracks easily through the forest.

"*Schnell, schnell,*" he said to Messner and Gettinger, looking impatiently behind him. It was clear that he didn't think they were keeping up the pace.

Dietzel's finger practically itched on the trigger as he held the rifle at the ready. He still wasn't happy that the American sniper had managed to pin him down during the fight at the château. It had only been a bit of luck that had enabled Dietzel to escape.

He could sense skill in another, and the man had been a fine shot, which surprised him. In Dietzel's experience, the Americans all saw themselves as frontier marksmen. He also knew from experience that this couldn't be farther from the truth. Most American soldiers he encountered were only mediocre with a rifle, at best.

However, this American with the Confederate flag on his helmet certainly seemed to be an exception. Dietzel kept his eyes peeled as they moved through the woods, not wanting to find himself in the American sniper's sights.

When Dietzel finally caught up to him, he would prove with finality which man was the better shot.

* * *

As Cole's group moved through the forest, it was hard not to feel another enemy catching up with them—the cold and exhaustion. They had been moving most of the night, and now it was daylight. Tired and cold or not, they walked on because there was little choice but to keep going.

Although the gray morning was not exactly encouraging, Cole thought it was better than being trapped inside the old château. While the place made a good fortress, it was not where he wanted to make his last stand. He always preferred to be free and out in the open.

The Ardennes Forest was not all that different from the mountains he had grown up in back home. In fact, he wouldn't mind coming back someday to do some hunting here when there wasn't a risk of being shot at by the Krauts.

Then again, he reminded himself not to think too far ahead. They had to survive the next hour, let alone the rest of the day.

Get your head right, he warned himself.

He shook off his exhaustion and forced himself to be completely alert.

Even in the midst of winter, the rolling hills and hidden fields had a kind of rugged beauty that appealed to something deep within him. Maybe it was that rugged spirit or the feeling of individualism that dwelled at his core.

After another half hour went by, Cole was almost surprised when they reached a road through the forest. Lena offered a satisfied smile and nodded. "This was where I was bringing you," she explained. "This road will take you to your headquarters. Now you must follow it."

"Aren't you coming with us?" Vaccaro asked.

The girl shook her head. "No. I must return to my mother and make sure she is all right."

Cole and Vaccaro looked at one another. This sounded like a terrible idea to Cole, considering that somewhere behind them were murderous German soldiers and angry American ones.

"You had better stick with us," he said.

The girl shook her head stubbornly, her mind apparently made up.

Lieutenant Rupert gently took hold of Lena's arm. "You can't go back," he said. "Your mother will be fine. You heard her say that she knew where to hide herself, where the Germans would never look for her. She wouldn't want you to place yourself in danger."

Lena seemed to waver but then took a step back from Rupert. "She is my mother," she offered, as if that were the only explanation needed.

To everyone's surprise, the German spoke up next. "Excuse me, Fräulein," he began, then continued once he had her attention. "Please listen to your friends here. It would not be wise to go back alone through these woods. From what I saw of your mother, she is quite the resilient woman. No, you had better come along with us. I know that Lieutenant Rupert, in particular, will not be disappointed by your company."

Finally, the girl relented. "All right," she said. "This way." Lena started down the road.

Cole glanced at the German, who once again seemed lost in his own thoughts. He still wore the Webley revolver tucked into his belt. Cole didn't ask for it back. In fact, he had hardly given a second thought to the notion that Bauer might run for it. During the fight at the château, Bauer had more than held his own, displaying just the sort of courage one might expect from a German officer. Having come this far, he didn't seem to be about to make his escape. Then again, maybe he was just waiting for the right opportunity.

Cole had mixed emotions about Bauer. Not long ago, he had been ready to shoot him on sight. But somehow Bauer had redeemed himself. His words to the girl had shown that Bauer did have a heart, even if it was branded with an Iron Cross.

They continued down the road, moving faster without logs to step over and low-hanging branches to duck under. Cole kept his eyes roving in every direction, especially in front and behind them. There was no telling who else might be on this road.

In the forest, they had managed to leave the war behind, surrounded only by trees, snow, and the occasional sound of an animal or bird. But here on the road, the signs of war were unmistakable. They came across the frozen body of a German soldier dusted with snow. It looked as if he had been wounded elsewhere and reached this lonely spot, where he'd either given up the ghost or his companions had left him for dead.

Cole shook his head, looking at the youthful face of the soldier. His smooth, beardless cheeks confirmed that the dead German couldn't have been much more than a teenager. Someone had taken his boots, leaving his white feet exposed to the elements. For some reason it seemed worse than leaving him naked.

Cole knew that scenes like this had been repeated dozens, if not hundreds, of times that very day across the battlefield. *It was much easier to love a dead enemy than a live one,* he thought. He reminded himself that more than a few of the dead they had passed were Americans.

They saw multiple tracks where men and vehicles had passed this way. Some of the boot prints bore the hobnails of German shoes, while others had the rubber soles of American GIs. They passed the wreckage of a panzer, scorch marks showing where it had been struck by a shell. A single dead crewman hung half-in and half-out of the hatch. It was a gruesome tableau of death, considering that the soldier's face was scorched and his short blond hair was singed. Lena stifled a gasp at the sight. Cole had to admit that none of it was easy to look at.

They continued walking, passing the wreckage of a smashed jeep, although thankfully there weren't any bodies around it. Then they came to the wreckage of a Kübelwagen that had gone into the ditch, probably because the driver and passenger were riddled with bullets.

"Look at that, Herr Barnstormer," Vaccaro said, pointing to the body of a German officer. "He might be one of your friends. Maybe you knew him."

Bauer shook his head. "No, I'm afraid that I do not know him."

"Maybe there's something valuable here," Rupert said. Although Cole had been ready to walk on, Rupert approached the vehicle and, to their astonishment, after a brief search he pulled out a black leather attaché case.

"Well, what have we here, gents?" Rupert said. His fingers were obviously cold because it took him a few moments to jiggle the latch. Once he got it open, he pulled out several papers and maps. None of it meant anything to Cole, but beside him, Bauer also leaned in for a look, and Cole could feel him stiffen.

Must be something, Cole thought. He glanced at Bauer, who stared at the documents intently.

Apparently Rupert knew a little German, but Lena knew more. The two put their heads together and pored over the documents. Bauer remained circumspect and tight-lipped.

When Rupert finally looked up, his eyes glowed with excitement. "You won't believe this," he said, "but this is some kind of battle plan. I think these marks on the map here are showing supply depots, and these other marks are showing bridges across some of the mountain streams. So clearly this is the route that the Germans plan to take."

"I'll be damned," Vaccaro said. He looked at Cole. "Who's lucky now?"

"All right," Cole agreed. "I guess we'll have more than just Herr Barnstormer to drop off at headquarters. Maybe they'll even give us a hot cup of coffee for that information."

Vaccaro said, "I wouldn't count on it."

Bauer didn't say anything, but for the first time he looked troubled to Cole's eyes. It hadn't seemed to bother him to shoot at Messner and the other Germans, but that was almost like a personal feud. These maps and documents were something else altogether. They were closer to what Bauer might think of as treason by allowing them to fall into American hands.

"All right, let's keep going," Cole said. "Lena, you've done a good job, but you'd best let me lead the way from here on out. We've seen way too many dead Krauts along this road, and I'm worried that we're going to run into some live ones before long."

Lena nodded and let Cole take point. He set a rapid pace, telling the others to follow behind him. If he went around a bend and walked into some Germans, at least the others might still have a chance.

They hadn't gone far when he heard Lena cry out behind him. Cole stuffed the maps and documents into his haversack and looked back to see that Lena, clearly tired and exhausted, had stepped into a frozen rut and twisted her ankle. Lieutenant Rupert knelt, rubbing her ankle in concern.

"Damn it all," said Cole. "Just figures." He slipped off his haversack and leaned his rifle against it to look at Lena's injured ankle. "Try to put some weight on it," he said, tightening her boot laces as much as possible to give the ankle extra support.

Lena gamely straightened up but released a cry of pain when she put weight on her foot.

"Hold on," said Cole. He slipped into the woods beside the road and spent a couple of minutes searching. Having found what he was looking for, he drew his bowie knife and cut a sapling with a Y fork at one end so that Lena could use it as a makeshift crutch. When he returned to the road, he noticed that something wasn't quite right. Tired as he was, it took him half a beat to figure it out.

Somebody was missing.

"Where the hell is Bauer?" Cole wondered.

Vaccaro also looked around in surprise. "I'll be damned. He was right here a second ago."

Cole glanced at his haversack and rifle. His rifle was just where he'd left it, but the haversack had clearly been opened. When he went over to it, he saw that the captured documents were gone.

And Bauer was nowhere in sight.

CHAPTER TWENTY-EIGHT

Cole scanned the area, but there was no sign of the German. Bauer had disappeared so quickly that Cole half expected him to suddenly materialize again out of thin air.

But no such luck—the German was truly gone.

"Son of a bitch," Cole muttered.

"He took off, didn't he?" Vaccaro wondered.

"Unless you've got him hidden in your pocket, then I'd say he made a run for it."

Cole considered what to do next. Tracking Bauer down seemed straightforward. The snow would make locating his trail easy enough, and from there it was only a matter of heading into the forest after him. Yet, as Cole contemplated the inevitable chase and confrontation, a twinge of reluctance crept in. He wasn't sure that Bauer would give up without a fight. Despite his initial willingness to shoot the German, the thought of potentially having to pull the trigger on Bauer was now less appealing. It was a hard truth to swallow, but Cole had grown to respect the man, even if he couldn't bring himself to like him.

Cole had to admit that if the tables had been turned, he would have long since tried to escape. You couldn't blame Bauer for finally making a run for it. Their discovering of the documents seemed to have pushed him over the edge, which made the value of what they had found only more apparent.

"We have to go after him," Vaccaro declared, breaking into Cole's thoughts. "He took those documents and maps, knowing full well that they were important."

Lieutenant Rupert chimed in, "And don't forget, he still has my revolver with him."

"That's why I'll let Vaccaro go first," Cole said.

Another choice would've simply been to let Bauer go, but for Cole, that was not an option. Considering that Bauer was the reason they were all out here in the first place, they really had no choice but to go after him.

As they readied themselves to head into the woods in pursuit of the German officer, a distant shout halted them. Turning toward the sound, they were taken aback to see a trio of American soldiers approaching.

"Look, it's some of our guys," Vaccaro observed, perplexed. "What the heck are they doing out here? They must be lost."

Cole wished that was the case but decided that there was something familiar about the three figures. "Or maybe it's the guys who attacked us back at the château," he said.

Cole's grip on his rifle tightened instinctively. His suspicions were soon confirmed as the soldiers drew near enough for their features to become discernible—it was Brock and his cronies.

They hadn't yet aimed their weapons at Cole's group, so Cole kept his own rifle pointed toward the ground—for now. He eyed Brock warily.

"Well, well, looks like we've caught up with you," Brock announced, a smug smirk playing on his lips. "Seems you're not as quick on your feet as you thought."

Cole finally got a closer look at the man and realized he was imposing—a real brute. Taking him down in a fistfight would be a challenge, but that was where guns came into play; they leveled the playing field. "I reckon you did catch up to us," Cole mused. "Not so bad."

Brock's gaze shifted from one face to the next, his confusion apparent as he noticed the German officer was no longer among them.

"I hope you've done the smart thing," he said. "Maybe you went ahead and shot that damn German."

"We sure did," Cole replied smoothly, the lie rolling off his tongue. "Got tired of dragging his carcass through these woods. Who's going to know the difference, right?"

Brock stared at him, suddenly skeptical. "I've got to say, you don't seem like the type," he countered. "Back at the château, you were fighting tooth and nail to protect his sorry Kraut ass. What did you really do with him?"

Before Cole could respond, Lena blurted out, "What happened to my mother? Is she all right?"

Brock's face was hard to read. "Tell you what, little girl. You tell us what you did with the German, and I'll tell you about your mother."

Rupert made a gesture to stop her, but it was too late—Lena was already spilling the beans. "The German ran into the woods," she confessed. "We were just about to go after him."

Brock smiled with satisfaction. "That sounds more like it," he said. "He ought to be easy enough to find. Just follow the tracks. Why don't you let us go ahead and follow him and finish him off? We'll save everybody a lot of trouble."

As Brock started toward the woods, Cole raised his rifle, holding it at hip level. At this distance, there was no way he could miss. Simultaneously, Vaccaro and Rupert raised their weapons, pointing them at Brock's men.

Lena began darting toward the woods but was brought up short when Brock fired a burst into the ground ahead of her. "Not so fast, little girl."

Lena froze.

Cole had held his fire, seeing that Brock was firing only a warning burst. Still, the man was only a finger flick away from getting a bullet.

Lieutenant Rupert now had his carbine trained on Brock, the expression on his face making it clear that he was struggling not to shoot the man.

"Easy there, Lieutenant," Cole said, not taking his eyes off Brock. He had decided that there were too many guns pointing at too many people for this to have a good outcome.

Slowly Brock turned his submachine gun and aimed it directly at Cole. "I guess we have a situation here," Brock stated into the ringing silence that followed the burst of fire, his voice steady.

* * *

IN THE COVER offered by the woods, Obersturmbannführer Bauer grappled with his decision to seize the documents and flee. His sense of honor was at war with itself; he had surrendered willingly and fought alongside the Americans, who had reciprocated with trust, leaving him unbound and armed. Yet, in the throes of war, how far did that trust go? His duty as a German officer gnawed at him, compelling him to secure the vital plans and maps to prevent them from falling into American hands. To Bauer, allegiance to the Reich outweighed any debt to the Americans.

Suddenly the crack of gunfire pierced the silence around him, then ceased. The firing had come from the direction of the road, where he had left the others behind. Bauer's heart raced. Should he continue his escape, or had something gone awry on the road?

Compelled by an inexplicable urge, he sighed and turned back, retracing his steps. He realized that he hadn't gotten very far. He was sure that the hillbilly sniper would have caught up to him in no time at all. His revolver would not have been much use against a sniper rifle. He chided himself for making his escape attempt purely on impulse.

Reaching the road, Bauer peered through the dense foliage, taken aback by the sight of a small band of American soldiers in a standoff with Cole's squad, weapons drawn. The gunshots made sense now, although it didn't appear that anyone had been shot—yet.

"What on earth is happening?" he murmured, curiosity winning out over caution. With another sigh, this one of resignation, he stepped onto the road, his sudden emergence startling the Americans. They hesitated, unsure where to direct their aim—except for Cole and Brock, whose weapons remained steadfastly trained on each other.

Several guns now targeted him, but Bauer, with the satchel of documents in hand, slowly raised his arms in a gesture of surrender. "What is going on here?" he inquired calmly, as if walking into the midst of a standoff between rival Americans was a normal occurrence for him.

"These boys want to shoot you for what you did to their buddies," Cole replied, his voice firm. "They sure as hell tried, back at the château. But I can't let them, tempted though I may be. My orders are to bring you in, and that's just what I aim to do."

Bauer gave Cole a nod of acknowledgment. "I respect your sense of duty, Private Cole," he said, "but perhaps we can negotiate."

Brock seemed to sense that he had the upper hand and scoffed. "Negotiate? What terms could you possibly offer, aside from a bullet?"

Bauer's gaze never wavered from Brock as he spoke, his voice steady. "In my hand, I hold documents of great importance—maps and plans salvaged from wreckage we found on the road. What if I were to hand them over? Everyone could lower their guns. You could present them to your superiors and be hailed as heroes for capturing invaluable enemy intelligence."

A flicker of interest crossed Brock's face as the German's offer sank in. The Obersturmbannführer had cast his line, and it seemed Brock was considering the bait. "And what about you?" Brock asked. "I suppose you think we should just let you go?"

"Let Cole escort me to headquarters, as he's so determined to do," Bauer proposed. "What do you say to my proposal?"

Brock's brow furrowed. "It doesn't sit right with me," he admitted. "The men you've killed . . . you need to pay a price for that."

Bauer winced, as though the memory of what had happened to the American prisoners inflicted physical pain. "Yes, that was regrettable, against my wishes," he confessed. "Rest assured that there will be a reckoning. Once I reach your headquarters, I will face interrogation, and justice will prevail. The Allies will probably execute me, if not tomorrow, then after the war—which, should this offensive fail, could be sooner than we think. So, you see, there will be justice for your comrades. You will have your vengeance, albeit at the end of a rope rather than your rifle."

Everyone seemed to think that over. The standoff stretched on, weapons still aimed at one another with deadly intent, the air thick with tension, until one soldier spoke up. "He's making sense, Brock.

Let's just hand this bastard over to headquarters. He'll get what he deserves," he said, his voice betraying his anxiety amid the pointed weapons.

Brock pondered, then asked, "What exactly are these documents?"

"The maps detail supply depots as well as crossing points for the rivers, along with written orders and a timeline for critical objectives. With this information, your forces can thwart my countrymen's advance," Bauer explained.

Brock nodded slowly, turning to Cole. "Is this true?"

"It is," Cole confirmed. "That's why he fled into the woods with them."

Having reached a mutual understanding, Brock lowered his submachine gun, and Cole followed suit, pointing his rifle at the ground. The others did the same. Brock approached Bauer, who still held his hands high, and snatched the satchel.

But he also wanted something more than just the documents.

Stepping back, the big man landed a solid punch on Bauer's chin, knocking the German into the snow.

"That's a down payment on that justice you talked about," Brock said, sneering down at him. Then, hefting the satchel stuffed with documents, Brock turned to Cole and declared, "We'll take these and head back to Bastogne. As for getting this Kraut bastard to headquarters, you're going to need all the luck you can get. The woods are still crawling with Germans, and it's cold as hell out here."

As if to prove his point, Brock gestured toward the road winding into the dark, snowy forest. In the distance, the sounds of battle echoed—a cacophony of gunfire and the distant rumble of artillery. They'd had their moment of drama here on the road, but there was still much to worry about.

Brock and his men prepared to leave. Before Brock could depart, Lena's voice cut through the tension. "My mother—what of her?"

Brock paused, appearing oddly puzzled by the question, then replied, "You keep asking about your mother, little girl. But I have to tell you, there was no one in the house when we went through it."

Lena's expression relaxed, a silent acknowledgment that her mother's hiding place had been effective.

Cole and his men watched as Brock and his companions turned and disappeared up the road toward Bastogne.

"I reckon that's that," Cole muttered, realizing that his heart was thundering. He hadn't noticed it before, but it was no surprise. He had been a hair's breadth from pulling the trigger on Corporal Brock. Now, turning to Bauer, he wondered aloud, "What should I do with you? I should just shoot you."

Bauer gave him that annoying smile, which only made Cole want to shoot him even more. "Remember my words to the corporal," Bauer said. "Justice will be served, just maybe not today."

"I reckon you're right about that." Cole nodded, a grim agreement hanging in the air. Nearby, Vaccaro shook his head. "You don't always have to be so damn righteous, Cole."

Cole ignored him, his gaze fixed on Bauer, who just shrugged and looked away. Rupert chimed in, "Shouldn't we tie him up again? We should take back my gun, at the very least."

Cole shook his head. "He came back on his own, didn't he? He gave himself up to save our sorry asses from shooting one another. There's no need to tie him up again." To Bauer, he added, "Keep the gun. You might need it before the day's out."

Rupert spoke up. "Do you think that's wise?"

"He came back, didn't he?" Cole snapped, then added, "Sir."

Rupert didn't argue the point.

As they moved down the road, enveloped by the silent, dark woods, even the wildlife seemed to hold its breath. The encroaching woods offered respite from the wind, but there was no break from the cold, which crept up from the icy road into their feet. Snowflakes drifted through the branches, chilling their skin with a touch as cold as the grave.

Cole fell back behind Bauer to keep an eye on him. No matter what he had said before to Lieutenant Rupert, he supposed that it was better to be safe than sorry if Bauer changed his mind and decided to try to shoot him in the back.

He let Lena and Rupert lead the way. They had rounded a bend, approaching the charred remains of a truck, when movement caught Cole's eye. There was something, or somebody, hiding in the wreckage.

He swung his rifle up, but a gunshot rang out first. Rupert cried out in pain, then fell to the snowy road, blood flowing red.

Lena dove down beside him, a move that likely saved her life as more shots followed, snapping through the cold air.

Cole fired blindly toward the truck. "Off the road!" he yelled, but he stood firm, firing again.

Darting forward, Cole grabbed Rupert, dragging him to the roadside ditch, Lena following. Vaccaro and Bauer had already vanished into the woods. Bullets zipped past, and Cole knew the fight was far from over.

Cole spotted movement and recognized the distinct square shape of a German helmet. He aimed and fired, taking down the figure hiding behind the skeleton of a truck. But the gunfire continued, forcing them to take cover. "We need to get out of here," Cole urged. He asked Rupert, "How bad are you hit? Can you move?"

"Yes," Rupert replied through gritted teeth.

"Let's help him up," Cole said, turning to Lena. "You get his other shoulder." With their combined effort, they managed to drag the wounded lieutenant into the nearby woods, where Vaccaro and Bauer had already taken cover and were trading gunfire with the gunmen in the wreckage.

"I'll be damned," Cole exclaimed, catching his breath. "I reckon those Germans found us."

"Messner and Dietzel," Bauer confirmed. "They must have taken a shortcut at the bend in the road while we were unaware."

Cole couldn't argue with this theory; it seemed like the most logical explanation. They couldn't be more than a few miles from HQ at Neufchâteau. But now they had a wounded comrade and enemy soldiers on their tail, making the final leg of their journey even more harrowing. "Vaccaro, keep an eye on that truck and watch our back trail," Cole ordered. "I'll tend to Rupert's wound. We need to stop that bleeding before we do anything."

He quickly took out a first aid kit from his bag and treated Rupert's injury as best as he could. "I know it hurts like hell, Lieutenant, but we've got to keep moving," Cole said sympathetically. "We need to circle around those Germans. We don't have time to wait them out."

With Lena and Bauer supporting Rupert on either side, they made their way deeper into the woods, aided by an animal path that led them away from the road.

Despite his injury, Rupert was determined to keep going, but his strength was fading. In fact, he might not have made it at all if Bauer hadn't slung him over his shoulder like a sack of potatoes and carried him the last stretch up the steep incline. The German was certainly stronger than he looked.

The Krauts were tough bastards, even the officers, Cole admitted grudgingly.

Once they reached level ground again, Lena led them down a hidden path parallel to the road, keeping them out of sight from the Germans, who must surely now be on their trail.

They had left a trail wide as a highway through the snowy woods and up the side of the hill. Cole debated staying behind and making a stand against the Germans. He was confident that he had killed one of them, but the ambush on the road had rattled him, and he suddenly didn't like their chances, even if they technically outnumbered the Germans. War wasn't just a numbers game. Luck didn't seem to be on their side lately.

Cole spotted movement in the distance, confirming that the Krauts were indeed coming after them. They had to keep moving. "We can't stop yet," he declared. "Let's go." He fired a few shots in the direction of the pursuing Germans before continuing onward with his team. Cole hoped the shots would deter their pursuers, even if he hadn't hit them.

Their group pressed on through the dense woods until Bauer, breathless from the effort of supporting the lieutenant, insisted, "We must stop. He can't go on without a break." He glanced at Cole. "And frankly, neither can I."

Cole nodded, conceding to a brief respite. It risked giving the Germans time to close in, but they had little choice. He swiftly replaced the blood-soaked bandage on the lieutenant's wound with a fresh one. Then, settling on a fallen log, rifle resting on his knees, Cole took a deep gulp from his canteen. To his surprise, Bauer joined him, accepting the offered canteen with a nod.

The German then retrieved a flask from his tunic, offering it to Cole after a swift swig. "It's not poison," he assured him, "just schnapps." The sharp liquor eased the rawness in Cole's throat, the warmth cutting through the cold.

"It's a hell of a thing," Cole mused aloud. "Your comrades back there are relentless. They just won't let it go, will they?"

"That's Messner for you—determined, proud. The epitome of a German officer," Bauer said, a wry smile playing on his lips. Oddly enough, he sounded admiring of his fellow Germans, even when they seemed determined to kill them.

Cole shook his head in self-reproach. "I should never have let them get the drop on us."

"Do not be too hard on yourself," Bauer replied. "That Jaeger is quite clever. Without you, we'd have been captured, or worse, long ago. You are unlike any American I have met. Had we known there were many like you, perhaps we would have reconsidered the war."

Cole managed a half smile, but weariness and cold gnawed at him. Bauer's gaze sharpened. "Messner only wants me. If I surrender, he will spare you and the others."

"I'm not so sure about that. Anyhow, it's not an option," Cole said firmly. "We've been over this ground before. It wouldn't be right."

Bauer nodded. He tucked away his flask and checked his revolver, swinging open the cylinder, ensuring it was ready. "Then we shall face him together."

CHAPTER TWENTY-NINE

THE OBERSTURMBANNFÜHRER'S ASSESSMENT OF Hauptmann Messner being proud and determined was all too accurate. Like a hunting dog with the scent of the quarry in his nose, Messner hurried to follow the tracks in the snow. Behind him, Dietzel followed more cautiously, not as eager to walk forward into the woods. The Jaeger's eyes stared into the distance, as if willing the trees to part and give him a clear view of what lay ahead. He knew all too well that they might be walking into the other sniper's sights.

Messner didn't have the patience for caution. "Hurry it up, for God's sake! I don't want to spend another night in these godforsaken woods, not with so many Ami soldiers around. Besides, my toes are getting so cold that I can't feel them. The sooner that we catch up to them and put an end to things, the better. Then we can find a fire somewhere and some hot food."

"As you say, Herr Hauptmann," the Jaeger said, but he didn't walk any faster, much to Messner's frustration.

"You are moving like an old lady."

"Sir, you know that they outnumber us now?"

"Since when were two German soldiers outnumbered by less than twenty men?" Messner asked incredulously. It was a common notion that one good Soldat was worth several American GIs.

Dietzel remained silent, as if he wasn't so sure.

Messner was not about to slow his pace, but he had to admit that the American sniper, at least, was a formidable opponent. Gettinger was dead, having been shot in the head by the American sniper during the ambush. Gettinger's death had shocked him, first because the man had barely shown himself, not offering much of a target before being picked off, and second because Gettinger had been with him so long—longer even than Dietzel.

Gettinger had survived with him through thick and thin, almost like Messner's very own good-luck charm, a life-size lucky rabbit's foot. Messner would be lying if he didn't feel a pang of sorrow at Gettinger's death, but also anger that he had exposed himself.

The dummkopf should have done more to keep his head down.

Then again, the Germans had also taken their toll. Dietzel had managed to hit one of them—the British officer. There was blood on the snow, each dot like a liquid ruby, indicating that it was a bad wound. If nothing else, the wounded man would slow them down.

Unfortunately, it had not been Bauer who had been shot. Messner had pursued him this far; he intended to keep going until Bauer was dead.

Messner couldn't believe that the Americans were still defending Bauer. It seemed foolish at this point, almost insane. Why not just give up their prisoner?

For the same reason that the Americans had not surrendered Bastogne, he thought. They were a stubborn bunch.

No matter. At this point, there was no way that he would allow any of them to live, even after he killed Bauer. He owed Gettinger that much.

Moving through the woods, they reached a place where the ground rose sharply. The tracks went right up the hillside, although even Messner's untrained eye could see that their quarry had struggled, slipping and sliding on the snowy, frozen slope.

"I do not like the looks of this hill, Herr Hauptmann," Dietzel said. "I won't have my hands free to use my rifle if I need to."

"You worry too much," Messner said. "They are like scared rabbits, yet you expect them to turn and fight?"

The Hauptmann slung his MP 40 so that it hung across his back, keeping it out of the snow and forest debris. Dietzel had no choice but to sling his rifle in the same way, allowing him to pull himself up the slope using exposed tree roots and knobs of rock jutting from the snowy ground. Even so, he still slid down in places, making an awful racket as branches cracked and stones tumbled. If their quarry hadn't known they were coming, they did now.

Halfway up, Dietzel proved to be right when a couple of rifle shots shattered the stillness of the winter air. The rifle shots had come from above. Both men buried their faces in the snow and dirt.

"They are shooting at nothing," Dietzel announced after several tense minutes. "Those shots did not come anywhere near us."

And yet the shots did just what they had been intended to do, which was to slow them down and make the pursuers move more cautiously.

Finally, they reached the crest of the slope. The tracks continued into the forest.

Messner was panting from the effort of climbing the hill. But he wasn't about to slow down or give up. "Come on," he managed to gasp.

* * *

COLE WEIGHED their options and came up with a plan. He and Bauer would hang back to deal with the Germans. Vaccaro would go with Lieutenant Rupert and the girl, because at this point, the lieutenant needed to be helped along and Lena didn't have the physical strength to do it alone. To make matters worse, the ankle that she had twisted on the road still bothered her. Plus, if they ran into any trouble, they would need Vaccaro's rifle. He was the only one among those three in any condition to fight.

The trio would keep moving, sweeping around in a wide circle to reach the road again, hopefully skirting their pursuers in the process.

"I'm not gonna argue, but I don't like it," Vaccaro said, once he heard the plan. To his credit, he made no mention of simply turning

Bauer over to the Germans and being done with the whole mission. They had come too far for that.

"Let's finish this," Cole said. Then he took Vaccaro aside and added, "Listen here, city boy. If Herr Barnstormer and I don't make it, find that road and keep going until you reach our lines and get the lieutenant some help. Don't let that girl go back alone, neither, no matter how much she's worried about her mother."

"You'll make it."

"Sure we will," Cole said. "I'm just saying it as a count ten and see plan."

"I think you mean *contingency* plan."

"What I mean is, I'll see you when I see you. Now let's get a move on."

Cole gave a nod to Bauer, and the two men let the others head out, then they moved in another direction altogether.

"What do you have in mind?" Bauer asked. He touched the handle of the revolver jutting from his coat pocket. "I will need to be close to have any chance with this pistol."

"If this Jaeger of yours is any good at all, he'll see that those are German boot prints in the snow, and he'll follow our trail instead of the others."

"Ah, but then what?" Once again Bauer flashed him that amused smile. Cole was glad to see that the German didn't seem to have the least bit of fear.

"Then this," Cole said. They had reached a clear space in the forest. He intended for this to be where his own trail diverged from Bauer's, but first he needed to set a trap, using Bauer as bait.

Growing up in the mountains, Cole had learned to be a master trapper. He had often learned the hard way, once nearly drowning in a frozen mountain stream when he'd gotten caught in one of his own traps. He hadn't made that mistake again. From time to time he had put his trapping skills to use against the enemy. The question was, How much smarter was a German officer than a fox or a raccoon? He was about to find out.

They walked to a likely-looking tree with a fallen log nearby. The tree had created a small clearing when it had fallen. Cole nodded when he saw it, a plan forming in his mind.

"Give me your coat," he said.

Bauer hesitated, but then a look crossed his face as it seemed to sink in what Cole planned to do. He shed his officer's coat and handed it to Cole.

He cut a stick to fit inside between the shoulders, almost as if it was on a coat hanger. He then hung the coat from the stub of a broken branch jutting from a tree. He'd basically made a makeshift scarecrow. It wasn't perfect, but it might be good enough to trick someone at a distance.

"Trample the ground around here so it's not clear which way you went, then hide behind that log. I'm pretty sure they'll split up when they see we went in different directions. They won't want to take a chance that one of us can slip in behind them. They'll be wanting to get this over with sooner rather than later, anyhow."

"It is a gamble," Bauer said, but he nodded in agreement with Cole's plan.

"When one of them comes along to your hiding place, shoot him. Remember that if it's Messner, then he's got a submachine gun, so if you miss, he's got a lot more bullets to shoot back."

"What about you?"

"I'll keep going, and the other one will be on my trail. I'll bet it's that Jaeger fella, because Messner will want to go after you personally."

Bauer nodded, then asked, "What if they both decide to finish me off first, and then go after you?"

"Then I reckon you're a dead man."

"Fair enough."

But Cole had one more trick up his sleeve. He was betting that the two remaining Germans would indeed split up. The German officer would surely go after Bauer. That had been the whole purpose of his pursuit.

Leaving Bauer behind in his hiding place, he retraced their path. About seventy feet away, he reached a point where he would strike out on his own. He wanted to send a message to make certain that the Jaeger followed him instead of going after Bauer. He took a spent shell from his pocket and stuck it on the end of a twig. Then he started off into the woods, carving his own trail.

For the Jaeger, the spent shell from another sniper would be like a gauntlet thrown to the ground.

He wondered how he knew that.

Because I would do the same thing, that's why. I'd go after the other sniper. Let the officers settle whatever business was between them. When it came to snipers, one man had to prove himself better with a rifle than the other. It was as simple as that.

The question was, Just how good was this Jaeger?

They were about to find out.

Cole hurried, pressing deeper into the snowy forest.

* * *

MESSNER AND DIETZEL followed the group's tracks through the snow. To their surprise, the tracks separated. A blood-speckled trail led one way, while two distinct sets of footprints veered off in another—Bauer's German boots unmistakable among them. Without hesitation, they pursued Bauer's path, surmising that he and an American had split from the others to avoid being slowed down by the wounded soldier.

It seemed like a cowardly choice, abandoning the slower group to save Bauer's hide, which wasn't all that surprising where Bauer was concerned.

They would finish off Bauer first.

"They can't be far ahead," Dietzel said.

"Yes, let's make haste," Messner agreed, his voice tinged with anticipation. "The sooner we catch them, the better."

The two Germans quickened their pace, now almost running through the dense woods, eager to close in on their quarry. But soon the trail forked again. The American's tracks headed one way, while Bauer's went another. The different boot prints in the snow were as plain to read as a road sign.

"Bauer went this way," Messner pointed out, noting the difference in the boot prints, something that the Jaeger had shown him earlier. "We need to go after him."

Messner turned in that direction. However, Dietzel hung back. He had noticed a spent rifle shell stuck on the end of a twig, clearly left as a calling card.

Or an invitation.

"What about the American sniper?" the Jaeger asked. "It looks like he went in this direction."

"Who cares about him?" Messner snapped in reply. "It's Bauer that we're after."

Still, Dietzel hesitated. "Perhaps you should pursue Bauer alone, Herr Hauptmann. I have a score to settle with the American. He shot Gettinger. Besides, we would be better off knowing that he can't come after us in these woods."

Messner was hesitant at first, then nodded his approval. This didn't mean that he wasn't somewhat exasperated by the Jaeger's line of thinking. When he replied, he sounded impatient and annoyed. "Very well. I will track Bauer. It shouldn't be that hard in this snow. You hunt the American."

With a single nod, Dietzel disappeared into the forest. Messner, now alone, advanced cautiously. The trees seemed to conspire against him, closing in around him. Then he saw a glimpse of blue-gray—the familiar color of a German uniform—visible among the trees. Once he had spotted it, the uniform coat stood out plainly against the natural surroundings.

"I've found you, Bauer. There is no escape now," Messner whispered, his Schmeisser pistol ready, advancing silently, eyes fixed on the uniform ahead. This business of pursuing Bauer had taken far too long, and he would be glad to conclude it once and for all.

As he crept within arm's reach, he expected to savor Bauer's shock before pulling the trigger—but he stepped into the clearing to find only an empty coat, nothing more than a decoy propped up by a branch.

Confusion reigned as trampled snow obscured Bauer's escape route.

Where has the bastard gone?

Messner was not left wondering for long. From behind a log, Bauer stuck up his head, pistol aimed at Messner's heart. Messner reacted, but Bauer's shot rang out first. The bullet's impact never registered with Messner.

His finger hooked over the trigger as he died, sending a volley of fire from the submachine gun spewing harmlessly into the forest canopy overhead.

Satisfied that Messner had been alone, Bauer left his hiding place. He stood over the Hauptmann and shot him in the head for good measure.

* * *

Down the trail, Cole registered the solitary gunshot—a promising sign that one threat was neutralized. However, that had instantly been followed by a burst of automatic fire. It was hard to know what that meant. Had Bauer missed his chance and been gunned down? A final, single pistol shot signaled otherwise. He knew a coup de grâce when he heard one.

Now the final contest fell to him. Cole pressed on, aimless yet determined, as late-afternoon shadows began to claim the forest. He preferred to conclude this chase with daylight as his ally. Otherwise the two snipers would be playing a deadly game of blindman's bluff. How close was the German sniper on his heels?

Cole was certain the German would follow, because a challenge was irresistible to a man like him. After all, Cole understood the Jaeger, as it was like looking in the mirror. Pressing forward, he discovered a landscape feature that could turn the tables—a ravine, sharply cut into the hillside, almost as if by design rather than by nature. He entered, leaving conspicuous tracks, but it was a deliberate ploy. He wanted to leave no doubt where he had gone.

The ravine, narrow with rocky sides and a dusting of snow, resembled a cattle chute. He had the unsettling thought that it was how cattle were funneled into the slaughterhouse.

Emerging on the other side, Cole saw how the trees had fallen away to create a clearing, because the ground was paved with smooth rock where tree roots could find no purchase. Clearly the same natural forces that had been at work in carving the ravine had also been responsible for this clearing.

Unfortunately, there was no cover to speak of. Cole hoofed it across the rocky space, breaking into a run, feeling exposed at every step. He could almost imagine the German sniper coming out of the ravine, his crosshairs fixing between Cole's shoulder blades.

He said a silent prayer. *Not yet.*

He reached a ring of trees on the other side of the clearing and got under cover. *Far enough,* he thought. This was where the showdown would take place.

Now or never.

Cole rested his rifle across a log to steady it and willed his heart rate to slow down. He wouldn't be able to shoot worth a damn if he was shaking this much. A minute went by, then another, and he felt steadier.

Putting the scope to his eye, he saw the ravine spring closer, knowing that it was exactly where the German sniper would emerge. There was nothing to do now but wait. He supposed that the German couldn't be more than a few minutes behind him, but the minutes stretched out longer than they should have.

Cole was puzzled about what was taking the man so long. He took his eye away from the scope and studied the bigger picture of the woods across from him.

That was when he spotted the movement at the top of the ravine.

It was the Jaeger.

Cole's cold lips formed a grin. You had to hand it to that Kraut. The German had nearly outmaneuvered him, scaling the ravine's wall to avoid emerging right into Cole's firing zone.

But Cole was ready, and the German was in his sights, about thirty yards away.

It would be easy enough just to pull the trigger.

But first Cole wanted the man to know that he was about to die.

Cole shouted, "Hey!"

The German had been crab-walking across the top of the ravine, trying to get in position while also keeping an eye out for his target.

He froze when he heard Cole's shout. It was an old trick that hunters used to get a clear shot when an animal wouldn't stop moving, but the German didn't freeze for long.

In fact, Cole's ploy almost cost him the fight.

The Jaeger swung his rifle up and fired, faster than Cole expected.

Something supersonic and angry hissed nearby. Cole didn't know where the bullet had gone, and he didn't much care as long as it hadn't hit him.

The Jaeger had fired too quickly to aim accurately. The man worked the bolt of his own rifle desperately.

With his crosshairs firmly on the German's chest, Cole fired.

The German sniper sank to his knees, then fell over backward into the snow.

* * *

Some distance away, Vaccaro and the others had heard the shots, and they were left wondering what was going on. The outcome was anybody's guess.

It was hard to think of anyone getting the upper hand on Cole, but in Vaccaro's experience, war was always a gamble. For now they were still on their own.

Lieutenant Rupert was still struggling through the snow, supported by Lena and Vaccaro. Vaccaro had been left with no choice but to sling his rifle to leave his hands free for that effort. He couldn't help but think that a crutch would have been more useful than a rifle. They were on the run now, pure and simple.

"Those shots, what do they mean?" Lena asked.

It was a question Rupert would've asked as well if he'd had the breath to do so. The British officer looked weak and gray with pain, his face the color of plumbing putty.

"I don't know for sure," Vaccaro said. "I don't hear any more shooting, so that means it's over for them one way or another. It's not over for us, though. We need to get back down to that road, where we can get some help for the lieutenant. He's lost a lot of blood."

Lena nodded and said, "I know the way."

EPILOGUE

Slowed by Rupert's wound and the rugged terrain, it took them longer than Vaccaro expected to reach the road again, even with Lena's knowledge of the trails through the forest.

They still didn't know the outcome of the showdown between Cole, Bauer, and the German pursuers. Vaccaro's money was on Cole, of course, but he knew well enough that there were no sure bets in this war.

"Leave me here," Rupert said. He looked even more gray-faced from pain, and he shivered in the cold. "You two will have a better chance of getting out of these woods on your own."

"No way in hell, Lieutenant," Vaccaro replied, grunting with the effort of supporting Rupert across a section of trail covered by gnarled, icy tree roots. Lena continued to support him on the other side, nursing her own twisted ankle. Every step was an effort.

"I could order you to leave me here," Rupert said.

"That won't work, Lieutenant," Vaccaro said. "Besides, your girlfriend here isn't going to follow orders either."

"I suppose you're right," Rupert said. "Help me get back to the road, and then we'll see what's what."

There was no more discussion after that. Instead, they concentrated their energies on traveling the paths made by the deer and wild pigs that Lena had set them upon.

When they finally reached the road, they were met with a surprise. They had not gone more than a quarter of a mile when they heard a shout behind them. Vaccaro looked back and saw two figures gaining on them. He would have recognized the loping gait of the leaner man anywhere.

"I'll be damned," he muttered, then smiled.

Cole trotted toward them, with Bauer on his heels. He explained that they had reached the road sooner by cutting directly downhill through the forest. It wasn't a route that the other three could have managed.

"I reckoned we'd run into your sorry ass sooner or later once we got back to the road," Cole said.

"How did it work out with those Krauts?"

"Let's just say they won't be bothering us again," Cole replied.

"Glad to hear it," Vaccaro said. "They were starting to get annoying."

"You and the girl take point," Cole said. "Let me and Bauer lug the lieutenant for a while."

"You really must leave me," Rupert insisted.

"Shut up, Lieutenant," Cole said, not unkindly. "Let's go."

* * *

THEY REACHED the outskirts of Neufchâteau not long after dark, having navigated the last couple of miles groping their way along the road. Cole had been worried about running into more Germans, but it turned out that US sentries posed the biggest danger. They had materialized out of the gloom, rifles leveled.

"What's the password?" the sentry asked.

"Do I look like I know the damn password?" Cole snapped back, exasperated. "We just came from Bastogne to deliver this prisoner."

"Holy hell, all the way from Bastogne?"

The sentries lowered their rifles. Although they had been warned against German infiltrators, the battered group of misfits on the road

—an exhausted and half-frozen GI, a Belgian girl, a wounded British officer, a German POW, and a bad-tempered sniper—did not seem to pose much threat.

Without further delay, they were pointed toward headquarters. Meanwhile, Lieutenant Rupert and Lena were guided toward the field hospital.

"How about if you deliver Herr Barnstormer? I think you can handle it from here," Vaccaro said to Cole. "I'm gonna see if I can find some hot grub and coffee."

"Sounds like a plan," Cole said.

The army had taken over an entire crossroads village, with soldiers and officers hurrying from one small house to another. Only a few lights burned due to the threat, however remote, of a Luftwaffe attack. Nonetheless, a few desperately cold GIs had started small fires fed with scrap wood or broken-up furniture to keep warm. The fires were small enough that they could be kicked out or smothered with snow at the first sound of enemy aircraft.

There was enough light thrown by the sputtering flames to see the gray slush churned up under countless tire treads and tank tracks. The firelit faces they passed looked grim and determined. When they noticed Bauer's enemy uniform, some of the faces wore looks of curiosity while others scowled as if ready to shoot him. News of the massacre at Malmedy and the smaller murderous incident perpetrated by Hauptmann Messner outside Bastogne had spread, meaning that precious few German prisoners would be taken alive in the days ahead.

Word had also arrived that the fight for Bastogne was finally being won. Cole and Vaccaro would soon be returning to see for themselves how the fight was going. The worst of the German advance seemed to have been stopped, but there was still plenty of fight left in the Krauts.

An intelligence officer found them and told them to wait outside as he ducked back inside the house. He seemed excited by Bauer's arrival but not quite sure what to do with him. It seemed to be understood that Cole would continue to keep his prisoner under guard. Wisely, Bauer had already handed back his weapon.

The two men stood surrounded by the dirty snow, waiting for the officer to return. They faced each other, stamping their feet to stay warm. Their breath made clouds that hung in the frosty air, but no words passed between them. No one else was around, and nobody seemed to be taking much interest in them.

Soon the officer would come back out and Bauer would be thrown into the meat grinder of military justice. But for now it was just two soldiers who had survived an ordeal together.

"I could let you escape," Cole finally said. "It's not too late."

"You will do no such thing, Private Cole," Bauer replied. "You will continue to do your duty. You set out to deliver me to your headquarters for questioning, and that is exactly what you have done."

"If you get into those woods, nobody will find you."

Bauer shook his head. "The time for that is past, but thank you for the suggestion."

"What do you think will happen to you?"

"Don't worry, they are unlikely to hang me until Germany has lost the war. That may be months from now. At that point I will no longer be a prisoner of war, but a common criminal."

"For what it's worth, the way I see it, you aren't a criminal," Cole said. "You're just on the wrong side."

Bauer nodded. "Keep your head down, hillbilly."

The German straightened up, coming to attention. Cole did the same, and the two men saluted each other. The officer came back out with two MPs and took Bauer into custody. Then Cole turned and headed back down the snowy street to locate Vaccaro in hopes he had found some hot grub.

* * *

Before heading out for the return trip to Bastogne, Cole and Vaccaro stopped by the field hospital to check on Lieutenant Rupert. The hospital had been set up in a church. This was no cathedral, but a simple village chapel. A crucifix with an almost life-size Jesus overlooked the scene, and Christ's eyes seemed to watch the suffering with sadness.

The pews had been removed to make more room, so that the wounded lay on the cold stone floor. Portable kerosene heaters had been brought in, but they were struggling. Most of the warmth came from the collective body heat, which was a mixed blessing. Cole wished that somebody would open a window—the interior reeked of unwashed soldiers, fever sweat, rubbing alcohol, and a whiff of rotting meat. He wrinkled his nose against the assault of smells.

They found Rupert propped up on his blankets, letting Lena help him drink a hot mug of broth. He still looked exhausted, but some of his color had returned. Fortunately, his wounds weren't going to be fatal. What he needed was rest and hot food.

Some of the cases were far worse. Several men were so heavily bandaged that it was hard to tell where the gauze ended and the men began. In other cases, frostbite had turned the flesh of the victims' toes, fingers, even noses, black like bruised fruit.

"The sawbones tell me that I should be out of here in a few days," Rupert said.

"Don't be in a hurry, sir," Vaccaro replied. "I rushed to get out of the hospital so that I could get to Bastogne. What the hell was I thinking?"

"You weren't," Cole said. "And I told you so too. Don't make the same mistake, Lieutenant."

Lena smoothed a stray lock of hair and offered him more broth, showing the same intensity as when she had guided them through the forest.

"It looks to me like you're in good hands, Lieutenant," Vaccaro said knowingly.

"Lena is going to stay here and volunteer at the hospital as a nurse," Rupert said. "At least for a few days until the fighting around Bastogne is over. It's just too dangerous for her to head home right now, although she is more than a bit worried about her mother."

"Something tells me Madame Jouret will be just fine," Cole said. "She's one tough customer."

Lena laughed. *"Oui, c'est vrai!"*

Rupert had a question for Cole. "What about Bauer?"

"I delivered him to HQ just like we were supposed to, sir."

"If he had anything to do with those prisoners being shot, they'll hang him eventually."

"Yeah, I know," Cole said.

There didn't seem to be much more to say after that. Cole and Vaccaro made sure that the lieutenant had everything he needed. Then again, considering that he had his own personal nurse, he seemed to be well taken care of. They said their goodbyes and made their way out of the hospital. Cole was glad for some fresh air.

"Like I said before, the officers always get the girls," Vaccaro said.

"Aw, quit your bellyachin'. Let's see if we can find some more ammo. If we're headed back to Bastogne, we're gonna need it. The Krauts ain't licked yet."

* * *

AT THAT MOMENT, many miles away, a heavy tarp moved in the expansive attic of Château Jouret, as if stirred by a cold draft. There was certainly no shortage of those. As the tarp moved yet more, it revealed that the cloth had been draped over a heavy piece of furniture in such a way as to create a sort of tent.

Madame Jouret's face appeared at the gap in the fabric, peering out, as she listened intently to the house. She strained her ears, but the only sound in the house below was the distant scurrying of a mouse.

Inside the tent created by the dust tarp, there was a mattress, a washbasin, and a candle. All in all, it was a comfortable space, with the tent keeping in just enough body heat to make it bearable to sleep in the attic. It helped that Madame Jouret was rather plump, with plenty of middle-aged insulation against the cold.

There was also a double-barreled shotgun within her tent. If the Germans found her, she had planned on getting at least one of them.

But there had been no need. Having lived here for decades, she knew every creak and groan of the château. It was as if the old house could speak to her, verifying that it was empty. Satisfied that she was alone, she crept from her hiding place.

In the end, no one had even ventured into the attic. She had heard first the Germans and then the Americans venture into the house. There was a gap in the top of the walls that enabled sound to carry from the first floor. The words they had shouted to each other while searching the house had given them away. Madame Jouret understood the Germans well enough. She supposed that the words in English had much the same meaning.

But no one had been there since yesterday, so she had judged it safe to come out. Cautiously, she went downstairs.

Everything was a shambles from the fighting. Bullet holes pocked the walls. The shattered windows let in the snow and cold. Inexplicably, the searchers had slashed open the upholstered furniture. Who or what could they have thought was hiding there? Perhaps they were only being vindictive.

The lady of the house sighed. Windows could be boarded up. Walls could be repaired. The house had stood for a long time and wasn't going anywhere.

Her only real worry was that her daughter had made it to safety with the British officer and the Americans who were escorting the captured German. Then again, she had every confidence in her daughter. The two American soldiers had been tough and competent. Reluctantly, she also had to admit that the German officer had fought like a tiger to help defend them all.

In that short time, Lena had also taken a liking to the young British officer. Madame Jouret smiled at the thought. Perhaps something good would come out of this war after all.

**

Brock and his men returned to Bastogne, where the fighting was slowly winding down. Nobody seemed to notice that they'd been gone or asked where they had gone. There was simply too much confusion —not to mention that many troops had gone missing in the cold, dark woods. In some cases their remains wouldn't be found for decades.

It would have been easy enough to simply reappear and keep his head down, but he wasted no time getting the maps and documents that he'd "found" into the hands of his company commander, who immediately passed them up the food chain.

His CO found him later and announced, "You did good, Brock.

Word is that what you and your boys found was really useful. The colonel suggested putting you in for a medal."

"Just doing my part, sir."

"Keep doing it, that's for sure. Tell me again, where did you say you found those documents?"

"We killed some Krauts we ran across, and they had those documents on them." The story came so easily that Brock himself almost believed it.

"Well, that was lucky. Good job."

Brock didn't have a medal yet, but he puffed out his chest a bit as he made his way through the streets of Bastogne, Vern at his side. They'd already left Boot at the field hospital, where it wasn't looking good for his frostbitten toes. He'd looked for Charlie Knuth, to tell him that he'd found the German who had gunned down those GIs. Knuth had been too weak to ask for details, and Brock hadn't bothered to explain that he'd let the German officer go in exchange for the captured documents.

Anyhow, like that hillbilly sniper had said, the German would get what was coming to him.

Up the street, Brock spotted a soldier carrying a bottle of wine. The GIs had gone through Bastogne like a plague of locusts, looking for anything to eat or drink, but the soldier had somehow found another bottle in the ruined town. He moved to block the smaller soldier's path and "liberate" the wine, just as he'd done a couple of days before with a different soldier.

Beside him, Vern chuckled. "Same old Brock," he muttered.

The comment made Brock stop and think. *Was* he the same old Brock? He'd made good on his promise to get justice by hunting down the German, even if it wasn't exactly the justice he had first envisioned. He'd brought his men back, more or less in one piece. Hell, it even sounded like he was going to get a medal.

In the street ahead, the soldier found Brock blocking his path. "What's up?" he asked.

"Stick that bottle of wine under your coat before somebody tries to take it from you," Brock said.

The soldier nodded and took Brock's advice, then went on his way.

Vern was staring at him. "Hey, Brock, you know what? If I didn't know better, I'd say you've gone soft."

"Not soft, just older and wiser. Anyhow, don't push it," Brock growled.

* * *

Days after the dismal meeting in Verdun, General Dwight D. Eisenhower surveyed the map again, feeling a sense of relief. The Battle of the Bulge was far from won, and Ike had been forced to throw everything he had at the Germans to halt the advance.

However, the map reflected that Hitler's Operation Christrose was a fading dream. The wintry roads and lack of fuel had bogged down the German tanks. The snow-covered, rugged Ardennes didn't play favorites, however. The weather and rough terrain had been just as challenging for the Allied forces. But it was clear that the tide had turned.

Much of that success in stopping the enemy was thanks to General Patton and his Third Army. Patton's fighting spirit was exactly what had been needed, taking on the enemy panzers wherever his Sherman tanks and tank destroyers encountered them.

Soon the weather would clear enough for the Army Air Corps planes to resume flying. Once that happened, they would begin picking off enemy tanks and trucks like hawks swooping down on the chicken coop.

Then again, it hadn't been just Patton's troops who had stopped the Germans. No, each and every soldier who had shivered in his foxhole, holding his position, had done just that. Patton might get all the glory, but Ike was well aware that thousands of unsung heroes were responsible for this victory.

The stand made at Bastogne had also stopped the Germans in their tracks. They had not been able to advance any farther and had been forced to stop and fight once General McAuliffe had given his famous reply to enemy demands for surrender: "Nuts!"

Ike grinned, thinking about the consternation that response must have caused the Germans.

The Battle of the Bulge was being won, slowly but surely. Ike wasn't quite ready to relax, but he'd actually managed to get some sleep the night before.

He looked at the map, to what was next. Beyond the Ardennes lay the Rhine River.

Then Germany itself.

NOTE TO READERS

Many readers have asked whether there would be more adventures for Caje Cole, to the point where I was encouraged to see if I could go back and write another story or two. There seemed to be a gap in the timeline between the end of *Ardennes Sniper* and *Red Sniper* where at least one or two more stories could be set. The result is this book, although it's a little out of order, taking place well before Cole's stint in Korea or the events of *Sniper's Justice*. However, I hope Cole's fans will forgive that wrinkle in the reading order of the series in the spirit of allowing space for another tale.

Much of the final section of this book was written in a period that coincided with the eightieth commemoration of D-Day. The publication date also comes eighty years after the Battle of the Bulge was fought in the snowy Ardennes Forest. My heart still goes out to the soldiers when I imagine the cold and miserable conditions they endured. (Ironically, I was doing a lot of the writing during a summer marked by several record-setting heat waves.)

For many of you reading this, your fathers or grandfathers or uncles were suffering in that cold. I appreciate that some of you shared your stories about these heroes and what they went through. These stories must never be forgotten and perhaps, in some small way, these Caje Cole books will honor their memory.

The history of Bastogne and the larger Battle of the Bulge comes from so many sources that they are almost too numerous to list. That said, *The Battle of the Bulge* by Stephen W. Sears provided much helpful context about the overall campaign. Also useful for its detail, including maps and photographs, was *The Ardennes: Battle of the Bulge*, a Department of the Army assessment written by Hugh M. Cole. Finally, the scene describing the soldier who used his helmet to bring beer to wounded comrades at Bastogne is based on an actual incident related by Vince Speranza of the 101st Airborne in his book, *Nuts: A 101st Airborne Division Machine Gunner at Bastogne*, and in YouTube interviews. Be sure to read his book or watch the entertaining videos to learn more.

I want to thank the many people who have been understanding during the writing of what is one of my longer WWII stories. As always, a big thanks goes to Mike, Aidan, and Mary for moral support and for listening to me think out loud and occasionally gripe when things aren't going well, a small-but-mighty team of advance readers who road tested the story, Castle Walls Editing for correcting my errors and keeping the details straight, Streetlight Graphics for the cover design, Deny Howeth's photography, and the narration skills of Scott Bennett. Most important of all, thank you for reading and making these stories possible.

—DH

ABOUT THE AUTHOR

David Healey lives in Maryland, where he worked as a journalist for more than twenty years. He is an author member of the International Thriller Writers.

Check in with him on Facebook at
https://www.facebook.com/david.healey.books

Printed in Dunstable, United Kingdom